Puck Funny
Dani Galliaro

Production by eBookPro Publishing
www.ebook-pro.com

PUCK FUNNY
Dani Galliaro
Copyright © 2024 Dani Galliaro

All rights reserved.
No part of this book may be reproduced in any form or by any electronic or mechanical means, including information storage and retrieval systems, without written permission from the author, except for the use of brief quotations in a book review.

This is a work of fiction. Names, characters, businesses, places, events, locales, and incidents are either the products of the author's imagination or used in a fictitious manner. Any resemblance to actual persons, living or dead, or actual events is purely coincidental.

Cover design and illustration: Arbelle Jane Reisner

ISBN 9789655754766

Puck Funny

A Friends to Lovers Second Chance Hockey Romance

(Unintentional Puck Bunny Book 1)

Dani Galliaro

DISCOVERING THE NEXT BESTSELLER

Sign up for **Readmore Press'** monthly newsletter and get a FREE audiobook!

For instant access, scan the QR code

Where you will be able to register and receive your sign-up gift, a free audiobook of

Beneath the Winds of War
by Pola Wawer,

which you can listen to right away

Our newsletter will let you know about new releases of our World War II historical fiction books, as well as discount deals and exclusive freebies for subscribed members.

Dedication

For all the sports fans who felt sports weren't really for them, especially on the basis of gender or sexual orientation.

Sports are for everyone.

A Note on Accents

My writing has traditionally centered around Appalachian characters, whether they're still in Appalachia or not. As such, I've leaned toward capturing how characters sound phonetically on the page and haven't shied away from Appalachian regional phrases and dialects.

Puck Funny is new territory for me, as the two main characters come from places that talk very differently.

This book features Kitty, a West Virginian, and Guy, a French Canadian. I initially wrote this book with Eva and Guy's accents spelled out phonetically. However, that made for a tough read at times. In the interest of making the book accessible to more people, I'll instead tell you here how Guy's accent would sound, and you can use your own imagination to fill it in throughout the book where it works for you.

I studied numerous hours of interviews with French Canadian hockey players to figure out how to best capture how they talk. Credit goes to Marc-Andre Fleury, Yanni Gourde (the most tenacious and my very favorite hockey player, thanks for asking), and Jean-Gabriel Pageau, whose interviews I relied on the most.

Some consistent traits that I picked up on are as follows:
+ dropping the "s" from plural nouns
+ pronouncing "t" sounds very hard
+ making "th" at the beginning of words a "d" sound (dat, dere, and dese for that, there, and these), but still pronouncing "thank you" with a soft "th"

This is by no means meant to diminish their intelligence, as they all speak English very well. It's just with an accent. It is also not meant to fetishize them, "other" them, or have any sort of negative reflection on the character.

I mention Guy's accent a few times throughout the book as it stands today to remind you of how he sounds without lacing it into every piece of dialogue.

I hope you enjoy this wild emotional roller-coaster ride. And if you don't, it's just a silly little book about love, comedy, and hockey.

All the best,
Dani

A Note on Timeline and Triggers

I got a little goofy on some pop culture references. I tried to keep music references true to the time period when they would have fallen. I took artistic liberties here and there if something really made sense elsewhere.

There's one notable exception: I bumped up the release date of Emily in Paris by about four years. I'd say I'm sorry, but I'm not.

There's also a brief appearance from the villain of 2020, COVID. No one gets sick in my book, but I wanted to capture a little bit of that panic-for-your-loved-ones feeling that so many of us experienced. You can gloss over Chapter 29 if that's hard for you and know they briefly rekindled their friendship during the pandemic.

While speaking of less pleasant things, there is the on-page loss of a parent in this book. I know this occurrence is all-too-familiar to many, and difficult to read. If you want to skip it, it's in Chapter 6. Take care of yourself. You are so loved.

A complete list of triggers is at the back of the book.

Take care y'all,
Dani

Playlist

Music is a crucial part of how I create my stories. This one came to me while listening to a song on loop on a walk. Yes, I know some of these are covers, not the original artist. I chose these artists and their versions for a reason.

To find it on Spotify, search Puck Funny under my name Dani Galliaro.

I. The Crush

Kiss You – One Direction
Clarity – Zedd, Foxes
That Should Be Me – Justin Bieber

II. The Rush

Nice For What – Drake
Late Night Talking – Harry Styles
I'll Make Love To You – Boyz II Men
Mr. Brightside – The Killers
The Most Beautiful Girl In The World – Prince
Carried Me With You – Brandi Carlile
Out of the Woods – Taylor Swift
Can't Help Falling In Love – Kacey Musgraves

III. The Fall

The First Cut Is The Deepest – Sheryl Crow
Midnight Rain – Taylor Swift
champagne problems – Taylor Swift
I Will Always Love You – Dolly Parton
I Will Wait – Mumford and Sons

IV. Ghost

Ghost – Justin Bieber
Ghost of You and Me – BBMak
Holy Ground (Taylor's Version) – Taylor Swift
You Were Meant For Me – Jewel
Still – Niall Horan
When You Come Back Down – Nickel Creek

V. The Return

Save Tonight – Eagle Eye Cherry
Maroon – Taylor Swift

XO – Beyonce

In Your Love – Tyler Childers

VI. Coda

I Melt With You – Modern English
History – One Direction

Prologue

Kitty

Guy Stelle was new in town, and it was June. He and his mom moved into the one duplex on our street, occupying the second and third floors of an old house. I watched as mysterious items were unloaded from their U-Haul. Were those hockey sticks? My brother came up beside me to see what I was looking at.

"Ooh, is that a new boy for Bitty Kitty to have a crush on?" he teased.

"Shut up, Frankie," I hissed, slapping him on the arm.

I was turning fourteen that summer, and sixteen-year-old boys were very much of interest to me. Not as much interest as say, One Direction, but sixteen-year-old boys were slightly more tangible than Liam and Niall. The problem with sixteen-year-old boys, though, was that they were Frank's age, and thus, he would give me endless grief for having such interests.

"Quit gawking at 'em and go take 'em this chicken and tea," our mom, Heather, called from the kitchen. "Their U-Haul tags are Canadian. They've probably come a long way. Could use some supper."

"Supper," Frank and I mouthed at each other. We made a constant hobby of mocking our mother's country way of talking.

"I heard that," Mom jabbed. "Get out there. Have some manners."

"Yes, ma'am," we whined, sliding on our flip-flops before we headed out the door. Frank grabbed his basketball, presumably to shoot hoops before he committed to befriending the newcomer. He shoved the jug of sweet tea at me, which I rejected because I was already carrying the chicken.

"Don't make me carry this over there by myself," I protested. "They're from Canada. What if they don't speak English?"

"Canada speaks English, dummy," Frank said.

"Not in French Canada," I argued. Frank dribbled the basketball with his open hand, and I slapped it away from him, kicking it into our yard. He'd never admit it, but I was kinda better at basketball.

"Hi!" I waved my arm over my head to the mom.

"Bonjour," Frank muttered.

"Shut up," I mumbled under my breath.

The mom rested the basket she was carrying on the porch, turning to us with a smile. She yelled something into the house that sure didn't sound like English.

"Told you," I whispered to Frank.

She was petite, with an elegant bone structure, shoulder-length black hair pulled back in a low bun, and a charming gap between her front teeth. One look at her and I already knew I wanted to be her when I grew up. She exuded ease and friendliness.

"We brought you something!" I said, gesturing to what Frank carried.

"Oh, that's so kind. You don't have to bother with us," the mom said.

"No bother," Frank said, his voice strangely sweet. I knew that tone. He totally had a crush on her. I silently saved that information as ammo for pestering him later.

"I'm Eva," she said. "My son will be out here in a minute."

Frank and I introduced ourselves. Eva smiled, but something more complex hid in her eyes.

Then, her son emerged from the house, flopping his feet with a morose expression. His wavy brown-almost-black hair was a shade lighter than his mom's, long for a boy but not able to make it into a bun or ponytail. It poured over his forehead, and he flipped it to the side something like Justin Bieber. His eyes were a brooding deep brown that made me think of coffee grounds. His nose looked like it had seen some combat, but in an endearing way. Being a boy past puberty, he had some dark peach fuzz at his jaw. I knew Frank, who was still baby-faced, would be jealous. He was long and lean. I fought a swoon and hoped that my sweat could be attributed to the sweltering summer day.

How was I so lucky that *I* was the first girl he was meeting in Charleston? Dibs would have to be called as soon as I talked to my friends.

"Introduce yourself," Eva said, prodding him. "This is Kitty and Frank."

"I'm Guy," he said, with a thick accent. It sounded more like "ghee."

"How do you spell that?" Frank asked, scrunching up his nose.

"G-U-Y."

"Cool if I call you Guy?" Frank asked, pronouncing it "gai."

Guy shrugged, non-commital. I, however, committed mentally at that moment that I'd always call him by his proper name. I wasn't an uncultured rube like my brother.

"Frank and Kitty brought us some food. Isn't that nice?" Eva offered.

Guy gave a grimace of a smile for his mother's benefit. He was clearly miserable. But I could swear that when his eyes finally met mine, they softened just the slightest bit.

I was in trouble. Big trouble. This was going to be the crush to end all crushes.

Contents

Part 1: The Crush
page 17

Part 2: The Rush
page 57

Part 3: The Fall
page 165

Part 4: The Ghost
page 199

Part 5: The Return
page 219

Part 6: Coda
page 265

Part I:
The Crush

Chapter 1

Guy

"Here, here." I tapped my stick on the ice. Frank cut the puck away from Shane and passed it my way. Our little 3-on-3 game was going well.

The guys were starting to get the hang of some of the stuff I showed them. It was a winter afternoon where we didn't have any other practice and I could convince a few of the guys to come with me to the rink. I didn't know how long Maman and I would be staying in West Virginia. It felt permanent. I didn't want to lose hockey completely just because we moved. It was still my best chance at going to college and getting drafted.

Right as I went to pop it in the goal, my eye caught on Kitty. She was sitting in the bleachers, hunched over a notebook and scribbling something furiously. Probably working on one of her play ideas. My mind wandered to how she had that idea for monsters that—

"Shoot it, Stelle!" Frank yelled. Kitty looked up and raised an eyebrow at me. My focus came back to the ice just in time for Shane to swipe the puck back from me and break away. My cheeks, already red from the cold, went redder. Why was I distracted by *Kitty*?

After we finished our game, Kitty helped me put the hockey equipment away. Her arm wobbled as she lifted the other side of the goal, but I didn't bring it up. She always joked about her weakling status and theater nerd body.

"What were you working on?"

"Just an idea," she said, dismissing me. The door to the storage closet closed behind us. "Smells awful in here."

"That's hockey." I was trying to make her laugh. She wasn't having it. "What's wrong?"

Kitty shrugged. "Nothing."

"Kitty." I tugged her arm to get her to turn to me. Her breath stopped as her gaze met mine, shifting quickly between my eyes. Again, something stirred in me. Had I ever really noticed how pretty her eyes were? She'd recently gotten her braces off, and while she wasn't totally different, she definitely looked more grown up.

"What?" Her voice was barely a whisper.

"You can tell me what's wrong."

Her face flushed. "It's nothing, Guy." I softened my look, trying to convince her to open up. It worked. She shifted a step back, chewing at the loose skin on her thumb. She always picked there when she was nervous. "Your fan club is here today."

I knew who she meant. Some girls from school noticed that the guys and I went to the rink after school and followed, pretending to have a sudden interest in ice skating. The attention was flattering, but I wasn't all that interested, particularly when Kitty was around.

"They come for all of us, Kitty Cat."

"I hear them talking. They're after you." My gut turned. Did it bother Kitty that other girls were interested in me? Was she jealous?

And why was I interested in Kitty? We were *just* friends, right?

It's true that I didn't care about the other girls. They weren't Kitty. Kitty understood me. She knew how to make me laugh when I was down. She respected me. She was always kind when she corrected my English. She was the only person who pronounced my name the French way, and I liked that about her. She didn't treat me like an alien or an exotic creature like the other girls did. She saw me for who I was. I could be myself around her.

The realization came to me in a flood. Or maybe I'd known it all along and just denied it. Either way, something major changed inside me. I didn't fully understand it, but it was there.

Kitty wasn't just my good friend or my best friend's little sister. I wanted Kitty to be *mine*.

"I don't want them, Kitty."

It was a rare occasion that we were alone. A stray piece of hair had fallen out of her ponytail. Without thinking, I brushed it behind her ear. I didn't move my hand away from her face, though. I didn't know what I was doing but I knew without a doubt that I needed to do it.

My lips were on hers before I could second-guess myself. After a moment's hesitation, Kitty kissed me back, stepping more into my body as I held her tight. Her lips were soft, her scent a welcome change from the humid, dank air of the storage closet. Her lips were sweet, like she'd just put on her favorite strawberry lip balm, a smell I didn't realize I had memorized until that moment. We were both young and clumsy, but insatiable nonetheless.

I was just starting to think about how soft her skin under her clothes might feel when the door flew open. Shane and a girl from school stood with a hockey goal balanced between them. I shoved Kitty off me out of instinct, afraid it was Frank. I was kissing my best friend's sister. Who was also my best friend.

Kitty looked at the floor, face red. Shane and the girl stood dumbfounded.

"Not a word." I was panicking. Spiraling out. "You will say nothing. Do you understand?"

Kitty rushed out of the closet. I was too embarrassed to call after her. Frank would kill me if he found out I'd kissed his sister. But then, I'd just hurt my other best friend, too.

I was an idiot.

***

I hated that we had to move. I got why Maman wanted to start over. I got that she didn't want to live with Papa's ghost anymore. In Montreal, we were Gabriel Stelle's family, the ones he left behind. People either pitied us or wanted something from us.

But Maman and I knew the truth. Papa was no saint. And she couldn't live with the memories being around us all the time. So that summer, we left.

I was fifteen, almost sixteen. I had my friends. I had my team. I was even kind of partial to my school. And Maman was taking it all away.

I didn't get to say goodbye to my friends. She didn't want people asking questions. Maman told me my friends could visit when we got where we were going. When I asked where that was, she just responded with, "*Sud.*" South.

It wasn't hard for us to get visas into the U.S., thanks to my dad's former occupation. Hockey players have to be able to go freely between the U.S. and Canada, and we tagged on to those privileges. Thankfully, it hadn't been that long since he did some color commentary for the league, so we still had access to easy immigration.

I knew she didn't know where we were going. I was trying hard not to be a brat. It was hard for me, but it was harder for her. And I loved her. I wanted her to be happy. Some things were bigger than me.

One day in the middle of nowhere Pennsylvania, Maman sent me to the motel pool while she argued with Grandmere on the phone. When I came back, her eyes were red. She put on a big smile, gave me a silent hug, and we went to the nearby roadside diner. That night as we were falling asleep in the seedy motel room, I told her, "We're going to be okay."

"Yes. We are," she agreed, but I heard her quiet sobs after she thought I was asleep.

I'm not sure why she insisted on staying in crummy places while we went south. She got decent child support from Papa. Maybe she was determined not to spend his money.

I was furious when she stopped in that first mountain town. Didn't people make fun of West Virginia? Why did she want this to be home? I googled the nearest ice rink and convinced her to go a little farther south to Charleston. I wasn't about to lose hockey on top of everything else.

But once we met the Gattos, everything started to get better.

Mrs. Gatto, or Heather as she's always insisted I call her, was a lighthouse for Maman. They became best friends faster than Frank and I did. I remember the night Frankie and I were playing XBox. I kept hearing Maman and Heather laughing over wine in the backyard. We heard them singing Jewel and Prince. I acted horrified to Frank, but I hadn't heard Maman sing in years. She loved Prince and that one Jewel song was an old favorite of hers.

Later, when I went to see if Maman wanted to go home, our moms had their arms around each other's necks, tears streaming down both of their faces.

Mark Gatto steered clear when those two hung out, knowing he had no place but to keep their wine glasses topped up and the fire pit loaded with logs. That man is the real saint in the family. He knew Maman and Heather had something special and played his supporting role like a champ. I wished my dad could have been as sweet as Mark Gatto. But that wasn't my life. Kitty and Frank were the lucky ones to have Mark and Heather as parents.

And then there was Kitty. She acted shy at first, hiding her braces-filled smiles behind her hand. But she had a real cutting sense of humor. Once Maman started working at the restaurant and I had dinner at the Gattos more often, she'd make these really clever sidebars that only Frank and I could hear. Frank would roll his eyes, but I laughed. She wasn't my sister. I wasn't obligated to pretend like she wasn't cool or funny.

Sometimes Frank was cool with all three of us hanging out,

which was fine for me. I loved them both as best friends. But because Kitty was a little younger and a girl, we couldn't ever be close in the same way Frank and I were close. Those unwritten rules of growing up, I guess.

The three of us would watch stand-up comedians on YouTube or old funny movies. Laughing was important for me at that point in my life. Things had been rough, both before and after Papa left. The stable Gattos were a safe haven for me.

Other times, Frankie wanted his pesky little sister gone. He got a pair of rollerblades so we could play street hockey together. He was terrible at first, but I coached him into a pretty strong player. He convinced me to join the soccer team, so when August rolled around, that's how I made friends. Kitty tagged along to our practices for the ride home when she didn't have play practice.

I was nervous about being the new kid in school. I had a funny accent, but for better or worse, no one knew who my dad was. It only took a few weeks for the word to get around about me from the ladies, and then my social status took off. I didn't do anything to charm them other than be fresh meat with a French (to them) accent. That's all it takes when you're a junior in high school.

Once school started and I spent hours after school either at practice, at the rink, or at the Gattos, I got to see some of the unrest in the Gatto house. Even in a family as picture-perfect as theirs, things were still off sometimes.

Kitty was awful at math. Like, really bad. And her parents, especially sweet old Mark, didn't get why. They thought she didn't pay attention. I knew she was smart otherwise, but things were going so poorly with her and pre-algebra.

Heather had to take Frank to a doctor's appointment one day that first fall. Kitty and I were the only ones home at the Gattos. I could hear her crying in her room. I paced in the hallway, not sure what to do. Finally, I knocked on her door.

"Go away," came her quiet reply.

"It's Guy."

"I'm fine," she huffed, still not opening the door.

I knew I could help her if she'd just let me. I was a peer tutor in Montreal.

"I have M&Ms," I said, tempting her with her favorite candy. I didn't really have M&Ms, but I knew where Heather hid them from Kitty.

She honked her nose into a tissue, then the door creaked open. She walked back to the middle of her floor. There was a math test with a red forty-two at the top.

"Ouch." I nudged the paper with my socked foot.

"Dad's going to kill me," she sulked.

I nodded, chewing my lip. "What if you know how to fix your mistakes?"

She blinked up at me and narrowed her eyes.

"Come on, *ma puce*. Get a pencil and paper and I'll get the M&Ms." The term of endearment just flew out of my mouth and I couldn't take it back. *Ma puce*: literally, my flea. When it's said to someone younger, it's cutesy. When it's said to a girlfriend, it's very affectionate. I didn't know which of those Kitty was to me, but the name seemed to fit.

Kitty studied me and got a tiny smile. I fully expected her to question the French, but she didn't say a word about it.

We settled in on her floor with chocolate and math problems. I looked over what she'd done, and where she went wrong.

"It looks like you skip a couple steps every time. Does that sound right?"

"Probably, yeah." Her cheeks flushed.

"I'm pretty good with this stuff. I used to tutor back home. Do you want me to be your tutor?"

"Really?" Her eyes brightened. "You'd do that? I'm sure Mom and Dad could pay you."

I waved that off. "You're my friend. It's what friends do."

By the time Heather and Frank got home, I'd helped Kitty correct her mistakes on half of her test. Her smile had fully returned and she was back to throwing M&Ms at me every once in a while.

An inexplicable warmth ran through my veins. It was a warmth I sought out constantly.

But it was never quite the same if it didn't come from Kitty. And that one day in the storage closet at the rink, I screwed it all up.

Chapter 2

Kitty

"She is so pathetic. I heard she sucked him off but she was so bad at it, he made her stop."

My stomach dropped as two other voices laughed. I was in the bathroom before third period. No matter who they were talking about, it wasn't good.

"He pushed her off him like she was diseased. It was hilarious."

"She follows him around like a lost puppy. He only hangs out with her because he has to, anyway. If Frank weren't his best friend, he'd have no reason to be around her," another voice added.

My mind flicked through the roster of boys at our school. The only Frank was my brother.

Me. They were talking about *me*. And Guy. I'd never blown anyone, or offered, much less my brother's best friend. Guy kissed me in a smelly storage closet at the ice rink and Shane and Brooklynn caught us. It must have been Brooklynn with the diseased comment. I was mortified.

On that fateful day of the closet kiss, Guy and I couldn't exactly fight in the car on the way home, because Frankie was there. While I was waiting for him to come unlock the car, I got a barrage of texts from Guy.

GUY-GUY FRENCHIE
I'm sorry Kitty
So so sorry
Can we talk later?

I didn't respond to anything he sent me, tears blurring my view of the winter-brown mountains surrounding the rink. I was humiliated. *Guy* had humiliated me. One of my best friends. My buddy. Not only was it my first kiss from him, it was my first kiss from *anyone*. I could have forgiven it being in a stinky storage closet if it hadn't ended in him shoving me away, in front of other people.

I didn't respond to his texts. I didn't want to hear his excuses. No matter what he did next, I'd still be the pathetic slut that cornered him, and he'd still be Guy Stelle.

The rest of my freshman year was hellish. The names that went around were ever-so-clever, either Slutty Kitty, Hockey Ho, or Pussy-Kitty.

Guy and I never spoke about it directly again. I'm not sure how much he knew about my reputation after the closet kiss. Part of me wanted to ask him to date me, so I could at least have something to show for the accusations. But I was too afraid to ask. And I knew, in no uncertain terms, that he feared what Frank would do if we did. We couldn't break up our little friendship trio. The real miracle is that Frank never heard about the kiss from anyone else, or if he did, he never said anything.

To Guy's credit, he worked overtime to regain our friendship. The day we were due to work on my math homework next, he showed up right on time with a bag of M&Ms.

"Hey, Kitty Cat." He stood in my bedroom doorway, extending the twelve-ounce bag of candy my way. "Ready to math it up?"

I studied him for a long while before patting the floor next to me, where he always sat when we worked on my homework. Our meeting was stilted at first, like we didn't quite know how to be around each other. But before long, we were cracking jokes again, and he asked me to come over that weekend and watch one of our favorite shows together. It was an olive branch. Even though he'd hurt me, perhaps in ways he couldn't even know, he wanted to make it up to me. I missed being his friend, and it was harder to be mad at him than I thought it might be. So I took the proverbial olive branch.

Guy stayed for dinner that night, as he always did after tutoring me. When we got up to go help Mom set the table, he stopped me. He held my shoulders and watched me for a moment, but not like he did before he kissed me. His eyes held a more tragic kind of longing. Then he pecked a kiss on my cheek and pulled me into his arms. He held me tight, and I hugged him back.

"You're my best friend, Kitty Cat," he whispered.

"I thought Frankie was," I snorted.

"He is. But you are, too. And I can't lose you." His voice was serious, a rarity for him. I noted the muscle-over-bone feeling of his ribcage under my hands as he squeezed me one more time before letting me go.

The matter seemed effectively resolved.

Chapter 3

Kitty

My outer left thigh was plastered to Guy's in the backseat. And I do mean plastered. Shellacked. Completely stuck. We'd been on the road without stopping for four hours, with about as many ahead of us. It was unbelievably sweaty in the back of the rented van. No matter how hard my parents blasted the A/C in the front, it wasn't making it to the way-back where Guy and I were. I wondered how much of the sweat was his and how much was mine. As some sort of coping mechanism, Guy had been asleep for about an hour, his head leaned out and his mouth hanging open.

My friend Annie sat in the row in front of me, insisting on sitting next to Frank. It was no secret that she had a crush on him and that he couldn't care less. When she begged to sit next to him instead of me, I knew it would irritate him, so I let her.

Annie and I were going into sophomore year, while Guy and Frank were rising seniors. Like me, Guy had a summer birthday. That summer, he was turning seventeen and I fifteen. Eva had no problem letting Guy join us for our annual Outer Banks trip. It gave her some rare single mom solo time.

I was still pretending I didn't like Guy as anything more than a friend. Sometimes I was even mean to him. In reality, I was still obsessed with him. He was the last thing I thought about before I went to sleep and the first thing when I woke up. I thought about the way he talked. How his "th" sounds always came out like a "d" or a "t": dat, dere, tink. How he had trouble making nouns plural: "I have M&M for you, Kit-ty." I thought about him playing street hockey with Frank with sunlight in his dark waves. I thought about that one time I saw him mowing our neighbor's lawn without a shirt.

I thought about how he came to all of my school plays and gave a standing ovation at the end every single time. How he'd run lines with me to help me memorize. How he helped me with math, and listened to my writing ideas. How his goofy, honking laugh rang out when I really got him going: "A-ha! A-ha! A-ha!" I thought about watching him play hockey at the rink, though those thoughts sometimes came with a more painful reminder of what else had gone down under that roof. Still, he skated circles around everyone else. He was so natural in his body, it was almost poetic.

At school, sometimes he'd ruffle my hair in the hallway, or stop by my locker to tell me about a funny video he saw before sending me the link. I always thought that was cute, like he *had* to tell me about it so he'd make sure I opened it when he sent it. Guy's personal teaser. We always rode to and from school together. I felt like hot stuff every time we walked out of school side by side.

As time went on, I painted our closet kiss with rose-colored glasses. I replayed in excruciating detail everything that happened before we were interrupted. He basically admitted he had feelings for me. And he kissed me, dammit, not the other way around.

I fantasized that he'd make it all up to me with some You Belong With Me Taylor Swift moment. Writing each other messages between our windows when in reality our windows didn't line up like that. Then maybe one day, he'd take me to a school dance.

But he took some other girl to homecoming, and I faked sick when promposals were going around in the spring. I didn't want to deal with catching Guy asking someone else to prom. In general, freshmen couldn't go to prom anyway, but they made an exception if you were in a relationship.

Guy and I weren't in a relationship, though. I sometimes got viciously reminded of it. He'd get Snaps when we were in the same room. If he knew I could see his screen, he clicked it off immediately, but I'd catch him taking a peek later with a little smirk on his face. I had to assume he was talking to girls. My stomach dropped every time I saw him laugh at a message. I wanted the exclusive rights to make him laugh.

But on this beach vacation with my family, Mom mandated that we all only got one hour with our phones each day. Otherwise, they had to be in a basket in the kitchen.

While we were on the beach, Annie read her YA novels and I made notes for my screenwriting projects (all self-assigned). I was convinced I'd have a full screenplay by the end of the summer. Guy and Frank played frisbee and beach volleyball, and occasionally, us girls joined in. Annie was on the volleyball team, so she was quite good.

Days were long and filled with salty, sandy fun. I had that sun-drunk, heavy feeling at the end of every day, when we settled into long games of Phase 10 and Apples to Apples. Halfway through the week, though, there was what I internally refer to as The Incident.

We were all out playing in the water, and Guy and Annie got a little too cozy for my liking. I knew Annie liked Frank. It was a fact I knew well, as she often recounted to me how much of a hottie my own flesh and blood was. She'd never shown even a passing interest in Guy, but I knew just how easy it was to fall for him. I certainly had.

Did I mention that Annie was a bit of a knock-out? She had full C cups to my can-fill-out-a-B-cup-on-my-period boobs. While I was that kind of gangly teenaged thin, she resembled an Olympic athlete. And, as fifteen-year-olds often are, she was in a cute little bikini. I was, too, but the effect was entirely different. I know that when we compare ourselves, the patriarchy wins, but I'm only human. The facts were the facts. Annie was a smokeshow.

The Incident started with innocent splashing between Guy and Annie. Then Guy wrapped his arms around Annie and threw her. Then he picked her up like a freaking bride and sent her squealing into the surf, but not before using his cut, hockey-puck-shooting arms to lift her Olympic athlete stomach to his mouth for one of those raspberry tickles you do on little kids.

Guy put his mouth on Annie's stomach, in front of me. In front of my whole family. Frank looked the other way, and I focused on bodysurfing away from the scene so no one could see my face.

I was livid. I was upset with Annie, though in fairness, I'd never admitted to her that I still liked Guy. She thought I was forever mad at him from the closet kiss. But I was also upset with Guy. I hadn't given him permission to go touching *my* friend. And he was the one spilling his feelings in that closet, not me.

But those were just the lies I told myself. I was most upset because I wished it was me.

I busied myself with reading my book on the shore, claiming I was tired of being wet. Guy and Frank took up a game of catch on the beach. Annie knew I was pissed.

"You good?" She sounded genuinely concerned rather than confrontational.

"I think I'm just about to get my period," I lied. Annie knew I had tidal wave-aggressive periods and all the baggage that comes with them.

"Ugh. The worst," she said sympathetically. Then, like the really good friend she was, she added, "I've got some M&Ms in my suitcase."

"Hey, Kitty Cat!" Guy called as he came back over to our towel and umbrella home base. Little rivulets of water ran down his chest from his hair, making me both swoony and mopey. How dare he be attractive after what he did? "Wanna go look for seashells?"

I was lying on my stomach reading a book. Trying to show that selfish prick what he was missing, I squished whatever boob meat I had together as I looked up to respond. "No thanks. I'm kinda tired."

Guy puffed out his bottom lip. "I saw some kid with a really big one, though. You won't help me?" He cocked his head to the side. Why was he trying to be so playful with me?

"His parents probably bought it at a store and planted it," I said dismissively. "Take Frank."

Then Guy was shuffling next to me, moving the umbrella so I was in the shade.

"What are you doing?" I grumped at him.

"You're turning red. You'll burn when you nap." He put my bookmark in my book and closed it for me. "You'll look for shells with me tomorrow, yeah? Please?"

His brown eyes watched me with a puppyish optimism, like he'd laid a toy in front of me and was wagging his tail for me to throw it. I was still mad at him, but as usual, his cuteness won out.

"Fine," I huffed.

When Annie and I had showered and were getting ready for dinner, she sat on the edge of her twin bed, combing her wet hair. She eyed me nervously.

"You like Guy." My throat went dry.

"What are you talking about? He's like a brother to me," I managed.

"Kitty." Annie's freckles really stood out from her sun-stained face. "You can be real with me."

I couldn't say anything. I just nodded. My secret was out.

"Look, I got carried away with him today when I knew better. You're more important than him. I don't even really like him," Annie admitted, eyes trained on her cuticles. "But you do. You should be out there playing with him, too."

"I don't know if you recall, but we've kissed before and he famously shoved me off of him. He doesn't want me," I said miserably.

Annie rolled her eyes. "That was all because of Frank. And because your families are intertwined and he doesn't want to mess that up."

"You think?" I asked.

"Yes, I'm sure."

I groaned and fell back on my bed, wet hair sticking to my neck and shoulders. "I need to find someone else to like. Why does he have to be so, I don't know, perfect?"

"I'm sorry, Kitty. Life sucks sometimes."

"It really does."

Chapter 4

Guy

I woke up screaming. I'd been doing that a lot that summer. I went through a phase of it after one of Papa's particularly bad anger fits, but for some reason, the screams and bad dreams were back.

I knew the only way out of it was to get up and do something else. Laying in bed just made me replay the dreams on a loop. I decided to take advantage of the ocean-front property and go sit on the beach.

I sat, staring out at the whitecaps visible in the moonlight. I'd been out there maybe 20 minutes when I heard someone approaching. I looked just in time to see Kitty turning back to the house, a blanket in her arms and a single braid in her hair. She had on sporty shorts and a sweatshirt, looking all cozy.

"Hey! Where are you going?"

Kitty froze. "I-I didn't want to bother you," she stammered.

"You never bother me. Come sit."

I helped her spread out the blanket on the cold sand and sat on it with her. "Can't sleep?"

I gave her a wry smile. "Nightmare. You?"

"Something like that." She stared out at the water, chewing her lip.

We didn't say anything else for a while, sitting in companionable silence and watching the waves. Crash, roll, fizz. Crash, roll, fizz. The wind picked up a little and Kitty shivered. I turned to her, the moon lighting her delicate features. I studied the cupid's bow of her lips and the way her nose turned up ever-so-slightly at the end.

"Scooch up," I said. Kitty did, shifting to the middle of the blanket and hugging her knees to her chest. I moved with her and wrapped the blanket around our shoulders. I left my arm around Kitty. It felt so nice to hold her like that. It was how I wanted things to be, but they couldn't. Our families were basically one. Kitty even spent hours on the porch chatting with Maman on her nights off, sipping iced tea and bonding in that way that women do.

Kitty didn't turn her face toward me, but she didn't shake off my arm either. She was mad about something.

"What's bothering you? You've been grumpy all day," I prodded.

"Nothing."

I wiggled my arm against her. "Come on, *ma puce*. You're angry."

Kitty was silent for a while, but knowing her like I did, I knew she was just gearing up to talk. When she did, I almost couldn't hear her.

"I didn't know you liked Annie."

I sucked in a breath and held it. "I don't like Annie."

She pursed her lips like she didn't believe me as she looked over at me.

"You know it's you, Kitty."

She was silent, avoiding my gaze. A ragged breath came from her. "Then why did you leave me out to dry all year? Why didn't you date me? Why did you let everyone think I'm some kind of slut when it was you who kissed me?"

Guilt, shame, and a wave of nausea washed over me. I'd heard some people talk about Kitty here and there, but I didn't know if those rumors came from me or from somewhere else.

"Kitty, I can't give you what you need."

She scoffed. "Bullshit. Just because our families are close? Your mom would be thrilled if we dated. My parents love you. Frank would get over it."

"No, it's not just that. I'm not who you think I am."

She blanched. "What's that supposed to mean?"

I'd never told anyone the truth about my dad. Not friends back home, not Frank, no one.

"My dad." Those two words held so much weight for me, and that weight crushed down on my chest, constricting my breath. Kitty put her hand on my knee. She knew I was struggling. I fell silent.

"What happened with your dad?"

I looked over into her eyes. She was my Kitty. My person. And she might never see me the same way again after I told her. I covered her hand on my knee with my own, and she flipped hers and squeezed mine.

"You know I won't judge you. I know you, Guy. I'm here for you."

I took a deep breath. "He left for good maybe a year ago. He's always had a problem with getting mad, anger. You know?"

Kitty nodded and I went on. "He'd be fine for a while. Then he'd just get so mad about something. He never actually hit me or Maman, but he'd get pretty scary. Then it's like he'd wake up from it and just be mad at himself. He'd disappear for days and go drinking. The time before he left for good, he put a hole through our bathroom wall. Through the tile and everything. That was the only time Maman asked him to leave. She was worried for all of us. I think we all knew if she asked, he wasn't coming back."

Kitty squeezed my hand again and stayed quiet, waiting for me to say more. "He knew he couldn't be what we needed, so he left. It was hard when he was there but it's hard with him gone, too. Being in Quebec, his memory was everywhere. It bothered me, but it really got to Maman. She hated him for leaving us like that, even though she'd asked him to. I think we both wished he could have been better. We moved to get away from it all, have a new start."

"I'm so sorry, Guy. That's awful."

"Your family is so important to me and Maman, Kitty. But really, it's because I don't want to do all that to you."

"Guy, you're not your dad. You know that, right? I've never seen you mad once."

"I've been mad when people say things about you." It's true. I considered punching out anyone who said something about Kitty.

"That's not the same thing, Guy. Everyone gets mad. You're a good person." She held my arm for emphasis. "You're not him."

"Yeah, but he played hockey, too. Maman thinks his anger was from getting hit too many times." Emotion bubbled up inside me and tears pricked my eyes. "I still want to play. What if the same thing happens to me? I don't want to be like him. It's almost like I have to choose hockey or having a family someday."

Kitty pulled my head into her chest and held me there while I cried. I'd never cried in front of her. Hardly anyone, really. She was so calm.

"Didn't he play kind of a while ago?" she asked. "And aren't the rules different now?"

"Kind of. I don't know. People still get hit hard," I sniffed, sitting up.

"You're still not him, Guy-Guy. And you know what to watch out for. I don't think you should compare yourself. Or give up hockey. If it's what you want to do, you should do it."

My heart felt lighter. She understood how important the game was to me. I didn't really know what to say. Once again, Kitty just got me.

"Thanks." She rubbed my back. The warmth that we shared physically and emotionally thrummed between us. "I just feel kinda doomed."

"I can see why you'd feel that way." She drew shapes in the sand with her toes. "Wanna tell me about your bad dream?"

I inhaled and held it for a moment. "I was running. Couldn't stop. Something was chasing me. I've had problems with sleeping lately. I'm worried about Maman."

"What do you mean? Why?"

"I'm not sure. I think she's not feeling good. She's been taking medicine a lot, and when she comes home from work, she's always getting off the phone with my Grandmere." I winced. "She hardly talked to her before we left home. I'm afraid Maman is sick."

"Sick how?"

"I don't know," I said. "Something just seems wrong. I can't figure out what's making her hurt so bad to need medicine all the time like that. I've asked her and she just shrugs me off. 'Oh, it's just getting old,' or 'Oh, just a headache.' I'm afraid we'll have to go back to Canada."

"Guy, really?" Kitty's eyes were big, brow furrowed.

"I'm not sure how much longer her visa is. I can stay because I'm a student, but she might not be able to. Healthcare costs so much in America. At least at home, it'd be free."

Kitty let out a little whimper. "I hope that's not true. I love your mom."

"She loves you, too, Kitty Cat." A smile curved my lips thinking of how close the two of them had gotten. "The daughter she always wanted."

"I'm sorry," Kitty said, dropping her head to my shoulder and putting her arm around my back. I returned her embrace, tightening my arm on her side. We were hip to hip and wrapped up in the blanket. It was a bittersweet moment, but there was nowhere else I would have rather been. Time passed as we watched the waves in comfortable silence. Just being together.

"What's *ma puce?*" Kitty asked.

I shrugged, hoping she didn't feel the pulse of heat waft off my body. "Just a little name."

She pondered that answer. "Do you call anyone else that?"

"Never. Just you," I said seriously. "I can't call you Kitty Cat all the time. I can't believe that's your real name."

"It's Kitty Gatto."

"Which is Kitty Cat," I teased.

"My parents are sadists." She blew out a puff of air. "You know what's weird? I don't even like cats all that much."

I laughed. Not what I was expecting Kitty to say after all the serious stuff we'd talked about.

"Okay, then, Kitty Cat. What's your favorite animal?"

She sat, pensive. "I kinda like birds."

My face warmed at her sweet and simple answer. "Kitty Bird. That sounds nice. I'll call you Kitty Bird."

"Or KB for short," Kitty joked.

"Or Birdy," I countered.

"Birdy's nice."

"Or *ma puce*."

"That works, too," Kitty said. "What do you want me to call you? Guy-Guy Frenchie?"

"I like that one," I said, booping her nose. Then I went more serious. "I like that you call me Guy when no one else does."

"Then I'll call you Guy."

I sat watching her, my arm still around her waist. I wanted to kiss her, this girl who made me laugh, made me feel alive, and saw me for who I was.

I nuzzled her neck. She turned to face me then, letting me glide my hand along her cheek. I wanted to tell her just how much I felt for her, but words didn't seem enough. My fingers slid into her hair as my lips hovered over hers. Our breaths mingled, eyes trained on each other's mouths.

The space between us closed, her lips tasting faintly of her strawberry lip balm but mostly of her. Finally, I was getting to enjoy her the way I wanted to the first time I kissed her. Her hand clasped around my neck, thumb stroking the little bit of stubble on my jaw. My stomach tingled as her tongue met mine. I deepened our kiss, devouring her. She let out a tiny whimper that awakened something primal in me. I pulled her so she was in my lap, and she arranged her legs to straddle me.

This was fucking heaven.

Our kiss didn't break until I laid back in the sand. Kitty pulled the blanket up behind my head so I wasn't just in the cold sand. That little action to take care of me meant so much. We hardly ever got to show each other that we cared. I held her waist as she looked down at me.

"You're beautiful."

"So are you," she beamed. I reached up to kiss her again, pulling her down as her weight laid into me. My hand slipped under her sweatshirt, feeling the soft skin of her belly.

"Okay?" I asked.

"Yeah," she whispered, starting our bruising kiss over again. She felt so good on top of me, just kissing while my hand explored under her shirt. She moaned as my palm found her soft cotton bra, and I couldn't believe any of it was happening. Kitty Gatto, my best friend's little sister, his *beautiful* little sister, *my* best friend, was letting me touch her in a way that felt so foreign and natural at the same time. Foreign because it was her, and natural because it had always been her for me.

My thumb dipped into her bra, carefully stroking over her hard nipple. She pulled out of our kiss and held her face over mine, eyes wild and panting.

"That alright?" I asked again. I was pretty sure I had more experience than her and I wanted her to be comfortable.

"It is, but," she paused, looking down at my chest, "I've never gone all the way before."

I nodded, understanding. "I haven't either. Should we stop?"

She wrinkled her nose, looking disappointed. "Probably."

I kissed her. "I'm good with that. Wanna snuggle?"

"Hell yeah," she said with a smile. I flipped so we were both on our sides, facing each other. Our kisses rolled on with more tenderness. We fell asleep with her tucked against my chest, the waves and our own breathing our lullaby.

Chapter 5

Guy

When I got back from the beach trip with the Gattos, everything fell apart. Maman had drinks with Heather the night we got back, and she came home red-eyed and puffy-faced.

Maman sat me down the next morning and told me what was going on. I was right. She was sick. While I was at the beach, she had a number of medical tests done. She had Stage III ovarian cancer. The prognosis was uncertain, but with the cost of healthcare in the States, it didn't make sense for her to stay.

She told me I could stay if I wanted. Heather and Mark offered to take me in to finish high school. But I could never leave her alone to manage her sickness. If I was going to lose her, I was damn well going to be there with her every step of the way.

And besides, I didn't really have anywhere to keep up my hockey skills in West Virginia. That was my likely ticket to a good college. Going home to Quebec where I could sharpen my skills and get scouted made far more sense. Our life on the run was coming to a close.

So for the second time in my life, I was packing it all up and driving away. When Maman and Heather had wine in the Gattos' backyard that next night, they invited Kitty to join them. Frank and I snuck some liquor out of his parents' liquor cabinet and got drunk, too. Our moms knew, but they didn't care. Frank was a pretty tough guy, not really one to show a ton of emotion. We both lost it that night, though. It just wasn't fair, for any of us. Especially Maman, of course, but it was ripping all of us apart.

Kitty texted me that night while she was drinking with our moms.

> **KITTY BIRD**
> You should hear them singing
> It's hilarious
> Come up here
> > Me n Frankie 2 drunk
> lol
> I'm here for you tho Frenchie
> > <3

I hid those texts from Frank. I hadn't told him about kissing Kitty, nor did I act any differently toward her on our trip. Once I found out what was going on with Maman, I was glad I hadn't told Frank. No sense making him mad at me right before I left. It was selfish of me and unfair to Kitty. I wished I could have her out in the open without everything getting messy.

I was hung over the next day. Maman had to go into work, as she was determined to work her last few shifts at the restaurant. Around noon, I sent Kitty a message. I was still laying in bed, miserable.

> > Can u come over
> **KITTY BIRD**
> on my way <3

I heard the front door open and her climbing the stairs.

"Up here," I called from my third-floor room. It was a converted attic, and Maman was nice enough to let me have it all to myself. I sat with my head in my hands at the edge of my bed, not sure how I wanted to greet her. My bed was unmade, and I was still in my athletic shorts and t-shirt from the night before.

"Guy." The way she said my name held the weight of everything we faced. Her nose sounded stuffed up, probably from crying and being miserable like I was. I lifted my pounding head to look at her. Her hair was in a wet ponytail that left a damp spot on her shoulder. She wore her wandering around the house clothes: a big t-shirt, tiny shorts, and flip-flops. Her skin glowed from our time at the beach. That seemed like a lifetime ago, even though it had only been a couple of days. So much had changed.

She was pretty. So very pretty. She knew more about me than anyone in the world. And I was probably never going to see her again after we moved.

Kitty crossed the room and sat next to me on the bed, putting a tentative hand on my back. It wasn't nighttime like it had been at the beach. We weren't in a closet. We were sitting on my bed, alone in my house. Under different circumstances, I might have picked up where we left off on the beach. But I needed Kitty in a different way than that. I needed her as my best friend. I leaned into her side at first, then gave in and put my head in her lap. When my body shook with tears, she cried, too. She comforted me while grieving it all in her own way.

"I'm sorry," she whispered when my crying slowed. I nodded, letting her lightly scratch my scalp with her nails. It felt so nice.

"I have bad news," she said. I turned on my back to look up at her and raised my eyebrows. What could get worse? "You stink, Guy-Guy."

I coughed out a laugh. "Sorry. Your brother got me drunk." I sat up and wiped my face.

"Yeah, well, your mom got me drunk and I don't stink," she jabbed. "You eat anything?"

I shook my head. She stood up and offered me her hand. "Go clean yourself up. I'll make you some food."

I took her hand and stood, bending to kiss her temple. "I don't deserve you, *ma puce*."

Kitty's whole face flushed and her eyes went sad. She pretended to study some hockey sticks tacked to my wall. I didn't kiss her after our middle-of-the-night beach make-out, even though I wanted to. I dated other girls, but Kitty was always my favorite. I was so comfortable around her. I didn't have to put on a front with her. She was Just Kitty, and I could be Just Guy.

I just didn't want to taint her with my problems. I really *didn't* deserve her. If I was anything like my dad, I'd ruin her just like Papa ruined Maman. Better to keep it light and breezy with someone who didn't matter than ruin the one who mattered the most.

Then there's the fact that Frank might have killed me. I don't really get why. If Kitty was mine, I'd treat her so nice. I wouldn't screw her around like I did the other girls. I only gave them half my efforts because I really wanted Kitty.

The cycle went on: I half-assed with a girl, she got mad at me, Frank saw it, Frank swore I'd never be touching his sister.

Plus, what if we broke up and I lost Heather, Mark, *and* Frank, too? I couldn't lose my bonus family.

But none of that really mattered when Maman and I were going back to Canada.

Showered and teeth brushed, I entered our tiny living room. Kitty sat with two plates of grilled cheese and a foolish number of extra pickles on our plates, plus a couple of Dr. Peppers on the coffee table. She knew they were my favorite.

"Did you go to your house for those?" I asked. Maman didn't let us have soda. She said they'd rot my teeth.

Kitty nodded with a sly smile. "I can recycle them at my house, too. Hide the evidence."

"You get me."

"What do you want to watch?" she asked.

"That old UCB special?" Kitty, Frank, and I loved improv comedy shows. Upright Citizens Brigade was one of our go-to's. Frank and I were just there for the laughs, but Kitty seemed to absorb it in a different way. She was a student of the craft, dedicating herself to understanding how to form jokes. She said she wanted to study comedy writing at Alden. I thought she'd be perfect for it.

We sat on our respective ends of the couch and watched while we ate, laughing around our grilled cheese and pickle feast. When I was done, I decided it was now or never. I was moving away. I'd never see Kitty again after we left West Virginia. I knew how to be smooth with girls, but I found myself sweating trying to figure out how to get close to Kitty. I'd even kissed her before. Why was I such a mess? While I shifted in my seat and deliberated, she looked over at me.

"You okay? Why are you looking at me like that?"

"Like what?" I asked.

"Like you have ants in your pants or something."

I laughed nervously. "Ants?" My breathing went shallow and fast. My heart galloped in my chest. I wiped my sweaty palms on my shorts. "Kitty Bird, I . . ."

Our eyes locked, her deep brown studying me with X-ray like vision. Understanding washed over her expression.

"I know." Did she though? Did she know how much I loved her? As a friend, and as the person who just seemed to get me?

"I don't think you do," I said.

"I know you don't want to leave. But I know you have to. We can still talk."

She didn't know. She didn't know about the love. I went with her line of thinking.

"It won't be the same," I whispered.

She shook her head. "It won't."

We sat, watching each other for a long while. Then, after fidgeting with her hands, she looked back up at me and opened her arms. I scooted in and held her close to me. I almost couldn't breathe. Then the words finally fell out of me, so quietly I wasn't sure I said them at all.

"I love you."

Kitty nodded into my chest. "I love you, too. I always will."

I squeezed her tighter, tucking my head into her shoulder. My lips met the side of her neck for a soft kiss. I pulled back slightly and used my hand to lift her face to mine. We paused, some pain in her eyes.

"I don't want to leave you," I said. "I wish I could stay. I wish I could bring you with me."

Kitty gave a wry smile. "She needs you, Guy."

"But I need you, too."

Kitty's brow furrowed like I'd shattered her heart. Her mouth met mine. Tenderly, I showed her what she was to me, in a way I couldn't express with words at the time. Kitty was my person. I was sure of it, down to my bones. She deepened the kiss with a slant of her mouth, her tongue bringing a pastel light into the dark depths of my mind. I loved Kitty Gatto and I'd never get over it.

And that was the last kiss we had before I left for good.

Chapter 6

Kitty

Mom got the call from Guy's grandmere as we were about to leave for a school event one September evening. Eva was going to die soon. Our whole family threw clothes in bags, got in the car with our passports, and drove through the night to be there. Mom told off the school secretary in grand fashion when she argued that we'd be penalized for missing school unplanned.

We lived on gas station coffee and roller dogs. Mom, Dad, and Frank traded off driving. It was significantly more frightening with a caffeinated Frank behind the wheel. Mom kicked him out of the driver's seat after an hour.

When we got there, Mom went straight for Eva's room, while Frank and Guy hugged it out. I waited my turn. No matter what had transpired over the summer, I wasn't about to lay a big smooch on Guy. He gave me a big bear hug.

"Thanks for being here." His breath was warm against my hair. His accent was back to being thicker again. Through the year he spent in West Virginia, it had faded some. It was back in full force.

"I wouldn't miss it," I whispered under his crushing embrace. An hour or so later, Mom came out of Eva's room and ushered the rest of us in there. Guy took my hand as we went in. He was used to seeing her, but he knew I wasn't. Eva looked about as bad as you expect someone dying of cancer to look. Her face was gaunt, her already petite frame just skin and bones. But around her eyes, I could still see the soft kindness that was her baseline mood. We all took a turn giving her hugs.

"Kitty, I want to talk to you alone, *ma puce*," she said, her voice weak and crackly. I gave her a smile as everyone else shuffled out. Guy fussed over her in French before she shooed him away.

"How are you feeling?" I asked.

"Like death," she said, deadpan. We both laughed, not because her dying was funny, but because her honesty was. "I am so happy I got to know you, Kitty. I always wanted a little girl, and our talks last year gave me a taste of what it would be like. Thank you for that."

"Of course," I said. "I loved that time with you."

She took a breath. "We talked a little about boys and matters of the heart, but I think there was something you didn't want me to know."

I panicked. I'd told her I had an unwarranted bad reputation, but I never told her it was Guy's fault. I wasn't planning on leaking that while she was on her deathbed either.

I looked at her sidelong. "What do you think that is?"

"I think you and Guy are meant for each other. And I think you know that."

I was quiet for a moment. "I know he did you wrong, Kitty. And that you forgave him."

I nodded. "I did."

"I hate that he hurt you. He told me what he did and he feels terrible about it. But I really think he loves you."

I gave a soft snort. "He told me he does."

She exhaled and looked to the heavens. "*Dieu merci*. He's not as stupid as I feared. I was afraid he had too much of his father in him, a hockey boy screwing anything on legs. Guy dates all these girls, but they don't fit him like you do."

My stomach turned at the thought of who else he might be dating, but her words made me feel a little better. "But we live so far apart."

"Yes, *ma cherie*, but you might not always. You're young. You'll live your life and sow your oats, but I want you to at least try to come together at some point. If I'm wrong, I'm wrong. I'm on a lot of drugs. But I've known this for a while. Can you promise me you will try for each other?"

Her eyes were serious.

"Have you told him this?"

"He knows." She winced in pain and grabbed for my hand. I let her grip me tightly, until her wave of pain seemingly passed.

"Yes, Maman. I'll try."

"Good." She squeezed my hand.

"He calls me *ma puce*, too. What does it mean?"

"Oh?" Eva's eyes brightened. "He knows more than he shows. It means 'little flea.' You either use it to talk sweetly to a little girl or to a girlfriend who you love very much."

I laughed. "He probably thinks I'm just a little girl."

"I don't think so. But my boy has made mistakes with you before. He might be a stupid boy, too." We laughed together like we had so many times on her porch as the sun went down. The weight of the fact that she was almost gone pressed in.

"I wish you didn't have to go," I said, tears filling my eyes.

"I know. But it's my time. I know you and your family will look after my Guy," Eva said. "We almost stayed in a town north of Charleston, you know. Guy was the one who made me go more south. If we hadn't, we would not have you Gattos."

I got chills from her saying that. The two of them had been such a force since they entered our lives. I told her I loved her and left her to rest. When I went back into the living room, I found a face I didn't recognize. A girl. A very pretty girl.

"Kitty, this is Elise," Guy said. "My girlfriend."

The room felt hot. I wanted to puke. I wanted to run. Guy and I texted, but we always talked about stupid stuff: inside jokes, videos, memes. Never anything substantial like boyfriends or girlfriends. But I wasn't there to flirt with Guy, or kiss Guy.

I was there to be a good friend to him, and to say goodbye to Eva.

"Hi," I croaked, extending my hand for a shake. Her perfectly manicured hand barely held mine for a second. I did my best to make small talk. I was distracted by taking in her features. Of course Guy would go for someone so pretty and polished. She looked like she came from the Pretty Girl Store, not a hair out of place, generically beautiful. It almost made me want to be more of the gritty, sarcastic, biting person that I was. I wanted to cover myself in tattoos and piercings to prove how opposite I was of what he really liked. I wasn't even a tattoo or piercing person. I just felt like I had to rebel somehow to show my feelings were definitely, 100% not hurt.

Then I remembered what Eva and I had discussed and realized I needed to give it a shot. She was right. We'd go our own ways, and I had to accept it. We thought we'd never see each other again when he left West Virginia. He was free to date people, and so was I. But my heart felt like it could never love anyone but him.

Still, I breathed a little easier after Elise went home for the evening. She tried to kiss Guy inside, but he rushed to give her a hug and push her out the door. A small victory for me, even though I knew I had no right to him. We weren't really expecting to see each other again.

In the night, Guy came into the room I was sharing with Mom. Silent tears wet his face.

"I think she's going," he said, fear in his voice. Mom and I leapt up and ran to Eva's room, joining Guy at her bedside. Grandmere was already there, making continued signs of the cross as Eva's breathing got more labored. I'd never been there when someone died. I was scared. Mom sat next to Grandmere. Guy held one of Eva's hands, and I held his other hand. He whispered things to her in French, continually kissing her hand.

With one final gasp, Eva breathed her last. Grandmere led us in a Hail Mary in French. Mom and I mumbled along in English.

Guy laid his head on her bed and sobbed, not letting go of my hand. When he sat up, I pulled him into my chest and held him there. I wanted to absorb his pain, to somehow carry it for him.

Mom closed Eva's eyes and kissed her best friend's forehead one last time. Then she opened the window. I glared at her, confused.

"To let her soul leave," Mom said. "A country thing. I'll make the calls." She stopped to kiss Guy on the head and pat his back before quietly leaving the room. I started to stand to leave, too, but Guy pulled me down.

"Stay. Please." His eyes were so desperate, heartbreaking. And so I stayed while the undertaker came. I sat with Guy as he sat with his grief. Grandmere left the room when the undertaker did, leaving me with Guy and the empty bed.

"Do you want to go outside?" I asked him. He nodded.

It was cold. September in Quebec was a different affair than September in West Virginia. He draped a spare jacket around my shoulders as we sat on the top step of the porch. He pulled a pack of cigarettes out of his own jacket pocket.

"Those things'll kill you," I mused.

"Good," he grumbled.

"Guy." I took his hand.

"I know. I'm not going to do anything. I just have no one now. Papa left. Maman's gone. I have no parents."

"I'm sorry," I said, and let silence fall between us. "It's not the same, but you'll always have me."

He leaned into me, putting his head on my shoulder. I put my arm around him, letting him feel me as his cigarette's scent filled the crisp air. "I wish you could stay. I don't want you to go home."

"Me, too," I said. "I could watch you play hockey with people who actually fit your skill level. And brush up on my French."

He laughed softly. "Your French is terrible, *ma puce*. You'd be silent up here."

"Don't think I won't tell you to fuck off just because you're grieving," I said, flicking his leg. He chuckled and put his hand on my knee. I held out my hand for the cigarette. "Give me a hit of that."

"No. You have to stay healthy so you can wipe my butt when we're old," he said with a sad smirk.

"Who says you're not wiping my butt? You're the athlete. You'll probably be in better shape when we're old."

"Nah. I push my body too hard. I'll fall apart way sooner."

"Make a bunch of money playing hockey so we can pay someone to wipe our butts," I decided.

"Works for me."

It was a strange conversation to be having when someone too young had just died, not even getting the chance to grow old. And Guy had a girlfriend. I didn't want to bring up what Eva had asked of us, but his words implied we'd be together in the end. I was trying to go along with whatever he wanted to talk about. I was devastated, too, but it wasn't my mother. I still had both of my parents.

"I'm tired," Guy said finally, crushing out his cigarette.

"Let's get you to bed." I stood and offered him my hand. I headed for the door, but before I could open it, Guy pulled me to him.

"I don't want to be alone. I've been sleeping in her room every night," he said. "Will you come with me?"

"Sure." My parents might have freaked if they got up and found the two of us in bed together. I left a little note on the kitchen counter to say "I'm with Guy." We left Guy's bedroom door open so they'd know we weren't messing around.

We didn't bother brushing our teeth. We were both gross, but I followed Guy's lead. He was the bereaved. We faced each other again in bed like we had when we fell asleep on the beach before everything went sideways. Guy cried more, and I stroked his hair.

His body had stilled so much that I thought he was already asleep, but he cracked his eyes open.

"I love you, Birdy."

"I know. I love you, too."

His thumb brushed my cheekbone, holding my jaw, his barely-open eyes looking into mine. He planted a soft, cigarette-flavored kiss on my lips. I rested my hand on his cheek as we tasted each other. It wasn't going anywhere. Sweet and gentle. Just us showing our love. Just one kiss. Then another on my forehead. And then he succumbed to his exhaustion and fell asleep.

Part 2:
The Rush

Chapter 7

Guy

It was my junior year at Alden. It was all a bit of a sham anyway. I was already signed with the Seattle Sealpups and would be leaving at the end of the year. I'd stayed every summer to take extra classes so I could finish my degree early, hoping I'd get picked up by some NHL team. That sounds cocky, but I had scouts beating down the door all through my senior year of high school. It was overwhelming with just Grandmere to help me figure it all out.

So, I stayed on at Alden to prove I was worthy of my meal ticket after I signed.

Kitty and I fell out of touch over the years. She sent lots of messages in those first few months after Maman died, but I kinda hid from them. I still talked to Frank, or at least exchanged Snaps with him. Heather called me every once in a while to check on me, and sent me care packages full of my favorite goodies.

But sometimes talking to Kitty was too painful. Kitty was the one who held my hand and took care of me when Maman died. She held onto me as they closed the casket. She made sure I ate and helped me sleep until her family had to leave after the funeral.

I never told my poor girlfriend at the time, Elise. She was another case of a girl who I wasted time with while the one I really cared about was unreachable.

And I wasn't in a place where I could reach Kitty anyway.

It just hurt too much. Talking to her reminded me of Maman dying, and of the promise I made to her.

I still loved Kitty. I never stopped. But it was hard knowing she was so far away, and that I couldn't have her.

Frank told me that she wrote a play that was getting put on at her school during her senior year. I tried to figure out a way to go to Charleston to see it, but it just didn't work with my practice schedule. Instead, I found a little gold necklace of a tiny bird, the kind I'd seen on our street in West Virginia. I made sure it would arrive the day of her play starting.

My note read like this:

KB –
A little bird told me your play is opening tonight.
I know it'll be great, because you made it. I'm so proud of you.
Love, Guy-Guy

She sent a snap with a picture of her wearing the necklace and a thank you. Later that night, after the play had closed, she sent me a text.

Kitty Bird
I miss you

I sat on it for a while. I missed her terribly, but I was embarrassed about how bad I was at keeping in touch. That night, after I'd had many drinks to celebrate our win over Princeton, I broke away from the party to call her. I left a voicemail that I'm sure was a drunken mess. It was 2 a.m., so of course, she was asleep like a reasonable high schooler. I don't remember all of what I said, but it was something like this:

"Hey, Kitty Bird. I hope your play was good. You're a star. I miss seeing you. I love you forever."

She sent me a text reply in the morning.

Kitty Bird
You're a dork. Love you too

And that was about the extent of it. At that point, I assumed our I love you's had morphed into friendship I love you's. I didn't have the right to her heart, especially since I hadn't done anything to earn it and had left her hanging. Again. Just like I did when I didn't stick up for her after kissing her. I had my reasons, but I realized that I was in a pattern with her. Not a good one.

Frank told me she was going to Alden, but Kitty didn't mention it. I think she was secretly mad for all the time I spent avoiding her. Maybe mad's not the right word, but she understood that it wasn't our time to try like Maman had asked.

Then on move-in weekend for freshmen, the Gattos insisted I join them for dinner while they dropped Kitty off. Kitty was civil, but didn't say much. She was so fucking pretty, but there was a cool air about her that told me to back off. We had to wait at the restaurant, so Kitty and I stood outside while Mark and Heather sat to wait inside.

"So, Alden, huh?" I scuffed my shoes on the ground, hands in my pockets. "You get all moved in?"

"I didn't come here for you." The way she delivered it sounded like a mobster in a trench coat casually flicking her cigarette into the gutter. Our last interaction had been so friendly that I was somewhat shocked by her stormy mood.

"Yeah. I get it. You wanted to go here first. I had a full ride, so I went for it," I said, trying to warm her up.

"Must be nice," she scoffed. "Some of us will have debt for an eternity."

Kitty was truly like a cat hissing at me. Maybe she *was* pissed at me.

"Well, it's really good to see you again," I tried. "Your necklace looks good. How was your play?"

She softened the tiniest fraction, touching the tiny bird at the hollow of her throat. "It was good. You should've seen Mr. Bangor trying to manage it all."

She launched into the story and I did my best to encourage her and get her to smile. Luckily, our table got called, and we went inside. Heather ran the show, asking me about hockey and my schoolwork. Kitty was mostly pleasant until Heather asked me to give Kitty tips for school.

"Mom, I can settle in on my own just fine. Guy doesn't have to be my tour guide," Kitty insisted, cutting her salad into minuscule pieces. I'd never seen lettuce so small.

While it was good to see Mark and Heather, I couldn't tell if Kitty was embarrassed by her parents or just wanted space from me. It probably was awkward for her. People spread rumors about us in the past. The rumor mill was probably turning again saying she followed me to college. But I didn't see her much on campus, just a passing hello here and there. I got the impression she was doing her own thing. I figured when the time was right, I'd see her. I just hoped it was soon.

One fateful night in October, I got my wish. Oh, I got to see her, alright.

I was at a frat party. I wasn't a frat member, but being an athlete gets you invited to a lot of parties. It was a real raucous one, just the kind I liked for finding a good-enough chick to go home with. In fact, a look around the room showed a number of previous hookups that I needed to avoid.

I was, shall we say, extremely sexually active. But I rarely repeated a hookup. I never really dated anyone. I definitely never loved anyone. That title was reserved for one person.

My attention was drawn to the bar, where some of the elder frat bros were helping some girls stand up on the bar. All of them were clad only in underwear and white t-shirts. Some frat boys stood by with water guns. I could see where the night was going.

"Pathetic freshmen," Sonya, the girl who was hanging on me that night, said. "I can't believe they fall for it every year."

"Let's see who the winner will be, shall we?" some douche named Ross called out. "Ladies, are you ready?"

One girl, in particular, threw her hands up, drawing the t-shirt up to reveal a very tiny thong. Like, so tiny I could see the sides of her pussy lips. I wished that little scrap of fabric weren't there at all. Her legs were toned, meeting perfectly just after her knees. I could see the hint of her ass when she stepped her legs apart. She was hot as hell. My eyes drew upward and met a tiny bird necklace. And that's when I realized who it was.

I locked eyes with hers, and she smirked. "STOP!"

I charged toward the bar and the crowd parted for me as I pushed through.

"What the fuck, Guy?" Sonya yelled after me. I barely heard her and I didn't give a shit.

"Hi, Guy," the girl on the bar crooned. Her eyes were slightly glazed over.

"Kitty Bird, get down from there. Where are your pants?"

"Not sure," she said with a sly shrug. It set her off balance, and she almost fell off the bar. She had to be wasted, or close to it. I held her calves to stabilize her.

"I'm giving you one more chance to get down." My tone wasn't that far off from her dad when she was in trouble.

"Make me. Stop embarrassing yourself, Guy," she said, rolling her eyes. "I know what I'm doing."

"Okay, then." I took off my jacket. I wrapped my arm behind her knees, forcing her to bend and fall over my shoulder. I put the jacket over her bare ass that hung next to my face as she squealed and thrashed. "You sure you don't know where your pants are?"

"Let go of me, Guy Stelle! I can make my own decisions!" she screamed at me from behind my back.

"Not today, you can't. Where are your pants?"

She lifted herself bolt up to my shoulder, sliding down the front of my body. I ignored the fact that her bare ass passed through my hands. "What the fuck are you doing, Guy?"

"I'm keeping you from getting into trouble, that's what."

"Oh, and you're just rescuing me? What about all the other damsels in distress up there?" Kitty raged, flinging a hand toward the bar.

"*They're* not my best friend," I huffed.

"Best friend? Really, Guy? You stopped talking to me!"

"You've been mad at me! You haven't wanted to talk to me!" I objected.

"Before that, Frenchie!"

People were staring. One girl had her phone out, taking a video of the scene. I had to get us out of there if we were going to fight.

"We're leaving," I said. "We need to talk."

"Fucking clearly," she said, stomping off to a bedroom upstairs and hurling my jacket at me.

"Where are you going?" I demanded.

"To get my pants you want me to wear so fucking badly," she yelled. I watched her ass jiggle with every indignant stomp she made. I had to tell my body to behave. I didn't want to be attracted to drunk Kitty. Sober Kitty? All bets were off. But if I put moves on Kitty that night, I'd have been no better than the sleazebags downstairs running the wet t-shirt contest.

Kitty thundered back down the stairs a few minutes later in jeans, but no jacket.

"Aren't you going to be cold?" The outlines of her tight, dark nipples were visible through that white t-shirt. I'd seen way more of Kitty than ever in my life, all in the span of fifteen minutes.

"I'm fine," she protested with a shiver. I sighed and helped her into my jacket, then stepped us out on the porch and ordered a ride.

"You think I'm going with you? Don't think I don't know about you. Everyone knows what a player you are," she spat.

"I'm a player, but you were about to show your ass and titties to a room full of fucking predators? How does that work?"

Her cheeks flamed hot. "Don't slut shame me, Guy. And you were in that room, too. I can do what I want."

"Well, don't slut shame me, either! I can do what I want, too!"

"Fine, but you're the one who made me stop and dragged me out of there. How is that letting me do what I want?" she yelled, then hiccuped. Okay, that was a fair argument. But I still didn't like it.

"Because I love you and I don't want something bad to happen to you!" I snapped. "You're drunk and can't make good decisions right now. Those guys were primed to take advantage of you."

"Whatever," she sniffed.

I almost questioned my decision to pull her out of there.

Almost.

A few seconds later, she puked into the bushes off the porch. I rushed over to hold back her hair. I was in for a long night.

Chapter 8

Kitty

I woke up with a throbbing headache, a mouth the texture of the Sahara, a criminally upset stomach, and unfamiliar surroundings. I turned over to see the one and only Guy Stelle asleep beside me.

I looked under the sheets. I was wearing not my sweatpants and not my shirt. Guy was also dressed, so at least there was that. I was against the wall, so I'd have to crawl over him to get out and pee and/or puke, whichever came first. I'd have preferred to run from the scene entirely and do those things in the peace of my own dorm suite.

As I was laying there trying to figure out my escape route, my body forced the issue. I flopped over Guy like a fish on the dock and vomited into the trash can he had placed conveniently next to the bed. Guy sputtered awake, cussing in French. He held me in place by my hips as I hung almost upside down, puking. When I was done, he chuckled.

"Bonjour, ma puce."

"Where's your bathroom?" I squeaked.

"End of the hall. You need help?"

"No, no, I'll get there." I hurried out of the room with the dirty garbage can. I got myself and the trash can cleaned up and took a long, hard look in the mirror. I rolled the dice and used a random bottle of Listerine. Had Guy taken off my makeup? I looked surprisingly clean for someone who vomited a lot and didn't remember much. I could just run, but I probably owed him at least a thank you for putting up with me.

Fuzzy memories came flooding back. Oh, God. I'd asked him to make love to me because he's the love of my life. Not to fuck me. Not to have sex with me. I legitimately said "make love."

Oh no. Oh no no no no no no no no.

I walked back into his room. He had a glass of water, some pills, and a bottle of Pepto Bismol waiting for me on his desk.

I closed his door behind me and stood against it. "So, about last night," I started.

"It's fine. Come here, Kitty Bird," Guy said, scooting against the wall in his bed and leaving room for me. I lay down next to him, facing in like we always did. He reached over me to his desk, pouring me a dose of Pepto Bismol. I took it, then he handed me two Ibuprofen.

"Drink up." He held out the glass of water.

"Water is so harsh," I groaned after I swallowed the sip that I could stomach.

He laughed. "Been there before." I dropped back in the bed with him, facing in.

"I'm sorry I asked you to make love to me, Guy-Guy." I squeezed my eyes shut, not really wanting to see his reaction. I heard him crack a grin, and I knew without looking what that grin looked like.

"Why would you be sorry for that?"

"Guy, we haven't even really talked in years."

"I know. That's my fault. But it's time for us to start again," he said, patting my side. "I do still love you, you know."

"Obviously. You took care of my sorry ass last night."

He shrugged. "That's what friends are for. I'm glad I saw you."

I was nervous to ask my next question. "Guy, who changed me into these clothes? I don't have any underwear on."

"Nothing happened, *ma puce*. You puked on your clothes after we got out of the car. I had my roommate's girlfriend change you." He must have seen the fear in my eyes. "I would never let anything like that happen to you, Kitty. That's why I took you out of that party. I didn't like how those guys were looking at you. I wasn't trying to embarrass you. If you want to bang guys, go for it, but I want you to make that decision when you can speak for yourself."

Tears filled my eyes. How was he simultaneously like a big brother, a boyfriend, and a best friend all in one? "Thank you," I whispered.

"Hey, it's okay," he said, pulling me into his chest. His chest hair scratched under his shirt as I nestled in. "You're safe. Nothing happened."

"But it could have!"

"I made plenty of dumb mistakes when I was a freshman," he told me. "I'm glad you're okay."

"Please don't tell Frank. He'll kill me."

"Your secret's safe with me, *ma puce*."

Guy held me there while hang-xiety wracked my brain and body.

"Guy?"

"Yeah?"

"I love you."

His warm laugh rumbled through his chest where my head was still buried. "I know. You told me about a thousand times last night."

"Oh, God," I moaned.

"Don't feel bad. It was sweet. I feel bad for how long I waited to see you."

"It's fine. I knew you were here, but I wanted to get my own footing. I didn't come here for you."

"I know, sweetheart," he said, patting my hair. But instead of it being the condescending sweetheart that Southern moms use, it sounded like he really meant the endearment. Huh. "I didn't think you did. You hungry, or do you want to watch something?"

"Let's watch. I'm not ready for food."

Guy pulled his laptop into the bed and opened one of our old favorite comedy specials. He spooned me, resting his head on his hand behind me.

What an unusual relationship we had. We kissed, I got humiliated. He apologized. We stayed friends. We had some more kisses. We still said "I love you" in those few interactions we had between Eva dying and me seeing him at the party. I don't think either of us was sure if it was romantic or friend love. It was some bizarre hybrid of the two.

I was obviously attracted to him, but it was the dangerous kind of attraction, like a moth to a flame. I wasn't sure if he still cared about me the same way. His reputation on campus preceded him. He slept around constantly. I was a fool to hope for anything lasting with him. My little moth self was fixing to get her wings burned right up. So to keep myself safe, I assumed we were just friends, while still dancing that line of something more.

Snuggly friends. That's a thing that happens, right?

"No funny business, playboy," I warned. "I'm too fragile."

"No slut shaming, remember," he teased. "I'll be a gentleman."

We both dozed off again. Later, he borrowed his roommate's car to take me to McDonald's and back to my dorm.

"Don't disappear on me for three years," I said when I got out.

"Oh, Kitty Bird, you won't be able to get rid of me."

Chapter 9

Guy

I waited in the dark auditorium with Mikey, one of my best friends from the hockey team.

"So how do you know this chick?"

"We grew up together for a while. She goes here now. She's really smart and funny," I told him.

"Wait, is this the one who puked all over our place and Samantha had to change her clothes for her?"

I sighed. He was about to be a dick. "Yep. Same one."

"Ugh. Why are we here?"

"Shut up. You puked in someone's bed while you were hooking up with them," I pointed out. Mikey was notorious for that one.

"Touché, mon frére."

A Drake song kicked on and the improv group ran down the aisles of the auditorium to cheers from the crowd.

A busty blonde with a big dimple stepped forward, folding her hands behind her like she was an SNL guest host. "Welcome, welcome everyone to the Chainsaw Chatterbugs. To start our show, we just need a one-word suggestion from the audience."

"Damn," Mikey whispered, admiring the blonde.

Shouts came from the audience and she nodded. "I heard 'pebble.' Thank you, and enjoy the show."

I didn't tell Kitty that I'd be coming to her improv show. I'd seen a picture of her in the school paper that proved she was indeed part of this particular troupe. Pretty quickly, I recognized that they were doing long-form improv, something I was familiar with thanks to spending hours comedy nerding with Kitty and Frank. With three monologues and three sets of three scenes, they built a play from nothing. It was fascinating how quickly the actors molded to each other.

I hadn't seen Kitty act since high school, and she'd really improved. Not that she was bad to begin with, but she was so fluid in both her words and her physical comedy. She wasn't afraid to be raunchy, but she didn't rely on basic humor either. She was balanced, giving and taking from her team members. Even when her teammates made really wild choices, she supported it.

I'd always thought she was beautiful, but seeing her talents on display was just plain hot. It felt like the epiphany I had in the storage room at the ice rink when I kissed her. I was still crazy about her, not as a friend. There's nothing like seeing someone in their element, doing what they do best. I felt self-satisfied knowing I'd had the hottest girl on the stage in my bed, telling me she loved me. Begging me to make love to her. And God, I wanted to, but she was drunk and I didn't want to screw up years of friendship with one night of bad decision making.

"Your girl the brunette?" Mikey whispered. I nodded, not wanting to take my eyes off the stage to explain that she's not my girl. "Nice."

After the show, Mikey and I waited as Kitty got off the stage.

"Guy-Guy! Thanks for coming!" Kitty said, surprised and reaching up for a hug. "How did you know I'd be here?"

I loved the feeling of her body under my hands, and how I could cross my arms behind her back to hold her extra tight. I gave her a little peck on the cheek.

"Lucky guess. Told you you wouldn't be able to get rid of me," I said with a wink. Mikey cleared his throat. "Oh, this is Mikey. Mikey, this is one of my oldest friends, Kitty. Mikey's on the hockey team with me."

"Pleasure," Kitty said, her West Virginia accent peeking out.

"You were so, so good, Kitty," I gushed. "I haven't seen you act in so long. You're amazing."

"Yeah, you were funny as hell," Mikey added.

Kitty's cheeks pinked. "Aw, thanks, guys." I wanted to kiss her hot cheeks.

"I think Mikey and I were going to stop by a little get-together if you want to come," I offered.

"I actually have some math to do. It's due in the morning and I waited till the last minute," she said with a grimace. "Thought I'd get the core classes out of the way first so I can do all the fun writing stuff later."

"I could help you," I said.

"Bro!" Mikey objected, offended I was bailing on him.

Kitty smiled, good-natured. "It's alright. I managed the last three years without you. Y'all go on."

I fidgeted with my backward baseball cap. "Alright, well, since I came to your show, do you want tickets to our game Friday? It's the home opener."

Her eyes brightened. "Yeah, I'd love that."

"Bring your friend," Mikey said, gesturing to her blonde teammate.

Kitty laughed. "We'll see. I don't know that she's the blood-sport type."

"She could be," Mikey said.

"Okay, we're going," I said, ushering Mikey away. "You were lovely, Birdy."

We sat around at the main hockey house, drinking beers for a mid-week shoot-the-shit session. I'd had maybe two sips of beer when my phone buzzed.

KITTY BIRD
Help me solve an equation
    Sure!
If Guy leaves the party at 10:04 p.m., and Kitty leaves her dorm at 10:07, who will arrive first to that coffee and waffle shop on Mass Ave?
    Really? I can leave now
    I don't deserve you
    See you soon

When I got to the decided-upon coffee shop, Kitty had changed into sweats with her hair up in one of her signature ponytails. She already had her book open and was chewing on the end of her pencil.

"Hey," I greeted her, walking up to the booth.

"Hey," she said, not really looking up. "When the server comes, get yourself whatever you want. I already gave her my card since they're closing soon. I didn't realize that."

I got a hot herbal tea with a waffle when the server came over. Kitty was still in the zone. I grabbed her hand to get her attention.

"What do you want on top, *ma puce?*"

Kitty seemed surprised to see the server, then forced a smile at me. "You pick. I trust you."

I asked for strawberries and whipped cream. Strawberries made me think of her lip balm.

"Thanks," she mumbled. Her eyes screwed up in a pained, frustrated expression.

"Math still gets you worked up, huh?" I said, moving to slide next to her in the booth.

"I can't wait until I'm totally done with it," she sighed. "Just this semester and next and then I'm free."

"Good thing I'll be here to help you both semesters," I said, elbowing her side.

"Why don't you just do it for me?" she whined.

"Because then you wouldn't learn, Kitty Bird."

"I don't want to learn. I want to write comedy. This is a means to an end."

"Alright, let's break it down."

We fell into our familiar rhythm of how we work together. Kitty was prone to skipping steps and jumping to the end, so I had to help her slow down. She berated me the whole time like she always has. In a cute, friendly way. It felt nice to have a moment of normalcy with her. The last time we spent extended time together, Maman was dying. And over the weekend she'd been... unwell. We couldn't finish her homework before the waffle shop closed.

"Finish at my place? It's on your way back," I said. "Then I can walk you home."

"I can probably finish on my own. It's out of your way. I'll be okay."

I picked up her backpack for her. "It really wasn't a question, Kitty. Let's go finish at my house."

"Fine." She shoved the last piece of waffle in her mouth vengefully.

"I was saving that for you anyway," I pointed out.

As we walked, she caught me up on some of the high school gossip from people I'd remember. It was so nice to hear her voice again and be close to her. I had forgotten how her eyes lit up when she told stories, or how she watched me when I talked. Being back with Kitty was comfortable in a way I hadn't expected. Time had passed between us and there were things we didn't know about each other, but it still felt easy. I was grateful for that kind of friendship.

When we got in, I was still somehow starving. Practice had been a tough one earlier that day, and I still didn't feel caught up on calories. I dug through the pantry and fridge.

"Nothing looks good," I complained as I munched on a cheese stick.

"Hang on. Move," Kitty said, pushing me out of the way. She stacked ingredients on the counter. "Where's your candy?"

"What candy?"

"You're telling me you don't have candy or chocolate stashed anywhere around here?"

Sheepishly, I pointed to a drawer. Kitty opened it and gasped.

"You hockey boys eat this much junk? I'm telling your coach!" She fished around in the drawer. "Aha!"

She unearthed a bag of M&Ms and started mixing things up, turning on the oven.

"What are you making?"

"You'll see," she said, turning on the oven. We chatted while she mixed up what appeared to be M&M cookies. Colton and Mikey dropped into the kitchen, back from the hockey house party.

"Smells good," Mikey said. "What the fuck, are those my M&Ms?"

"I'll get you new ones," I said.

"And I'll share the cookies," Kitty crooned.

"I can't believe you let the freshman eat my M&Ms," Mikey grumbled.

"The freshman again, huh, Frenchie? I see our guest of honor is feeling better," Colton said, looking amused. I glared at him.

Kitty took it in stride. "I guess we must have met the other night when I was under the weather," she said gracefully. "I'm Kitty."

"Oh, I know," Colton said. "I'm wondering if you two have made love yet."

Kitty looked at me, mortified. "You told him?"

"No, Birdy. You told anyone who would listen that I was the love of your life and we were going to make love," I reminded her.

"Christ," she muttered, rubbing her eyebrows. "Not my finest night. Will delicious cookies make you forget that?"

"Nope. We were going to eat the cookies anyway," Mikey teased. "Hang on, let me put on some mood music."

He pulled out his phone and played "I'll Make Love To You" by Boyz II Men. Colton and Mikey started slow dancing. Kitty cackled, her face going red.

"Hey, Guy, if you don't want to make love to her, I could step in," Mikey said with a wink to Kitty.

"No. No. No one is making love to Kitty," I said firmly, shielding her from their view. Kitty saw how uncomfortable I was and piled on.

"I don't know. We could have fun, couldn't we, Mikey?" she suggested, peering around me. I shut it right down.

"Take your cookies and get out. Kitty's got homework to finish," I said, shoving a laughing Colton and Mikey out of the kitchen.

"Night, Kitty," Mikey sang with a flirty wave. I could have killed him.

Over cookies and milk, Kitty and I finished her last few math problems. Then we talked and did dishes. And couldn't stop talking. And then it was 1 a.m.

"What time is your first class tomorrow?" I asked.

"Not until 10. What about you?"

"Same. And I don't have practice until the afternoon. Wanna just stay over? I'm tired," I offered with a yawn.

"No, I can walk home," she said, packing up her backpack.

I put my hand on her backpack. "No, you can stay here. Spinninanight." I said it with a little smirk. I knew she'd cave to that. That's what she and Frank always called it in their West Virginia accents. It was years before I realized it was supposed to be "spending the night."

"I don't have a toothbrush or jammies," she protested, cracking a little at my joke.

"Colton's mom shops at Costco. We've got toothbrushes out our ears. And I'll give you some sweats again. Come on. Slumber party. It'll be fun."

Kitty laughed. "Fine, but I want your rattiest t-shirt and grossest shorts. I like soft things."

"Deal."

Kitty dressed in my worn-out clothes and waiting for me in my bed did nothing for my "are we still just friends" question. I was playing with fire. Kitty probably didn't remember, but the way she looked at me while we were together over the weekend was unmistakable. Something stirred deep inside me when she looked into my eyes and whispered, "You're the love of my life. We're meant to be together. Make love to me, Guy."

It wasn't like I wasn't attracted to Kitty or hadn't ever thought about what it would be like to fuck her. I totally had. For years. But even with our occasional kissing when we were in high school, it felt like we were in "just friends" territory in college. But I wasn't sure I wanted it to stay that way.

It was confusing. We'd even said I love you in our hungover haze, but as friends. Right?

And there I was, crawling in bed with her again. I loved torturing myself.

I got in the bed, facing her like we did.

"Hey."

"Hey. You still have chocolate breath," she said, booping my nose.

"I brushed my teeth! You're smelling your own chocolate breath," I objected.

"I'm a good brusher. You're a boy. You're probably not as thorough," she said, all smug.

"Yeah, okay," I said, reaching out to tickle her. She squealed and slapped my hand, squirming away from me. I grabbed her by the waist and pulled her back closer. Her eyes searched mine as her smile softened. Fuck, I wanted to kiss her. My heart took off and my stomach fluttered. But I got too nervous. I started blabbing instead.

"Hey, you know those skeletons they found in Pompeii? The ones that were curled into each other?" I asked.

"You mean how we snuggle?" Kitty laughed.

"Yes, that's what I always think of! We're just like those skeletons tucked into each other," I said, smiling at her.

"Wouldn't be a bad way to go," she said. "All at once. Just covered in ash. I mean, it was actually probably scary. I don't know. I wasn't there."

"But with someone you love," I added, folding our hands between us. "Wouldn't be so bad at all."

Kitty's expression turned more serious, not meeting my eyes. I wondered if she was thinking about us being something more, fulfilling our promise to Maman and growing old together. I wanted to see if her lips were as soft as I remembered. But her eyes started to drift shut, so I reached over to my desk and turned off the light.

"Goodnight, my fellow skeleton," I said, kissing her forehead.

"Goodnight, Guy-Guy."

* * *

In the morning, Kitty was up before me. She was the unfortunate soul to go in the bathroom after Mikey, which was bad on a non-drinking day and heinous after a night of drinking. When I realized what was happening, I tried to stop her. It was too late. I ran into Mikey in the kitchen.

"So, your girl stayed over. You never do that," Mikey said with a quirked eyebrow.

"She's not my girl. Nothing happened."

"She's not your girl, but you went to her improv show, left a party to help her with her homework, and let her stay over."

"It's not like that. We're old friends," I said, but again not really sure if that's what I wanted going forward. Mikey was right. I didn't let girls stay over. I usually went to their place and left as soon as it was socially acceptable. I didn't want anyone getting the wrong idea.

I wasn't boyfriend material. I hit and quit. I made it well-known. I always treated my partners right and made sure they had a good time, but I'd be gone just as soon as it was decent to go.

Kitty, on the other hand, had stayed over twice in less than a week. And the thing was, I wanted her to stay over more. I liked having her around, having our old rhythm back. Everything was so easy with Kitty. She didn't expect me to be a stud for her, nor did she treat my French-ness like a novelty or fetish. She knew the real me, and she loved me for it. She'd seen my lowest moments and loved me through them. I'd also had some of the hardest laughs in my life with her.

"Jesus Christ, Michael," Kitty said when she came out of the bathroom, her shirt over her nose. "You might want to get that checked out."

"My name's not Michael. It's Ben Miknevicius," Mikey objected. "And my doctor says I'm in perfect health, thank you very much."

"You hockey boys and your fucking nicknames," she laughed, heading back to my bedroom.

I watched after her, struggling to wipe the smile from my face.

Chapter 10

Kitty

"Um, excuse me. Whose sweatshirt is that?"

Violet and I met in the dining hall for breakfast before class on Thursday. Violet was my favorite roommate. We were lucky to be in a suite of singles at Alden. Of the four girls, Violet and I clicked the most. Her features were striking: piercing blue eyes, perfect full dark brows, olive skin, and gleaming chestnut hair. We first connected over our youthful shared love of One Direction and our disdain over certain slang terms. We could be found in each other's presence often.

I was a little low on sleep since Guy and I had stayed up so late talking.

"You can read. Whose name is on the back?" Guy had sent me home in his Alden hockey sweatshirt with STELLE 23 printed on the back. I noticed more people staring at me than usual in the dining hall.

Violet lowered her voice. "You fucked Guy Stelle last night? That's why you didn't come home?"

I laughed. "We didn't fuck. He's my oldest friend here. He helped me with my math and then it was late, so I stayed over."

"You're telling me you shared a bed with the infamous G-Spot?!"

I popped a bite of bagel in my mouth. "Is that what they call him here? Pretty clever nickname. His last name means 'spot' and his first name starts with a G."

"And I'm pretty sure he's a talented lover, French and everything," Violet said, wiggling her eyebrows.

"French-Canadian," I corrected. "And isn't that stereotyping?"

Violet ignored my question. "So wait, how is he your oldest friend? You didn't live in Quebec. You're West Virginia, through and through."

I explained our family entanglements, leaving out how his mom died and made us promise to try to fall in love. Guy and I hadn't even talked about that directly, ever. Who knew if he wanted to stick to it or not?

"Of course, I know he's hot, but we've always just been this weird kinda flirty, kinda family, kinda made-out-a-few-times relationship. He was the one who took care of me after the failed wet t-shirt contest."

"Um, you failed to mention that part of it," Violet said.

"Pardon me. I was a little embarrassed that I'd barfed all over myself, told him he was the love of my life, and asked him to make love to me."

Violet's jaw fell open. I went on.

"And then we cuddled in his bed the next day. But like, not romantically? I don't know. We're weird together. We're just friends, I think. He could make moves if he wanted to."

A moment from the night before flashed through my mind: the way he looked at me after he tickled me in his bed. And then held my hand when we talked about the lovers of Pompeii.

"You're out of your mind, Kitty Cat," Violet marveled. "I don't know what weird brother-sister shit you do in West Virginia—"

"Hey!" I objected, tossing a chunk of bagel at her. She knew West Virginia jokes were a sore spot for me and loved poking the bear. "If you can behave, I'll take you with me to his game tomorrow night. He gave me two seats."

* * *

Later that evening, I got a text from Guy.

GUY-GUY FRENCHIE
Get ur math turned in?
    Yeah thx
Got any more to do?
    Not til next week
Wanna come over and watch a show?
    It's 11 pm Frenchie. R u booty calling me?
No
    U just want ur sweatshirt back?
If ur not coming over wear it to the game tomorrow
    U just want me to wear ur name
Omg
Y r u making this so hard
    That's what she said :p
    I need more than good tickets to wear it
M and M?
    Now he's getting it

I sat in the library on Friday between classes, when I got a text from him again.

GUY-GUY FRENCHIE
Where r u
    Library
What floor
    3

Ten minutes later, Guy appeared in front of me with a sly smirk. He slapped a bag of M&M's down on the table in front of me.
  "There, you brat. Now will you wear it?"
  "Well, hello to you, too."
  "I met your demand. You have to meet mine."
  "You have to be quiet in here, Guy," I teased.

He ripped open the pack of M&Ms, shoved a handful in his mouth, and threw one at me. "I'll see you tonight."

* * *

Violet promised to be good, so that night, we took our seats at the hockey arena. Guy had given us seats right on the ice. On a normal day, that would be fine, but I wasn't feeling great. My periods were devastatingly bad, the killer combo of painful, long, and heavy. Sometimes the pain was so bad I threw up. This was day two, usually my worst day. I'd taken medicine, but sometimes that didn't cut it. This was one of those times. Thankfully, my bloating was hidden by Guy's giant sweatshirt, which I paired with some loose jeans and a winter hat.

We watched both teams take the ice to warm up. It didn't take long to find Guy. He stopped by our seats in a flash of sprayed ice and pounded on the glass, as if I wasn't already looking at him.

"HI, KITTY BIRD. YOU LOOK NICE," he yelled through the glass.

I giggled, tired, and waved back. "Hi, Guy-Guy. Thank you."

He must have noticed my drawn expression because he pulled off his helmet.

"What's wrong?" he mouthed.

I shook my head and waved him off. He stuck out his lower lip, then blew me a kiss before putting his helmet back on and moving on.

"See what I mean? We're weird together."

"That was insanely cute," Violet said. "He likes you."

"I don't know. That's just how we are. I'm getting popcorn and a soda. You want anything?"

Watching Guy play again was borderline enchanting. He was in the first line, not surprising. I'd forgotten the fluid grace with which he moved, and he'd gotten more aggressive since I saw him last. Watching him check a guy into the boards somehow got my blood moving, and for a while, I almost forgot my period misery. He really was professional grade.

His skating had gotten faster and smoother, his legs more powerful. I was happy for him that he'd gotten to go back to Quebec. Otherwise, he might have missed out on the chance to play at a higher level and get drafted. Though he'd loved his coach back home, West Virginia didn't have the resources to keep up with someone of his skill level. It's not hockey country.

In the second period, Guy stole the puck from one of Princeton's forwards, driving down the ice toward the goal. He netted it from way deep, lighting the lamp and setting off the crowd. I didn't notice that I was on my feet screaming too until he skated to where his teammates stood by our seats. He celebrated with his teammates, but before skating back to the bench for high-fives, he shot a wink and a "love you" over his shoulder to me.

"Did he just say that he loves you?!" Violet squealed.

"Yeah, we do that," I said, straining to be heard over the crowd.

"Okay, yeah, you two are weird."

Alden beat Princeton 3-1, with Guy getting an assist to go with his goal. We waited for him after the game for what felt like an eternity. Guy and his teammates trickled out of the locker room. His hair was still damp and tousled. I had to admit, he looked like a friggin' dreamboat. Plus, there was that whole suit rule, so he and every one of his teammates were also dressed up in their finest.

His smile was wide as he approached me. "Great job, Frenchie," I said, reaching up to hug him. He pecked my cheek, as he sometimes did, his stubble scraping my jaw. He pulled me off my feet, being so much taller than me and wanting to give me a real hug. After he put me down, I stepped back and flashed my hand to Violet.

"This is my roommate, Violet."

"Great to meet you. Thanks so much for coming!" Guy said.

"You two want to come to the after party? It's at the hockey house. You'd be guests of honor."

"Hell yeah," Violet said, but I hesitated.

"I don't think I can," I said slowly.

"What?" Guy and Violet both snapped their heads toward me.

"Why, Birdy?" Guy followed up.

"I just . . . I don't feel very good."

Guy pressed the back of his hand to my forehead, looking worried. "You don't feel hot."

The god-awful smell of his hands overtook me. "Guy, hockey hands!"

"You missed them," he teased, shoving them more in my face. I faked a gag, but it wasn't all that fake. "For real, why are you sick?"

"It's nothing. I just need to sleep it off, I think. Violet can go in my place, though, and take a friend."

"Yeah, yeah, you're welcome to come," Guy said to Violet, still not taking his eyes off me. "Want me to take you home, Birdy?"

"No, Violet can get me there," I said. "Really, it's nothing."

"Well, thanks for coming, even though you didn't feel good. You need anything?" Guy offered, pulling me to him again.

"No thanks."

And with a concerned look over his shoulder, he let us go.

Chapter 11

Kitty

When I'd settled into my PJs with my heating pad and trashy shows, I got a text.

GUY-GUY FRENCHIE
U get home ok?
    Yeah thx. Excited for ur party?
Kitty tell me whats wrong
I'm ur oldest friend here. I'm worried. U looked pale
    It's not a big deal
Birdy come on
    U really wanna know
Yes!!
    It's my period
Sorry ma puce
R u in for the night
    Yes
K

"K?" What the hell did that mean? Violet came in to check on me before leaving for the hockey party. Our other roommate, Sadie, flanked her. I had totally forgotten that it was Halloween weekend, thus I'd be missing the chance to go out scantily clad and hook up with some guy dressed like a goober. Sounds bad, but in reality, it would be fun. Sadie and Violet were dressed like the Powerpuff Girls. I was supposed to be Buttercup to round out the trio. Oops.

"Feel better, friend. We'll go get laid for you," Violet said, shaking her ass.

"Be careful. Hockey guys aren't necessarily the most upstanding gentlemen," I warned.

"We can handle ourselves, Dad," Sadie assured me before leaving me alone.

The suite was quiet, so I started one of my preferred methods for alleviating cramps: using my vibrator. Things were just getting good, when I heard a noise in the hall, footsteps and a bag rustling.

"Hello?"

"Kitty Bird? Which one of these is yours?"

"I'm in here," I answered, heart pounding as I turned off my vibrator and shoved it under my pillow.

And there was Guy, a knight in shining armor of sweatpants and a convenience store bag. The smell of cold air came in with him. His messy dark hair curled around the edges of a beanie, which he took off.

"Hi." He beamed, looking exceptionally attractive.

"How'd you get in here?"

"I saw Violet leaving. She told me where to go. You look like shit," he said, kicking off his shoes by my door.

"Thanks? Why aren't you at your party?"

"Because I wanted to party with you."

"Guy, you can't just show up. What if I had been asleep already?" I scolded him.

"Then I would have snuggled you," he shrugged. "Or waited for you to get up. Or dropped the snacks and left. I don't know. I didn't think about it. You just looked really bad earlier. And now."

Man, he couldn't stop bringing up how bad I looked.

"So you've said. Does my period not scare you off?"

He got a funny look on his face. "No. You're my friend, and you're sick. You're not going to bleed on me. You already puked on me last weekend anyway. What's a little blood?"

"Suit yourself."

"Move over. Let me show you the snacks I got."

I paused the TV and scooted to make room for him on my bed.

"Okay, so we've got," he extracted each item from the bag, "Salt and vinegar chips, those lime tortilla chips you like, M&M, Dr. Pepper, and fizzy water. What do you want?"

"Salt and vinnies," I said with a grin. "Guy, this is too sweet. You didn't have to do anything."

He looked at me with a pout. "I don't like seeing you sick. What are we watching?"

Guy opened the bag of chips for me because he knew sometimes I pulled too hard and blew up the whole bag. Then he cracked the Dr. Pepper, took a swig, and wiggled to get in bed behind me.

"Did I say you could get in my bed?" I asked.

"Do you not want me to?"

"I mean, yeah, I want you to, but you don't even ask," I argued, sitting up at the head of the bed with my chips.

"Oh, so at my place, you can get right in, but I have to ask at yours?"

I tipped my head to the side, weighing that question. "Point taken. You played really well today, by the way."

"Thanks. I was glad you came. What were you going to be for Halloween tonight?"

"I was Buttercup from the Powerpuff Girls."

"Clever. That explains what your roommates were wearing."

"What about you?"

"Dracula. Same costume every year, so I'm not missing anything by not going out."

"Let me guess, so you can suck on girls' necks?"

"Ugh, Kitty, you have the worst opinion of me," he scoffed, offended. "And yes, you're right."

"So my opinion is justified," I said, feeling righteous.

"But you know, I don't make love to any of them."

I snapped to look at him. "You don't have sex with the girls you get with?"

"Oh, I have sex with them. I just don't make love to them. That's reserved for the love of my life." He said it deadpan, but I could see he was imploding from trying not to laugh. His accent was loud and proud in that statement: "sex wit dem," and "de love of my life." He could be simultaneously charming and infuriating.

"Fuck off," I said, slapping his chest. "I can't be held responsible for what I said last weekend."

"Oh, yes, you can."

"Guy, stop," I whined. "Not only do I have crippling cramps and bleeding, but now I have anxiety, too."

"I'm sorry, I'm sorry," he said quickly, attaching himself to my side for a hug. "You know I love you."

"But am I the love of your life?" I asked, gesturing to him with a chip.

Guy took a breath, thinking. "To be determined."

I grabbed a tissue to wipe the chip grease off my fingers and burrowed back down in the sheets.

"I think you're on my heating pad," I said. Guy started moving his body, looking for the heating pad. Then, to my absolute horror, he shoved his hand under my pillow and pulled out my little purple vibrator.

Guy froze for a second with it in his hand, mouth slowly going into a wide O and his eyes growing round.

"Kitty," he said like he was uncovering a scandal. "Were you touching yourself when I came in here? Is that why you were mad when I got here?"

"It helps with my cramps," I huffed, snatching the vibrator out of his hand and shoving it in the bedside drawer. "Getting off is sometimes better than painkillers."

"Did I interrupt? Do you need me to leave so you can finish the job?"

"No!"

His eyes went sinister. "Do you want me to help?"

"Jesus, Guy!"

"Okay, forget I asked. But the door's open if you need me," he said airily. "I'm pretty good at it."

"I'll keep that in mind," I scowled, finally finding my heating pad and turning it on. "I was watching Emily in Paris. Should we do something else?"

"Whatever you want, Birdy. I'm just here to keep you company and make sure you don't bleed out or cramp to death."

"That's not quite how periods work, but I appreciate it anyway."

Guy sat up in the bed, pulling me between his legs to lean into his chest. He wrapped his arms around my waist to hold my heating pad. Even though he was a wall of hard muscle, it was surprisingly cozy and warm snuggling into him. At first, Guy acted like he didn't care about Emily in Paris. He was annoyed at the French stereotypes and the ridiculous cutesiness of it all.

By the third episode, he was furious. "Why is she even fucking with Alfie when she's in love with Gabriel?!"

"Gabriel's with Camille!" I argued.

"Well, he shouldn't be. These people ignore their feelings!"

"I think that's the point."

"And you like watching people torture themselves?"

"I mean, they're pretty people and it's more angst than torture," I pointed out.

"True," Guy sighed.

"Do you want me to turn it off?"

"No," he sulked. "I'm invested now."

We both took a bathroom break, then got back into bed. Guy readjusted so he was spooning me.

"Can I get you anything? You comfortable?"

"I'm actually pretty tired," I said.

"Do you want me to leave or keep you company?"

"Whatever you want. I'm cool if you stay."

"Good, because I'm tired, too."

And so we fell asleep like that, with Guy's breath on the back of my neck and his warm, heavy arm holding my heating pad in place.

It was strange, and I knew it. Guy and I were snuggly friends. That day had been the first time we'd ever discussed anything remotely sexual, other than our slut-shaming conversation and the time he had his hand up my shirt in high school. I wondered what he would have done if I'd told him to get me off. Was he just joking? Or was he for real? Luckily, my body was too worn out to keep me up analyzing it.

Until it wasn't. A few hours later, I woke to intensely painful cramps. My stomach roiled and I feared I'd throw up from the pain. It felt like my uterus was trying to physically leave my body. I curled forward and writhed as the waves of pain came over me. I let out a little cry. Guy stirred awake.

"Birdy?" he asked softly. "What's wrong, *ma puce?*"

"It's really bad," I gasped.

"What can I do?" His hand ran over my hair, kissing behind my ear.

"What time is it?"

"3:30."

Enough time had passed that I could take medicine again. "Pills."

"Okay, okay. Shh, it's okay. I'm here," he said frantically, scrambling to open the pill bottle on my desk. "How many?"

"Four," I said, going full prescription dose for how bad my pain was. Guy handed me the pills and opened my water bottle. He reached down and turned my heating pad back on, then got back in bed behind me. His big body was so cramped against that wall, but he didn't say a word about it.

"Is it always this bad?"

"Most times, yeah. It's getting worse the older I get."

"Poor Birdy." He kissed my hair again. "That must be so hard."

I turned over to face him, and he held me tight to his chest. I was shivering and sweating from the exertion of the searing pain.

"Have you seen a doctor for it?" Guy asked.

"Not really. I just figured it was my curse."

"Will you promise me you'll go see someone? I'll take you if I have to. I don't think this is normal, Kitty." I heard the fear in his voice and knew he was thinking of his mom's ovarian cancer.

"Yeah. I'll go."

"Thank you. I can't stand that you're hurting this bad." Silence passed between us as I waited for the meds to start kicking in.

Guy stroked my hair and nuzzled my forehead, pressing kisses between my eyebrows. His voice was quiet and gravelly when he spoke next. "Would it help if I touched you, Kitty?"

He was already touching me in almost every way, his body completely surrounding me. His legs tangled with mine, his arms a tight hug around my upper body. His lower bicep was my pillow. It would seem he didn't mean just physically putting his hands on me. He meant putting his hands on me *there*.

"I want to help you feel better. If that will help, I'm glad to do it, Birdy."

But what would it mean? Would he kiss me? Did it mean he loved me more than as a friend? Would it mean he wanted me to touch him, too? I did want to. This would be crossing a line that our friendship may never come back from.

"Do you want to touch me like that?" I asked, barely a whisper.

Guy sucked in a shaky breath. "Yeah, Kitty. I do."

I took an equally wobbly inhale. "Then yes."

Gently, Guy shifted me so I was on my back. "Okay if I touch you other places and kiss you?"

"Yes."

Guy's mouth suspended over mine for a moment, giving me a chance to change my mind. Then his lips dropped to mine for the first time in years, sweet and soft. I gripped the back of his neck, drawing him into me as our lips sampled once, twice, then he stayed with me, our tongues meeting. Guy's hand traveled down my body to the hem of my shirt, then crept up my bare skin.

"So soft, Birdy," he whispered against my lips. His mouth worked against my throat as his fingers grazed the underside of my boob, my nipples puckering immediately. His touches were feather-light, maddening. He dragged his fingers lightly around my nipples before giving me the touch I craved. He peeled my shirt up to have full access to my breasts in the dark, teasing his mouth over the pebbled peaks. Under the cover of the dark, it was easier to accept what we were doing. Completely sober. We'd worked ourselves into a place where we couldn't do something so intimate, yet there we were doing it.

Every nerve ending in my body was on full alert as his touch drew me out. I knew I was wet, and not from blood. His tongue flicked over my nipple again and I breathed out his name. He gave a tortured growl.

"Okay if I take my shirt off? I want to feel your skin," he said.

"Fuck yeah." The shape of him rose up on his knees and swiped his shirt off with one clean pull. I leaned up and let him yank my shirt off, too. When we crashed back together, the reality of what we were doing and what it meant faded, driven only by our bodies and need and years of wanting. His hair tickled my cheek as we kissed again, his body lined up over mine. My bare breasts smashed into his chest and though they were sore, it hurt so good. I curled my hips out of instinct, finding him hard in his sweatpants. He rubbed back against me, his erection hitting me just right. Guy moaned my name into my ear, pulling my earlobe into his mouth and pinching it between his canines. One hand was lodged under my neck, thumb stroking my throat, while the other explored my bare skin.

"My legs are hot," I said, my sweatpants suddenly suffocating me. Guy sat back and tore them down my legs, shedding his own as well. We were down to just underwear. Somehow we went from friends who cuddled to friends who ripped off each other's clothes in the throes of passion. He quickly arranged himself on top of me.

"You okay, Birdy?"

"Yes," I panted, wrapping my legs around his hips. "More."

He groaned again, grinding his erection along my seam. Even the thin layers of our underwear seemed like too much. I needed all of him. Nothing would be enough until I had him inside my body. Moisture pooled where precum leaked from his tip. Or maybe that was my own wetness. He continued rolling his hips slowly, his cock against my clit. I made my hand into a fist and captured his tip in it as he pressed forward.

"Fuck, Kitty." He picked up the pace, the sensation of our bodies together intensely satisfying. He slowed down, bringing himself back from being lost in the moment.

"If I put my hand down there, will I get blood on me?" he asked. Not disgusted, just curious.

"No, I have a tampon in. Unless you pull it out and fling it across the room, you should be good."

Guy stopped his grinding and gave a hearty laugh into my ear. "You have a way with words, Kitty Bird."

He leaned on one elbow and palmed my breast, then slid his hand into my underwear. His middle finger parted me, dipping into the wet we'd made. My chest heaved, head falling back on the pillow as he dragged the wetness up to my clit, applying the lightest pressure to tease me. I moaned.

"That feel good?" he asked, the glint of his eyes in the low light hanging over mine. "Yeah?"

"More," I begged.

"So greedy," he said, keeping his touch light. I pushed my hips up into his hand. "So. Very. Greedy."

"I need to come," I whined.

"Oh, you're going to come, sweetheart." His voice was as dark as the velvety black around us.

"I want you to come with me."

Guy let out a feral sound. "You first, *ma puce*."

"Then let me have what I want," I argued.

He did, smashing his mouth to mine as he sped up his circles around my clit and pressed harder. His mouth moved back to my breasts, sucking on one nipple and flicking it with his tongue.

"So fucking sexy when you want it, Birdy," he gritted out, not really for my benefit, but more like he couldn't help himself.

"Guy, I'm going to come."

Just then, he backed off his touch. He was fucking edging me. "Tell me who this pussy belongs to, Kitty."

I panted and writhed, desperate not to lose that edge. "Please," I whimpered.

"Tell me," he said playfully. I'd heard rumors of how fun he was in bed. This was certainly proving it.

"It's mine." I was unable to play his game.

"Oh, Birdy, that's true, but you know that's not the answer tonight. Who's taking care of you?" The pressure from his fingers got lighter and lighter. I squirmed, seeking more.

"You."

Guy rewarded me with increased speed and pressure from his hand. I clutched his wrist, desperate to keep him there.

"Good girl. Now come for me." His voice was low and commanding, while also being encouraging. In the dark, I felt everything. His skin on mine, his breath on my neck, his hard length pressed into my leg, the intensity of his perfect touch.

And with that, I released with a cry, my pussy pulsing against his fingers.

"There you go, Birdy. That's perfect," he cooed, like he was genuinely proud of me for coming. His smile shined through as he covered my neck in kisses. "Feel better?"

He ran his fingers through my wetness, giving me light touches as my orgasm ebbed. I heard him suck his fingers, a hum as they left his mouth. Holy shit, that was hot.

"Much," I laughed. We lay there, catching our breath, until my sweat started to cool. I reached over to Guy's middle, slowly sliding my hand toward his dick. He put a hand on me to stop me.

"You don't have to, sweetheart."

"I want to," I said. "Unless you don't want me to?"

"You need to rest, Kitty. Your body's been through a lot tonight."

"So you don't... want me to touch you?"

"No. I don't," he said. A sick feeling dropped into my stomach. I immediately regretted letting him get me off. He had just been doing me a favor. He wasn't attracted to me. That wasn't him wanting me. That was him taking pity on me.

He was rejecting me, just like he had in high school. But my pride was too big to let him know just how bad that hurt me. How much it ripped that scab open and dug into the wound all over again.

"Oh. Okay," I said softly. Was that why we did it in the dark? So he didn't have to look at me? I worked very hard not to cry, but I knew he was allowed to say no for any reason.

That didn't mean it didn't hurt, though.

"Come on, Birdy. Let's get some sleep." He turned me in to face him and planted a kiss on my forehead before passing out.

Chapter 12

Guy

The sun peeked through the blinds in Kitty's room. I'd stayed the whole night. I'd also made her come with my hands, and it was really fucking hot.

The way she rolled her body under me, how she used my dick for her pleasure. Her nipples under my tongue, knowing how dark and pretty they were from the night of the wet t-shirt contest. Her little moans and begging. The way she gripped my wrist as I brought her over the edge. Her sweet pussy pulsing into my fingers. The way she tasted when I sucked my fingers clean. The way she begged to please me, too.

But I couldn't let her. I didn't want her to think I came over just to get laid, or that I expected anything from her. She was worthy all on her own, whether it was for pain relief or just for the pleasure. Plus, she'd just been writhing in pain in my arms. She was probably in *less* pain, but I didn't want to put her to work while she was suffering.

And there was the fact that I'd done her wrong in high school. I owed her a bonus orgasm for her trouble.

Kitty glowed in the morning light, looking almost angelic sleeping next to me. Still just in her underwear, her hair mussed from our activities in the middle of the night. The sheets pooled at her hips, her perfect handful tits exposed. The sight and the memory of how good they felt in my mouth had me achingly hard. I admired her sweet belly that she always had no matter how fit she was. The delicate lines of her collarbones. Her hand on my bicep holding me as she slept.

I was seeing my best friend, who could very well be the love of my life, undressed for the first time. I pressed a kiss to her forehead to see if she'd wake up, but she remained asleep.

I wondered if things would be different between us after what we'd done, if we'd start moving into more-than-friends territory. Was that what I wanted? It was getting harder to think of other women, and even harder to think of her being with other guys.

I leaned over to check my phone and found a sea of notifications. That wasn't unusual for a party night after a game, especially when I wasn't there to partake. Half of them were people looking for me. Some girls hoping to repeat hookups. Little did they know I was in bed with the one that I'd forever compared everyone to.

And then the team chat was completely lit up. There was a warrant out for our goalie Pete's arrest. He'd stolen his townie girlfriend's dog in the middle of a fight. Kara was twenty-four, a Bostonian who hadn't gone to Alden. Pete and Kara had gotten their ridiculous chihuahua, Bowser, together, but it was *her* dog. Pete showed up to the hockey house looking enraged with Bowser tucked under his arm, and everyone pried the truth out of him.

Because I was the alternate team captain, the actual captain Colton was looking for me to figure out how to smooth it all over. We needed to convince Kara to call off the police and get Bowser back where he belonged.

Not exactly how I wanted to spend my Saturday morning. I'd rather have stayed until Kitty got up and we could get breakfast together. Maybe fool around again if she was feeling better. She was still fast asleep. I carefully crawled over her and out of bed, rushing to put my clothes back on. I had that anxious, hungover, pissed off feeling, even though I hadn't touched a drop of alcohol. I didn't like my time with Kitty being cut short.

She stirred as I pulled on my hoodie, but she didn't fully wake up. I hated to leave like that, but I didn't want to wake her when she'd had such a rough night. I looked back at her one more time to see if she'd wake up before I left. When she didn't, I walked out the door, sending her a text so I wouldn't be totally gone without a trace.

> Sorry I'm not there. Team emergency.
> Hope u feel better

Walking into my apartment was like walking into the eye of the chaos hurricane. The living room was packed with the team, filling the huge sectional couch and the floor in front of it. Bowser was dozing, nonchalant, on Pete's lap, unaware that he was the center of all the drama.

Kitty's roommate Violet scampered out of the bathroom, Powerpuff googly eyes in one hand. She kept her eyes down and rushed for the front door. A Saturday morning walk of shame. I wondered whether Colton or Mikey hooked up with her. Our other roommate, K-Gar, had a girlfriend, so it wouldn't have been him. Considering how long Colton stared after her, I suspected it might have been him.

"Bout time," Mikey said as I sat on the floor. "Where have you been?" He was from Detroit, but he sometimes carried his mom's country accent. When he asked me a mom question like that, he sounded like his own mom.

"It's only 8 a.m. I was gone like nine hours," I argued.

"Did you hook up with Kitty?"

"It's complicated," I shrugged, not really wanting to share that I got her off to relieve her period cramps, she offered to reciprocate, and I declined. It sounded pretty bananas when I stopped and thought about it.

Colton sat on the arm of the couch, ready to hold court. "Alright, let's get started. I'm calling Coach after we figure out a plan. Pete, if you took Bowser back now, would Kara call off the cops?"

"I'm not giving him back! He's mine, and she's out of her fucking mind," Pete huffed.

"Pete," Colton warned.

I rubbed my forehead. I couldn't believe I'd left a mostly-naked Kitty for this. "What are you two fighting about now?"

"She said I was looking at one of the Powerpuff Girls at the party," Pete whined.

I normally would have questioned it, but it was Halloween, so I knew who he meant. Why a twenty-four-year-old was coming to our parties was a bit disturbing to me anyway, but that was Pete and Kara's odd relationship. It was decided that Colton and I would drive Pete over to Kara's with Bowser to apologize. Colton and I had to act like hostage negotiators to convince them to kiss and make up.

It was well into the afternoon by the time we were done with Operation: Bowser Return. Luckily, the cops didn't have to be involved, so neither did Coach.

I still hadn't heard from Kitty, so I texted her again.

> U ok?

KITTY BIRD
Fine

> U wanna have dinner tonite

Have plans, sorry

Yikes, okay. No "Thanks for coming over, Guy-Guy?" No "How about a rain check, Guy-Guy?" Why was this weird? I didn't want this to be weird. I loved touching her, but maybe she thought we crossed a line. It kind of hurt my feelings. I'd thought about what Maman said about us being together a lot, particularly after Kitty drunkenly alluded to it and told me I was the love of her life. Was Maman right? Was it time for me and Kitty to try being together?

I saw her from a distance on campus a couple of times that week, her ponytail swishing behind her as she burrowed down into her coat. She was always too far away for me to catch up to her. I opened and closed my text app constantly, trying to think of something to make her want to talk to me, but came up blank. I didn't see her up close again until a frat party the next weekend.

Kitty was gorgeous, her long, dark hair in waves swept over one shoulder, and a loose green sweater that showed her entire back. I knew how soft that skin felt and I wanted to put my hands on it again. She couldn't have been wearing a bra, because there was absolutely nothing on her back. Just miles of smooth, creamy skin. My lips ached wanting to kiss every inch of that skin. I wanted those sweet nipples back in my mouth. I wanted the taste of her pussy on my tongue again. But first, I had to break whatever awkwardness made us stop talking for the past week.

She was talking to one of the frat bros. I strode across the room, ready to break it up, just as the guy stroked his hand down her spine and whispered something in her ear. She had the sexiest smile as she listened to what he said. I wanted to be that guy. I wanted to be the one turning her on.

Kitty turned to face Generic Frat Boy and when I was about ten steps from them, his tongue was in her mouth. I stopped in my tracks, feeling like I'd been punched. Now I really wanted to be that guy. Or smash his face in.

The room blurred. My throat went dry. I scanned my surroundings, looking for a girl who might soothe my sore feelings. There were beautiful women everywhere, but none of them were the one I wanted. I turned to find Mikey, told him I was leaving, and got the hell out.

I cursed myself on the way home. I must have fucked it all up if Kitty was out hooking up with other guys after she'd been with me.

Or did she not consider it being with me? Did she think it was just some kind of favor for a friend? Was that a friends-with-benefits thing I did?

I'd never gotten jealous seeing my past hookups moving on at a party. I never wanted anything lasting with any of them, though. But why didn't I? Some of them were pretty cool. I might have had fun in a relationship with them. I'd had a couple of girlfriends in high school. But I'd never been in love.

Or had I? That didn't make any sense either. Kitty and I had never *really* been together. I loved her, like as family, as my best friend, and I think before I left West Virginia, I really loved her. All the way. But did that ever fade? I was so young then. Was it just puppy love?

I didn't really know how to name how I felt. I just knew that I wanted to throw things whenever I saw her with another guy.

Kitty hadn't spoken to me the whole week before. Likewise, I guess I didn't ask her to do anything with me when maybe I should have. I told myself I was giving her space, though it killed me. And space resulted in her going home with someone else, so look where that got me.

The day after I saw her go home with Generic Frat Boy, I knew I needed some advice. Normally, I'd talk about my problems with Frank, but that would entail fessing up to having fooled around with his sister. Colton would have to do instead.

We went to the gym together and had lunch after. He was the captain for a reason. He always knew what to do. I explained to him who Kitty was to me: a lifelong best friend who I probably would be in love with if we gave it a chance. I told him what happened that night in her room and he slapped his hand over his face.

"Bro," he scolded me. "You didn't call her after that?"

"No. Should I have? I thought she needed space. She didn't want to talk to me."

"Look at it from her perspective. You got her off. She asked to do the same to you and you said no. Did you at least kiss her goodbye?"

My cheeks burned red. "No. I left to deal with Bowsergate and sent her a text to say I had an emergency. I texted her to ask if she was okay later."

"Bro."

"What?"

"She probably thinks you don't like her! You turned her down and bailed on her, then disappeared. Of course she's out hooking up with other people. She thinks it meant nothing to you! Hell, she may have hooked up in front of you just to spite you," he pointed out.

"Fuck." My mind flashed back to high school, when I'd pushed her away, too. She probably thought I was a real piece of shit.

"Yeah, fuck. You need to take her out for coffee or something and talk about it. Tell her why you did what you did. Tell her you like her."

"Is that what you do? I don't know how to date people, Colt. I'm a wham-bam kinda guy. Most girls know that though."

"Well, now she thinks you wham-bammed her and she doesn't want to be your friend anymore," he said. "You need to fix it. I'm into her roommate. I don't need to be taking sides out here."

"I knew it!" I said, grateful for the topic change. "I thought you two hooked up."

He chuckled. "Yeah, she's pretty fun. Fuckin' rocket, too. Jesus."

"Happy for you, man."

Later, I sat alone trying to figure out how to get Kitty back in my life. I worked myself into a headache wondering if I even had any business trying to have a relationship with anyone. Thoughts of my dad and his rage issues haunted me. Could I even be a good partner for Kitty?

But I remembered that Maman had faith in me and Kitty. She knew us both well and still thought we needed each other. Maman knew me better than Papa did, and I'd spent far more time with her than with Papa. I was my mother's son, not my father's. At least that's what I hoped.

I texted Kitty to try and make it right.

> I miss u. Can we talk?

KITTY BIRD
Ok. When?

> U free now? I'll take u for coffee

Can't now. Kinda busy this week

I tried again and again with her, Kitty never offering another alternative. Finally, I had to force the issue.

Chapter 13

Kitty

The Chainsaw Chatterbugs show was a mess. Brian insisted on rhyming everything he said. That was funny for about one scene, but then he wouldn't give it up. Nothing worse than a selfish player in your group, especially when they're not even funny. It's hard to "yes and" shitty choices. Plus, I'd been in something of an on-and-off shitty mood since my accidental orgasm with Guy. He kept trying to talk to me, and I was sure it was just going to be to friend zone me and remind me why I wasn't like that to him.

I didn't need that slap in the face. He'd already dealt me one by just leaving in the morning and not waking me up to say goodbye. And turning down my offer to get him off. And not kissing me after the deed was done. My stomach turned every time I thought about it.

So I avoided him like the plague to avoid that conversation. I didn't want to be mad at Guy. We'd just started hanging out again. But if he was going to play me, his longest friend, then yeah, I was mad. I focused my anger on disliking certain members of my improv group.

"Can you believe Brian?" I asked Cassie after the show. "So annoying, right?"

She rolled her eyes. "I don't know, Kitty. You kinda left him hanging."

I screwed up my face. Something wasn't adding up. Cassie was almost always game to talk a little well-deserved shit after shows. "You fucking him or something? You always talk shit about Brian."

Cassie's face instantly went red. "Oh, shit, Cass! I wasn't serious! I, uh, I'm sorry. Uh, how's it going with him?"

Her face softened, the embarrassed red going to a more enamored pink. "He's pretty sweet. Enthusiastic."

"I guess you can say that for him."

"Hey, I think someone's waiting for you," she said, gesturing to the back of the auditorium. A tall, lanky figure leaned against the wall. I waved goodbye to Cassie and headed toward the person, knowing damn well who it probably was. Once the lights were out of my eyes, my suspicions were confirmed.

"Hi, Guy." He gave me a sheepish smile.

"You did great, Birdy." He opened his arms. "Hug?"

I sighed and stepped into his embrace. "I know that's not true. Tonight was a flop."

"I thought you were wonderful," Guy said, kissing my hair. I inhaled his cologne. Deodorant? Whatever it was that made him smell so damn good. "So are you still busy now? Have some math homework I can help you with?"

I took a deep breath and looked up at him. His eyes were so hopeful. He had been trying to get me to hang out a lot, and I kept shutting him down. It was easier to shut him down when he wasn't standing in front of me, and he knew that. I did have homework and could use his help. "Tea and waffles?"

"Sounds perfect."

We walked out into the November cold. He seemed to be angling to put his arm around me, so I busied myself with walking apart from him and cracking jokes.

"Kitty, we should talk about last weekend," he said, brown eyes earnest under the brim of his beanie.

"Do we have to?" I groaned.

"Yes, Kitty. I don't want to lose you because of it. You don't need to feel awkward about it."

"Then why did you leave without even saying goodbye?" I was skeptical. Once a fuckboy, always a fuckboy.

"Kitty, I really did have an emergency," Guy started. I leveled him with a sharp look. "I did! One of my teammates stole his girlfriend's dog and had the cops out looking for him."

I cackled. "Can I use that in a script?"

"You really should," he said, laughing. "Looking back, it's pretty funny."

I worried my lip between my teeth, wanting to rip off the bandaid. "I know what happened between us was kinda weird, so can we just pretend it didn't happen? You're a hookup boy, and I know you don't settle down with anyone."

"I mean, that's true, but Kitty—"

"I miss being your friend. We've been apart for so long and I think we need to find our footing again." I was desperate to beat him to the punch on *let's be friends* and keep one shred of my dignity intact.

Guy got a funny look on his face. His voice cracked when he spoke next. "Yeah. Yeah. Probably a good idea." Wait, did he want it to mean more?

Neither of us said anything for what felt like an eternity. "Hug it out?"

"Okay." Guy held me close to him, tucking his head to mine and kissing the top of my head.

"I love you, Kitty Bird," he said, pain in his voice as he squeezed me tight.

"I love you, too, Guy-Guy."

We walked on to the waffle shop, where we both got tea and a waffle to share. Guy was just as much fun as he always was when we did homework: patient, not condescending, and making me feel smart. He cracked jokes, and the warmth that we'd shared for years returned. We were still such good friends no matter how much time passed between seeing each other. We were two instruments tuned to the same key, playing perfectly together, complementing each other.

That warmth was what I protected at all costs. We couldn't lose that warmth by playing with fire together.

Chapter 14

Guy

The Friday before Thanksgiving break, I got to see Kitty do standup at an open mic in Cambridge. The crowd was packed with her supporters: her roommates, some people from her improv group, Colton because he was doing whatever Violet wanted, Mikey because he wanted to tag along, and of course, her number one fan, me. No sign of the frat bro from Kitty's last hookup, which I was a little too happy about. Probably a third of the bar was crowded with Kitty's fans.

Kitty stepped on stage to loud cheers.

"Wow! Cambridge really loves to see the funny white girl show her stuff!" she joked as the applause died. "Thank you, thank you. I'm Kitty Gatto. For those of you who don't speak Italian American wop, that translates to Kitty Cat. And yes, Kitty is my real first name. Not Katherine. Not Kate. Not Kit. Just Kitty."

Violet let out a loud, "WOOOOO! We love you, Kitty!"

"Thanks, Mom," Kitty cracked, making the room erupt again. "So my parents had trouble having kids." The room went ghostly quiet. "That's not funny, though. That's not the joke. Could you imagine if it was? And I was just standing here waiting for you to laugh at that? I'd be a monster. And like, one of you would give me a sympathy laugh." The laughter broke again. That was a format I'd seen Kitty play with over the years: dropping something morbid and then following up by acknowledging that it's not funny. It put crowds in the palm of her hand, building trust in seconds.

"What's funny is that after all their trials and tribulations, they finally had a son. And my darling older brother is named Frank. Standard American name, right there. Frank Gatto. Totally normal, right? But my mom still wanted a little girl. And they tried, and tried, and finally got their wish. I came along!" She put her hands on her hips to milk the crowd. She got what she wanted.

"But instead of a normal standard American name like Frank had gotten, they said, 'No. She will be Kitty Gatto. We want our daughter to be Kitty Cat.' But the thing is, if they had wanted to make Frank's name into a cat pun, they could have. They completely left Felix Gatto on the table." She looked out into the crowd, absorbing the laughter. "Frank Gatto instead of Felix Gatto. Could have had Felix the Cat. It never ceases to amaze me."

The laughs kept coming. Kitty told a story about a wild trip to a sex toy shop in the suburbs where she had to pee behind a dumpster filled with raccoons. My sides hurt from laughing and I felt extra special to have met one of her apparently many vibrators.

I was so happy to see Kitty shine like that. Nerves weren't even part of the equation. She was just natural, beautiful. In her element.

After her show, we all went to a party on campus. I wasn't drinking because I had a game the next day. Kitty had asked us to be friends, and I respected that, but I wanted to be available in case she changed her mind. While I was waiting for the bathroom, I heard some bros talking.

"You gonna be a chuckle fucker tonight?" one asked.

"The fuck is that, bro?" another responded.

"You know. You fuck comedians. Funny people. I guess half the people here are from the comedy scene," the first said.

"Hard to fuck a funny person when women aren't funny," the third said. I gritted my teeth and fostered a fantasy of snapping that idiot's bones like a twig. Still, I laid low. Kitty probably wouldn't like me beating the tar out of someone to defend her honor.

When I finally made it out of the bathroom, I saw Mr. Women Aren't Funny chatting up Kitty. She looked decently tipsy but not drunk. I didn't want her hooking up with anyone but me, period, but I definitely didn't want her hooking up with that guy.

I walked toward them, running my finger down Kitty's arm when I got there.

"Oh, hey, Guy. What's up?" she drawled.

"Can I talk to you for a minute?"

Her expression went dark almost instantly, eyes shooting out daggers. "Now?"

"Yes, now," I said, trying not to show how agitated I was as I pulled her toward the door.

"Are you cock-blocking me, Guy?" Apparently, hell hath no fury like a cock-blocked Kitty.

"You don't want to hook up with him, Birdy."

She huffed, turning to square up with me. "That's rich coming from you."

"What do you mean, coming from me? I'm trying to help you!"

She glared at me, her hands balling into fists at her sides. "Why do you care who I hook up with? You didn't even want me to touch you. You may as well have shoved me off you again."

My stomach dropped. This was unexpected. "Birdy—" I started, taken aback.

"Don't 'Birdy' me," she snapped, eyes filling with tears. "You pity fucked me in the dark so you wouldn't even have to look at me. Or I guess not even pity fucked. Pity finger banged! And then, you ran off. You think I'm disgusting. Just your best friend's little sister to fool around with when you feel sorry for her. Your ugly secret. It's just like high school again, Guy." Her voice caught. I couldn't believe how much pain was in her tone.

"Kitty, *you're* my best friend," I said, trying to get through to her. I put my hands on her shoulders. She instantly wrenched out of my grasp.

"You didn't even kiss me after it was over." A single tear fell down her cheek. I wanted to die. Something I did was making Kitty cry. How could I? I grabbed for her hand, desperate to make her pain stop. She whipped it out of reach.

"Kitty—" I protested again, but she held up her hand to stop me, not looking directly at me when she delivered the next part.

"I get it if I'm just another notch in your bedpost like everyone else, but don't get mad when I move on."

Her eyes flashed back to mine for a second. Then Kitty turned on her heel and stormed back into the party, swiping at her cheeks as she went.

I stood, stunned. Kitty thought I didn't like her. She thought I didn't care about her, when she's the only one I ever cared about. I thought I'd been caring. I thought I'd conveyed that I wanted to see her again.

But I'd never told her how that night in her bed made me feel. How it was the most precious night I'd ever had. How it felt insulting to call it just fooling around, because it was so much more to me. How much self-control it took not to let her finish the job with me, but I wanted to go slow. I wanted her to feel good when we did that again. I wanted her to really want me, not just feel like she owed me one.

I didn't tell her how being with her made me think it was time for us to try.

Fuck. I had my work cut out for me.

* * *

About an hour before we had to go get on the bus to go to Yale the next day, my phone rang. Heather Gatto flashed on my screen. I panicked, thinking something was wrong with Kitty and she was calling to tell me.

"Heather? What's wrong?" I answered in a rush.

Heather's warm voice filled the line. "Oh, nothing's wrong, babe. Why do you sound like that? You alright?"

"Oh, yeah, Mrs. Gatto. I'm fine. I just thought maybe you were calling about Kitty."

"Why? Something wrong with her?" Heather asked, surprised.

"No. No. I just saw her yesterday. I think she's fine," I said, trying to calm my voice.

"Good. Well, Guy, do you have plans for Thanksgiving?"

"Actually, I don't. I usually stay on campus."

"I've got a better idea. We waited too late to book a flight for Kitty, so we rented her a car. She'll be driving back and we'd love it if you came with her. Stay a few days, then you can go back together. We'd come get you but we're driving to Michigan to pick up Frank."

I hadn't talked to Kitty since the night before when she told me off.

"Does Kitty know?" I asked.

"Oh, yeah, she told me to call you so you wouldn't think she was making it up," Heather said with a laugh. "It's a long drive, but you two are getting to be two peas in a pod again. Road trip with your old buddy!"

Did Kitty actually want me to go home with her for the break? It didn't sound right given how she and I talked the night before, but I was glad for any chance to spend more time with Kitty.

I laughed nervously. "Yeah. Really fun. Um, yeah, that sounds great. Count me in. Thanks for the invite, Mrs. G."

Chapter 15

Kitty

"You did what?" I seethed. I was on the phone with my mother.

"Yeah, Guy said he'd love to come! He's looking forward to the road trip with you," Mom said. "I told him it was your idea."

I rubbed my forehead. "Mom!"

"What? Are y'all not friends anymore or something?"

I really didn't want to get into it. *Well, Mom, he came over when I was on my period and rubbed my clit until I came, but not until after he felt me up, dry humped me a little bit, and let me feel his mostly-naked body and seemingly monstrous cock. But then he ran off like the room was on fire and acted like I was the weird one for thinking that was a bad response.*

"No, we are. I just wish you'd asked me first."

The following Wednesday morning Guy waited for me on the bench outside my dorm. I busted out the door, wrestling my too-big suitcase in the snow.

"Let me get it," he said cheerfully. "Wanna get a Dunkin? My treat!"

So this was how he was going to play it. The "nothing happened" card.

We rode the bus to the car rental place, and somehow got the car without incident despite us both being under twenty-five. God only knows what sorcery Mark Gatto worked to make sure we could get home. We ended up with a cheap four-door sedan with a suspicious odor to it.

"Really fresh smell." Guy's eyes danced with mirth. He knew I was weird about smells. "Hey, there's a Dunkin right before the highway. Pull over."

I did, and as promised, Guy went in and got my Dunkin order. I may or may not have added extra words to my order so he would have to work hard for it. He returned with my drink, exactly to spec, plus a giant iced coffee for himself and a big box of Munchkins to share. He put the goodies down and shuffled around in his backpack.

"I can't believe you're drinking iced coffee," I grumbled.

"My life is on the ice, *ma puce*. May as well be in my drink, too," he said with a wink.

I guffawed. "You're such a nerd."

"I made us a playlist," he said, wiggling his eyebrows.

"Can it wait until I've had at least half of this coffee, Frenchie? You're killing me with the endless optimism this morning."

"Sure, grumpypants." He busied himself with staring out the window and reading every road sign and billboard. He added commentary like, "Oh, that's interesting!"

I knew what he was doing. He was trying to make me break. I was determined to stay grouchy. He had wronged me, again. And tried to act like he didn't. He wasn't getting off that easy.

But I loosened up about an hour outside of Boston. The caffeine and sugar hit my bloodstream, and his unrelenting goofiness broke through the tiny cracks in my heart of stone. I let him turn on his playlist. There was all kinds of nostalgic stuff, like songs our moms liked. Prince. Jewel. Some One Direction that I knew he put on to appease me. He did his best high-pitched Prince voice to go with his awful off-key singing. He changed lyrics to have my name in them.

How was I supposed to stay mad when I had the silliest pile of lean muscle and brawn in my passenger seat? I admired his profile: full lips and his many-times-busted nose. Dark eyes and floppy, wavy dark hair. Randomly perfect eyebrows that I knew for a fact he didn't groom. They were just like that. Lucky bastard.

About a half hour out of the New York City bypass, a light snow started to fall. It quickly developed into a full-on snowstorm. I was only eighteen, and though Dad had done his best to train me on driving in mountain snow, I was still inexperienced. The snowflakes dashing at the windshield were dizzying, like watching stars go by when jumping to hyper speed. The roads were pretty packed, being the day before Thanksgiving. It seemed like a good portion of my fellow drivers were tractor-trailer drivers, adding to my tension. My whole body was rigid from concentrating. I did that thing where you turn down the music to be able to see better.

"You okay?" Guy asked, noting my death grip on the steering wheel.

"Fine."

"You'll let me know if you need a break from driving, right?"

"Do you even have a driver's license?" I asked, wrinkling my brow further.

"Not an American one, but I know how to drive. And especially in the snow," he rebutted.

"Right. Because you always know better than me," I snarled.

Guy went still, in motion and sound.

"Kitty," he said, putting a hand on my leg. He watched me, taking in air like he was going to speak a few times, but not saying anything. "You're my best friend. We're better than this. Talk to me."

"Sorry. It's true, though. You do know what's best for me sometimes. You were right about that douche from the party," I admitted, briefly lifting my hand from the steering wheel to show my exasperation.

"I'm sorry," Guy said quietly. "I wish I wasn't right about that. Did he hurt you?"

I thought back to that night a few days prior. The guy I'd met at the party after my standup set wasn't outwardly bad. I consented to everything we did, but he really didn't seem to respect me. It was just a shit hookup. He could have cared less if I got off. He all but shoved me in an Uber immediately after he was done with me. An Uber that he made me order and pay for.

"No," I sighed. "He was just a dick."

Guy winced. "You're going to kill me, but you were wrong about something else that night."

I flashed him a quick look before locking my eyes back on the road. Guy went on.

"You said I think you're disgusting. That's just not true, Kitty." He paused, drawing a shaky breath before going on. "I think you're the most beautiful girl in the world. I always have, Kitty. I'm sorry I've ever made you feel anything less. It's been eating away at me."

"Then why did you do it, Guy? Why didn't you want me to touch you when we messed around?" I panted, having just spit all that out. "Why didn't you say something, all these years?"

"I was scared, okay?" he snapped. "I have always wanted you, Kitty. From that first day. I told you that at the beach! It's always been you! You were so sweet to me when I was so lost, so far from home. You called me by my real name. You kept me laughing when everything was falling apart for me. We were just kids, but you saw me, Kitty. And I saw you, too. You were smart, and funny, and so much more than that awful reputation you had. I don't want to fuck this up with you."

"Well, you kinda did fuck it up. *You* were the reason I had that awful reputation in high school. *You* repeated high school shit and made me feel like some kind of cheap favor," I said, getting more wound up with each part I admitted. "*You* pushed me away, Guy! You just disappeared after you got me off. You didn't kiss me after you made me tell you my pussy belonged to you. What the fuck is that, Guy? You're allowed to say no to sex, but that fucking hurt!"

"I didn't want you getting me off when you'd just been in so much pain. I didn't want you to feel like you owed me anything. You're worth it all on your own."

Tears blurred my vision. Fourteen-year-old me would have heard Guy's words and been screaming and crying like I was front row at a One Direction concert. Eighteen-year-old me wasn't buying it.

"Why would you think I don't want you, Kitty?"

My next words were brittle. "I was practically begging you to let me touch you."

"We were entering new territory. I didn't want to rush after we spent years dancing around it, Kitty. I loved touching you."

Silence rang through the car. The only sound was the grind of snow on the tires and the wind whipping by. I couldn't fully comprehend what he was saying.

"Because you love women. I was just another woman," I argued.

"No, it was because it was you, Kitty!" Guy burst out, staring at me. "What are you not getting here? Why is it so hard for you to believe that I want to be with you?"

"Because you've always hidden me away!" I shouted. "You've never been willing to say that I'm yours. I've always been your dirty little secret."

Another tense silence crackled between us. Guy removed his hand from my thigh. "I'm sorry."

The tears that had been threatening their arrival started to spill. My hands wobbled on the steering wheel. I sniffed. "I need to focus on the road."

"Let me drive, Birdy," he said. "Pull over."

The roads had become so white that it was hard to see the lanes, much less where the shoulder might be. "I can't see the side of the road," I said, panic tinging my tone.

"Right," Guy agreed, looking around. "Fuck, Kitty, look out!"

Guy barely got the sentence out before I had to swerve.

Chapter 16

Guy

Kitty's arm clamped over my chest at the same time that mine clamped over hers. The human seatbelt is a funny instinct like that. Our car barely missed the jack-knifed truck, but went into a spin, sailing off the side of the road into a ditch. The car came to a stop when the rear passenger bumper crashed into the guard rail, both of our heads jerking.

"Kitty, baby, are you okay?" I scrambled to reach for her, my body charged with adrenaline. She sat, staring ahead and shaking.

"Daddy's gonna kill me," she whispered.

"No, he's not, sweetheart. He won't. It was an accident."

"Are you okay?" Kitty turned to me with wild eyes.

"I'm fine, baby." That's when I noticed the trickle of blood coming down the other side of her face. I see plenty of blood in hockey, but seeing it coming down my best friend's face, sweet, innocent Kitty, almost made me throw up on the spot. "Kitty, baby, you're bleeding."

"We have to get the car out of the snow," she said, cutting the wheel back and forth.

"No, baby. We need to go get help." I couldn't stop saying 'baby.' Seeing Kitty so vulnerable broke something inside me. She'd endured so much with me. She never cried in front of me about people calling her names. She never even mentioned it. She cried with me when Maman died. She cried because I'd hurt her recently. But with everything we'd seen together over the years, she didn't break easily.

There was no way my door was opening, as it was lodged against the guard rail. "Open your door and we'll both get out, okay?"

Kitty put her foot on the gas and pressed, snow flying everywhere. I put my hand on her arm.

"Kitty, I need you to listen to me. We can't get out of the snow like that. We need to go get help for your head and check on that truck driver. My door won't open, so I need you to open yours. Turn off the car and open your door, baby."

She turned off the car but didn't open her door. I stripped off my coat and took off my t-shirt, then put my coat back on and zipped it.

"Let me see your face, Kitty Bird." Kitty still wasn't crying, just shaking. I didn't realize how bad I was shaking too until I went to zip up Kitty's coat, then pressed the t-shirt to the cut on her head.

"This is bad, isn't it, Guy-Guy?"

"It'll be okay, sweetie. I'll get us out of here." I don't know how I was holding it together. I knew I needed to check her for a concussion. I knew we needed to make sure that truck driver was okay. I needed to call 911. We needed to get out of the car. I was overwhelmed.

Luckily, a man appeared at Kitty's window. It was the truck driver. He kept apologizing when we all knew it was just shit road conditions. He said help was on the way. He helped Kitty out of the car, and I climbed out after her. Snow swirled around us. Kitty was having trouble standing, so I held her close.

Other people were stopped since the road was blocked and got out to help us. Another car had wrecked, too. A different truck driver had us wait in his cab where it was warm. I carried Kitty there, her legs too weak. I held my shirt on Kitty's head that whole time, afraid if I let go, I'd lose her somehow. Heads bleed a lot, even with not that serious of cuts, and I knew that. Still, this was my Kitty. She was too precious to lose even one drop of blood on my watch.

When the ambulance came, I hesitated to let her off my lap. If she was in my arms, I could feel that she was still warm, still breathing, still alive. It could have been so much worse, and that thought terrified me. What would I have left if I lost Kitty?

They loaded Kitty into the ambulance and had me get our essentials out of the car. I just grabbed whatever I could stuff in my backpack, a change of clothes for each of us, and our toiletries. Then I got in the ambulance with Kitty. While the paramedics finished up outside, I started crying. We were safe and with real help, but I was haunted by what almost happened.

"It's okay, Guy-Guy," Kitty said, looking pale. I'd been the one reassuring her all along, but now it was her turn.

"What if I had lost you, baby?" I sobbed. "I can't lose you."

Her lower lip wobbled. "I can't lose you either."

"I love you, Kitty Bird," I said, gasping through my tears. "Like, really love you."

Her eyes flooded as her hand found mine. She nodded and her face crumpled into tears. I kissed her forehead, then tenderly held her uninjured cheek and kissed her lips. Her big brown eyes found mine when I pulled back. She pulled at my nose to wipe it, and I laughed a little. "I don't want to fight with you, Guy."

"Me either." I drew in a breath. It was time to pitch. "I know I've screwed a lot of things up with you. You have no reason to give me another chance. But I meant what I said. I think all this time, I've just been waiting for you. I'm ready to try with you. I don't want to see you with other guys anymore. I want to love you out loud. No hiding. I want to give us a try."

"I want that, too," she whispered. "Let's try."

I kissed her hand and watched over her as she closed her eyes and rested.

* * *

We got out of the hospital later that night. I called Mark and Heather to fill them in, who were not at all mad, just worried. Kitty got 20 stitches at her temple and into her hairline, but she didn't have a concussion that they could tell. A social worker got us a ride to a hotel room. We were apparently in Bethlehem, Pennsylvania.

We were both exhausted by the time we got to the hotel, and we didn't have much of our stuff. We stripped down to our underwear and flopped into the single king bed. I held Kitty all night, careful to keep her freshly stitched-up head comfortable. Hearing her breathing in her sleep was the ultimate comfort, knowing that my girl was safe and mostly well.

I woke up to her watching me with sleepy eyes. "Happy Thanksgiving, Guy."

"Happy Thanksgiving, Kitty Bird." I rolled to my side to face her. "How are you feeling?"

"Sore, but okay. How about you?"

I stretched, testing my muscles. "Sore, too, but I think I'll be okay."

We lay there, looking into each other's eyes in the morning light for a minute. "I meant what I said yesterday," I told her. "I want to be with you."

"I meant it, too," she said. "What do we do now?"

I propped my head into my hand, raising up on my elbow. "I think," I said, tracing shapes over her collarbone, "I finally make love to you."

Kitty laughed, and it was the first time I'd heard her laugh in days. "Now?"

"If you're up to it," I said, kissing her shoulder.

"I'm gross," she groaned. "I feel like I should shower."

"Can I help?" I asked with a wolfish grin.

Kitty bit her lip with a smile. "Sure."

She got up first, taking turns using the bathroom and brushing our teeth. Nerves fluttered in my stomach. This was really going to happen. I was going to have sex with my best friend. I was rarely nervous with sex, and it's not like we'd never done *any-thing* before. I knew just how sexy she sounded when she came, what she tasted like. Still, this was Kitty we were talking about. Would she like the way I fucked? Neither of us were virgins, but the anticipation was like it was the first time.

She bent to turn on the shower, and I stood behind her, both of us still in our underwear. I stroked her hair over one shoulder, kissing softly at her neck.

"You are so beautiful, Kitty," I whispered in her ear. "So fucking beautiful."

Her hands reached behind her, running from my hips down my thighs. She scratched her nails over the fronts of my thighs, instantly getting me hard. I turned us so we were facing the mirror in the bathroom. "Look how gorgeous you are, Birdy."

"Guy." She laid her head back on my chest as she met my eyes in the mirror. I spun her around and put her butt on the bathroom counter. We kissed, slowly at first. Her lips were soft and tender, testing, exploring. Long, sensual pulls at each other's lips, my hand going to her jaw as I used my tongue to coax her mouth open. With a moan, she gave me what I wanted. I devoured her, finally having what I'd wanted for so long. Kitty, with me, understanding what I wanted and wanting the same.

My hands fumbled for her bra clasp for so long that I had to pull out of our kiss. She laughed and undid it herself, pulling the straps down her arms and revealing herself to me. Steam covered the mirror, just the color of her skin on mine visible. I palmed her breasts, the perfect shape and weight in my hands. I squeezed and stroked my thumbs over her taut nipples. Kitty rolled her hips toward my aching erection, opening her legs wider as my mouth moved over the dark buds, tongue flicking. I trailed my mouth down to her belly button, finger tracing her pussy in her panties.

"So perfect," I cooed, feeling her drenched and taking in the scent of her pussy. The most intimate scent of a woman, and hers was my very favorite.

She breathed my name, raking her fingers through my hair. "I need you."

I stood, lifted her off the counter, and dropped my boxer briefs to the floor, kicking them away. I dropped to my knees to pull down her underwear, unveiling her center that I'd only felt in the dark prior.

"Gorgeous." She shuddered as my breath hit her skin. I stood, taking her hand and leading us into the shower. Kitty stopped for a moment, getting a hair tie from her makeup bag to pull her hair up, along with some body wash.

"I don't want to get my wound wet," she said, and I nodded.

"I'll take care of you, sweetheart. Don't worry," I said with a kiss. The water cascaded over our shoulders as I held her to me, my cock pressing into her stomach. The heat felt so good on my sore muscles. I groaned loud, taking in the relief.

"Feels nice, doesn't it?" she asked. "We've been through hell."

"We have," I laughed. "All the more reason to feel good today."

I soaped up Kitty's body, admiring the slip of her skin under my hands and finally getting to know every glorious inch of her. "I've wanted to touch you like this forever, Kitty."

That's when her soapy hand met my cock, working up and down the shaft. "Holy shit," I gasped.

"Good?" Her eyes held an evil glint.

"Fuck, Kitty, it's so good," I said. "But I want to get you first."

"You *are* going to let me touch you, though, right?" she asked, referring to our last rendezvous.

"Oh, you're gonna fuckin' touch me," I growled to her excited giggle. I quickly washed my hair, soaped my body, and rinsed, then dropped to my knees again. "But right now, I'm starving."

I ran my hand to her ankle, lifting it to place her foot on the side of the bathtub. I kissed the inside of her lifted thigh, licking and biting up to where I wanted to be. As my tongue sank into her, Kitty dropped her head back and cried out.

"Oh, God, Guy," she moaned, grabbing her breasts. Her clit

was already so swollen, so I circled it with my tongue, giving it light strokes that made her twitch.

"You taste so fucking good," I said as I pulled back. "So fucking sweet."

I sucked on her, one of her hands slamming into the shower wall while the other pulled my hair. I kept at it, sliding a finger into her pussy. She bucked against my face, seeking more, using my nose as another source of friction.

"Guy, I can't. It's too good," she whined.

"You want me to stop?"

"No!" she objected.

I gave a low chuckle. "That's what I thought. You can do it, Birdy. Come all over my face, sweetheart."

She squeaked out my name one more time and that was the last intelligible sound she made. I moaned into her flesh as my tongue worked her sensitive bud, my finger pulling at the swelling tissue inside her. Her pussy tightened, and then on a shout from her, she pulsed into my face, clapping her hand over her own mouth as she whimpered through her orgasm. I lapped up all the extra arousal her body put out, savoring the taste of her and hoping I got to taste it every day for the rest of my life. I sucked, desperate for more of her, looking up to find her completely melted over me.

"That was incredible," she breathed.

"*You* were incredible," I told her as I rose to my feet, kissing her hard. "You taste that? You see how fucking good you taste?" Kitty panted, stunned and sated as she gazed at me.

I turned off the water, stepped out, and grabbed our towels. I wrapped my towel around my waist, my dick making a tent out of the material. I dried Kitty off as she stepped out, her chest and cheeks flushed from her orgasm and her hair a little frizzy. She grinned as she knocked my towel off, taking my cock in her hand.

"You're fucking huge, Guy," she mused as she drew my foreskin over the head.

"I bet you can handle it," I told her with a smirk.

"We'll find out," she said, eyebrows raised as she lowered herself to the floor.

Kitty's tongue shot out of her mouth as she looked up at me, barely licking some precum off my tip. She hummed as she tasted it, then pulled back my foreskin and swirled her tongue around the head. She was teasing me, giving me the tiniest touches that felt so unbelievably good. Her tongue danced up the underside of me, pulling just the head into her mouth.

"Ah, God, Kitty," I gritted out. "So good. You're killing me."

She popped her lips off the tip, sending a shock through me, then went back to teasing.

"More," I begged, taking my base in my hand and offering my whole dick to her. "Take me to your throat, baby. Please."

"What was that?" she asked with a devilish grin. "I'm not sure I heard you." She was playing games. She wanted me to get nasty.

"Be a good girl and take this cock in your mouth or I'm not letting you come later," I growled.

She stifled a satisfied smirk. "Oh, well, we don't want that," she said in an innocent voice. Then with one slick move, she sucked me to the back of her mouth, letting me hit her throat. She gagged around me, her mischievous eyes watering.

"You comfortable?" I asked, stroking my fingertip along her jaw. She nodded. Even though I'm a little rough sometimes, I'm not a monster. I'm not having fun unless she's having fun. "Tell me if it's not feeling good, alright?"

As if to prove it *did* feel good, she got to work. Her mouth traveled up and down my whole shaft, working the base with one hand and my balls with the other. She pulled back and spat on my dick at one point, her sordid eyes watching me.

"Beautiful, filthy girl."

She moved faster, eyes watering, hands working, tongue sliding until I was at my edge.

"You want my cum in your mouth, sweetheart?"

"Mmmhmm," she moaned around me, pulling me to the back of her mouth. I gave a few thrusts into her, then melted down her throat, my vision going black at the edges. I held her head in my hands as I stilled, coming down from my high.

"So fucking perfect, Kitty Bird," I breathed. "So goddamn perfect."

Chapter 17

Kitty

My throat was raw and my jaw ached, but I was as turned on as ever. Guy helped me off my knees, kissing me when I stood.

"Thank you, baby," he cooed. We walked out into the bedroom, where I got a glimpse of the clock. It was almost 10 a.m.

"Shit, we're going to miss continental breakfast," I said. "Nothing else will be open today."

"Shit, you're right," Guy said. "Intermission? I can throw on some clothes and go get some stuff. You can stay here and wait for me just like this."

He walked me backward until my knees met the bed, his wet hair falling over his forehead. He pushed me back on the bed, crawling on top of me to kiss me. I giggled as he nuzzled my neck and tucked me into the sheets. He tapped the bandage on the side of my face lightly. "This doing okay?"

"Think so."

He pulled on a hoodie and some sweatpants and headed for the door. "Stay there. I'll bring sustenance for round two," he said, shooting me a wink before the door closed behind him.

While he was gone, I called my mom. Guy had already talked to her while we were at the hospital, and texted them when we got into the hotel the night before.

"Kitty Cat? Are you alright?" Mom sounded frantic.

"I'm okay. I'll probably have a cool scar to show for it, but Guy and I are alright. We're just sore today. And carless."

"Daddy's going to come get y'all on Saturday and take you back to Alden safely. The last thing we need is the two of you driving."

"That's about the last thing I want to do, anyway," I confirmed. "It'll be a while before I want to drive again. Not too thrilled with snow at the moment, either."

Mom tsked. "Where's Guy right now? Can I talk to him?"

"He went down to get us breakfast. He's letting me rest."

"Love his heart. That boy is just the sweetest thing," she said, her voice finally calming.

"He's been taking good care of me," I said, remembering how he carried me through the snow after the accident. And ate me out with a skill I'd never encountered before.

"Well, have a happy Thanksgiving. Daddy'll Venmo you so you can have enough money for food and hotel while y'all are stuck there. I saw the Bob Evans nearby is open so y'all can get a proper meal. We'll be missin' you today."

I got a little emotional. Even though I had Guy to dote on me, I hadn't seen my parents since they dropped me off on move-in weekend. I missed home. Annie was home for Thanksgiving break and I wanted to be there with her, too. And after the accident, all I wanted was a hug from my mom and dad.

"Miss you, too, Mama," I said, trying to keep my tears out of my voice but failing miserably.

"Oh, sweetie. It's alright. I know yesterday must have been scary."

"I was afraid we'd both die, Mama," I said, hiccuping as I cried. I smoothed the hotel duvet, tucking myself more into the sheets. "It was so scary."

"I bet it was," she said. "I'm glad you have Guy with you. Why don't you two both video call us later?"

I agreed, we said our "I love you's," and hung up.

Guy came back in as I was wiping my tears, carrying two to-go cups of coffee in the crook of his arm and two over-stuffed plates of different breakfast foods. His face instantly went concerned.

"What's wrong, *ma puce?*" He kicked off his shoes, put the plates and cups on the desk, and sat on the bed next to me.

"I just got off the phone with Mom. I was just telling her how scary yesterday was," I said, starting to cry again.

Guy's arms surrounded me as he pulled me to the soft fabric of his hoodie. It smelled of laundry detergent, and him. "It was really scary. I'm glad we're safe now."

"I'm glad you came with me, Guy-Guy. Even though I almost killed you."

"Me, too, sweetheart. I'd never want you to go through that alone. And I'm fine. For better or worse, it brought us together," he said. "Let's get some food in you, no? They had that flavored creamer you like. The Irish cream or whatever."

He brought the food over to our bed and let me have the first pick of what I wanted.

"I eat anything. I'm a garbage disposal," he joked.

We flipped on the TV and watched the Thanksgiving Day Parade while we ate. It was nice. Comfortable. Even though I was naked under the covers and he was in sweats, it made sense for the moment. I caught Guy looking over at me.

"What?"

"Just looking at how beautiful you are," he said with a smile. "I'm happy we're trying this out."

"Does that mean you're ready to be exclusive?" I was nervous to ask but knew we should clear everything up in the temporary just-us bubble we were living in.

"Absolutely," he said, sliding a hand under the covers. "I'm not sharing that delicious pussy with anybody else. In fact, I think I need another taste."

I put our plates and cups on the nightstand and turned off the TV. "Oh, you do?"

Guy peeled off his sweatshirt and got up to drop his pants.

He grabbed a condom from his backpack, giving me a chance to admire his thick hockey butt and thighs. He threw it on the nightstand with a flourish. "Yes. I do."

"Come here, potential love of my life," I teased as he crawled over to me.

Guy's naked body hovered over me under the warmth of the covers. I ran my hands over his chest and abs as he leaned down to kiss me, the defined muscle rippling under my fingers. Guy hit me with a burning hot kiss, sucking on my lower lip.

"I don't know when I'll get enough of these kisses," he sighed. "I've been stupid jealous of anybody who got to kiss you."

He nibbled my neck before stopping at my breasts, cupping one in his hand while he engulfed my other nipple. His cock teased my entrance, so I rolled my hips to let him feel how wet I was. A shiver went up his spine.

"Jesus, Kitty," he groaned. "This is supposed to be for you, but you're driving me crazy."

"Maybe that's what I want to do. Exert my control over you."

"Oh, you think you're the boss, do you?" he said. "I could go back to not letting you come if you make me go too fast."

"You keep threatening that, but I don't know if I believe you," I taunted. "I think you should stop making threats and make love to me already."

"Patience, *ma puce*. I've got a good handful of orgasms to give you. The lovemaking's just beginning."

I gasped as he rubbed two fingers over my clit, then dipped down to my pussy and thrust two inside.

"*Guy*," I rasped.

"There's my girl," he cooed, flipping the covers back and lowering his face between my legs. "Gotta get you good and stretched out so you can take me."

With that, his tongue fell into my slit again, teasing, tasting, almost constantly edging me. He added a third finger to my pussy and I cried out.

"That's it, Birdy. You can take it. Let go for me, love," he said sweetly. "I want the taste of you on my lips when I push my cock inside you. Let me hear you come for me."

And with those dirty words and his tongue working its magic on me, I fell over the edge. My stomach hollowed out. I couldn't find my breath. All I could feel was the searing intensity of my orgasm: Guy's breath on my skin, his slick tongue working over my most intimate spaces, his hand gripping my ass and pulling me close. He sucked on me as my throbbing slowed, genuinely drinking me up. I'd been eaten out plenty of times, but no one had been nearly as talented or enthusiastic as Guy. He smiled up at me from between my legs.

"Good?"

"You fucking know it was," I said, nudging his shoulder with my foot.

"Doesn't mean I don't like hearing it." He grinned as he muscled his way to the top of the bed. I pulled him close, kissing him deep. I pushed him to his back, climbing on top of him and straddling his hips.

"You ready for me?" I drawled in his ear. Guy rested his hands on my ass and sighed as I bit his earlobe, kissing my way down his neck. But the longer I stayed on top with my face looking down at him, the more my stitches hurt. Guy reached up and pulled me in for a hungry kiss, but I squirmed to break away.

"Sorry, Frenchie. My stitches are sore. You'll have to be on top."

"Oh, jeez. Yeah, we don't want you hurting. Pleasure only, *ma puce*," he said, helping me roll to my back and coming with me. I reached down and dragged his cock through my slit.

"So fucking wet," he groaned.

"You did that."

"I fucking love it. You ready to do this?" I nodded, handing him the condom from the nightstand. He tore into it with his teeth, sheathing his length and kneeling over me, his intimidatingly large dick standing out. I let myself take him in: thighs where I could see every individual muscle, hands with long, thick fingers, corded arms leading to muscular shoulders, a chest with flat brown nipples and raised pecs, and most importantly, his gorgeous coffee-brown eyes, loose waves of dark hair falling over his forehead. His eyes dragged over my body, his expression turning serious. "You're so beautiful, Birdy. I'm so fucking lucky."

I was honored that he'd been admiring me, too.

"I think I'm the lucky one," I grinned. "Come here. Show me how I'm yours."

A sweet softness came into his eyes. I'd never really been in love before, but I imagined that's how someone in love with you would look at you. Guy held himself above me, taking his time kissing me. It was during that kiss that he notched himself at my entrance.

I flinched, preparing for impact. "Birdy, look at me. I won't hurt you," he said, holding my eyes as he pushed the first couple of inches inside me. Just starting, he was so thick. But still, it felt so perfect, so right. "Breathe, baby."

I did as he asked, overwhelmed by the stretch and fullness of him.

"You're doing so well," Guy told me, sliding in a little more. He laced his hand with mine and pinned one arm to the mattress, looking down at me adoringly. "You were made for me, Kitty. And I was made for you, too."

"I know," I whispered, heat pricking behind my eyes. The mood was lust-filled but still sacred and sweet. No sex I'd ever had before could compare. Maybe Guy meant what he said about loving me. Maybe this was what it felt like to be loved by a man.

"Can you take a little more? We're almost there, sweetheart."

"Give me all you got," I told him, wrapping my legs around his hips. With one final push, he was all the way in. I put my head back, so completely full of this man who'd possessed me for years. I squeezed his length inside me. And from there, we were off. Guy worked my neck as he thrust inside me, slow but hard, pushing down to hit my clit just right. His eyes met mine and a smile curled one side of his mouth. "It feels so good, Guy."

"That's right it does. You're mine, Kitty Bird," he panted, taking my leg in his hand and pinning my knee to my torso. "All fucking mine."

"Faster," I begged, and he gave, driving into me.

It was surreal. I felt like we'd always been destined to end up at this point, at least in my dreams, but it was actually happening. We connected in the deepest way two people can. It did feel like it was perfect, that we were made for each other. We'd teased each other about making love since the night I blurted it out, but that's really what we were doing. And something a little more raw than that, too.

"So pretty when you take it like that," he gritted out as he picked up a merciless pace.

I yelped out desperately. "I'm so close."

"Me, too, baby. I need you to come," he urged. "Fuck, I'm close."

"Harder, just a little harder," I cried, curling my hips to meet his strokes.

"Come for me, sweetheart. Show me who makes this perfect pussy feel good." And just as he choked out my name into my ear, another orgasm ripped through me.

I shouted, a lot. I'm not sure it was coherent. Half phrases, half words, my brain complete mush. Was that true what they said about having your brains fucked out? That felt like a real thing. Sweat made us sticky where our bodies connected. We watched each other, smiling, disbelieving. His arms caged me in with a snug embrace. Guy gave me the softest, most delicate kiss while he was still buried deep inside me.

"I love you, Kitty Bird. You're my always."

Chapter 18

Guy

Kitty and I caught our breath, facing into each other like we always did. This time, though, we were naked with our legs wrapped around each other.

"What did we just do?" she said on a laugh, turning to face the ceiling.

"What we've been meaning to do for years," I said, tilting her chin back to me. "I made love to the love of my life."

Kitty was clearly going through some doubts, her lower lip caught between her teeth. "Guy, we're just getting started. Anything could go wrong."

"But it's you and me," I argued. "We already know each other."

"Not like this, we don't. What happens when we get back on campus and girls are all over you again?"

"I'll tell them I'm with you, and that will be it."

Kitty looked at me, skeptical.

"I'm serious," I said. "I've never loved anyone but you. Everyone in between was just me killing time, Kitty."

Her eyes were sad when she turned to me. "Then why didn't you call all those years? If you loved me so much, why did you let people think I was something I wasn't in high school? Why didn't you try to hang out with me as soon as I was at Alden?"

I tugged at her waist to get her to face me fully again. "I can apologize until the day I die for hurting you in high school and it'll never make it okay. I know that."

She nodded. "I know."

"But I hope you know what I was up against. That doesn't make it alright, but you know how worried I was about being my dad. I still worry about that."

Her lower lip quivered. "How do I know you're not going to leave me like that again?"

"I don't want to. I don't ever want to live with this kind of regret again, knowing I hurt you. I want to be the man that you deserve, Kitty."

She took my hand. "I think you can be. Maman thought you could."

"That's the other thing. I couldn't talk to you for a long time after she died, because you reminded me of that loss. Not on purpose, but you were the one who carried me through it. We didn't get a chance to be normal again after that, you know? It made me too sad to talk to you."

"I get it," she said quietly, not mad, just like she understood.

"I never said thank you for that, Kitty. Even when I wasn't responding to you after you went home, it still meant so much to hear from you. You're a better friend than I am."

She blew a raspberry. "I wouldn't say that. We've both screwed up here and there."

"I should have talked to you, though. I needed you, but I didn't know how to separate you from the sadness."

"Are you able to separate it now?"

I traced a finger over her cheek. "Yeah. Seeing you at that party forced me to see you as a whole person again. You've lived a whole life between her dying and now." I swallowed a lump in my throat. "Kitty, I know you didn't come to Alden for me, but I came for you."

Kitty's brow furrowed, her eyes darting over my bare chest. "What do you mean?"

"I knew you wanted to go there for comedy. I had offers from other places, but once I had an offer from Alden, I knew that's where I had to go. I came hoping you'd get in and we'd get our shot at being together."

A sea of emotions passed over Kitty's face: touched, disbelieving, irritated. "And you didn't seek me out, knowing I was there?"

"Yeah. Chicken, I guess. Afraid I'd think of Maman. Afraid I wouldn't give you space to be your own person," I said. *Afraid to commit to the best relationship of my life.*

Kitty nodded slowly. "So when you say you love me, is it as a friend?"

I thumbed over her lips. "It's as my everything, Kitty. You're the person who gets me. You're my best friend. You're family. You're my love. All of it."

She narrowed her eyes. "You're so sure about this."

"I am. It's okay if you're not. I've put you through hell. That's why we're trying."

"I wasn't even sure you liked me like that until . . . yesterday? Particularly after the period incident. I don't know." Kitty flopped on her back and poked around her stitches. "I'm happy. It's just a lot to process."

"I'm sorry I didn't make you feel as loved as you are until now. That's my mistake. I should have been clear the night you were sick," I said, kissing her collarbone and letting my eyes roam her breasts. "I'm willing to make up for lost time, though."

Kitty met my devilish grin as I grew hard against her leg. "Again? Seriously? I'm sore! My stitches hurt! And my parents want to FaceTime us later. We'll have to get dressed and out of this bed at some point."

"What, you don't want Mark and Heather to see us naked in bed together?"

"Do you want Mark to murder you when he comes to get us Saturday?" she quipped.

"Mark wouldn't. He loves me," I said, smug.

"He loves you until you're dicking his one and only daughter." Kitty yawned. "And I think I need a nap before I can take more dicking."

"I can get behind that," I agreed, snuggling up to Kitty and kissing her until we dozed off.

The rest of the day was dream-like. We spent most of the day naked and in bed, napping, laughing, exploring, and zoning into each other. We blew right through lunchtime and raided the vending machine for snacks to hold us over. I got Kitty ice for her head. We showered off all our sex sweat and got dressed for our Bob Evans dinner and FaceTime call. In all, it was a nice way to kick off our relationship, although it was under bad circumstances.

Heather cried when she saw Kitty's bandage and the bruise around it. Mark's arm went around his wife, and though it was sad, it was heartwarming. It was how I wished my parents had been growing up. I could see Kitty and me being like them when we were older: loving and comforting each other, loving our children. Being a family.

Frank got on the call, too, asking about my hockey season. I asked about his soccer season, which had just ended.

"Your parents are sweet together, Birdy," I told her when we got off the call.

She got a wry smile. "They really are. They love you, too, you know."

"Oh, trust me. I know," I said with a laugh. "Your mom never lets me forget."

We walked through the snow to Bob Evans. Kitty said she wasn't ready for cars yet, and I was fine with stretching our sore muscles a bit. I wasn't majorly hurt in the accident, but it did mess with my muscles a lot. Between that and going down on Kitty many, many times, my neck was extra stiff.

Kitty's cheeks and nose were tinted pink from the cold, and with no makeup on, she looked more like the Kitty I grew up with than college girl Kitty. The snow had stopped, but there was still plenty to sift through. I noticed Kitty limping about halfway to the restaurant.

"You hurting?" I asked.

"Just sore," she said, brushing me off.

"You're limping, Birdy," I pointed out.

"Fine, I think my boot is hitting where my driving foot hit the console."

"Say no more," I said, scooping her up like she was my bride, carrying her again for the second time in two days.

"Guy, no! You're sore, too!"

"But I'm not limping, *ma puce*." I snuck a kiss into her neck. I mostly got a faceful of her scarf, which carried her light, girly scent.

"I'm not happy about this," she pouted.

"I am." A few blocks later, we were at Bob Evans. I booted the door open, still carrying her.

The hostess looked like she didn't know what to do with us.

"Put me down," Kitty hissed.

"Table for two," I announced proudly. Kitty squirmed and wriggled until she fell out of my arms, landing hard on her feet with a quiet "ow."

"See? You should let me carry you," I said, self-satisfied.

The hostess led us to our table, eyeing us like we were diseased. Kitty slid into the booth across from me, stripping her many layers.

"Only my second American Thanksgiving ever."

"Aw, buddy, did you not celebrate the last two years?"

I shook my head. "Ramen noodles and porn."

Kitty stuck out her bottom lip. "Don't tell Mom. She would have driven through a hurricane to come get your ass for Thanksgiving if she'd known you were alone."

"Oh, I wasn't alone. I had many moaning women to keep me company," I said with a grin.

Kitty rolled her eyes. "Definitely leave that part out if you're talking to Mom. I hope I'm not disappointing you. Sounds like the last two years were pretty hot."

I laced my fingers with hers across the table. "They were, but this year wins. I wouldn't change a thing. Except maybe the car accident. I'd rather be charmingly stranded than desperately stranded."

"Fair," she said, looking at her menu. "Ready to eat until you're sick? I don't know how you Canucks do it, but that's how we do it in America."

I'd loved the Thanksgiving Maman and I spent with the Gattos in West Virginia, but this one had it beat. Kitty was mine, after all that time. I gave her a piggyback ride back to the hotel. I iced up her leg and head, curling up around her. We fell asleep to the drone of football on TV. I was with my family, my best friend, and my love all at the same time.

Chapter 19

Kitty

"That's it, Birdy."
I lowered myself fully onto Guy's cock. We were in a chair in front of the mirror in our hotel room the day after Thanksgiving. We still had another day to kill until my dad came to get us, so we killed time the best way we knew how: marathon fucking. Once we ripped off the bandaid of our physical attraction to each other, there was no stopping us. I couldn't get enough, stitches in my face or not.

I faced away from Guy, sitting in his lap while he filled me. He kissed my back as his hands reached around, one toying with my clit while the other played with my breast. The slap of skin and moans filled the air.

"So fucking pretty riding that dick." Guy's gaze flicked from my back to our reflection. It was so deeply erotic to see how he watched me, his eyes devouring me voraciously.

"Oh, God, Daddy," I spilled out, not really sure where that came from. Guy was a little older than me, so I guess that qualified him for daddy status? We'd said so many dirty things to each other in the prior twenty-four hours that I think I was just looking for something new to say.

He seemed to like it well enough. Or at least, he supported my choice like any good improviser would.

"Ooh, am I your daddy, baby?" Guy said, going with it. "You Daddy's good girl?"

"Yes," I said, the pleasure building. I bounced up and down as Guy's hand worked me. It felt blindingly good.

A knock sounded at the door. We froze. I looked over my shoulder at him.

"Did you put on the do not disturb?" I hissed.

"I thought I did," Guy said, panicking.

"Busy!" I shouted. "No service needed!"

Footsteps shuffled in the hallway and I thought they silenced. We resumed our activity, the slapping of flesh on flesh picking up again.

"Fuck, Kitty, this pussy feels so good," Guy moaned. "You're gonna make Daddy come."

"Kitty!" came a voice at the door with more knocking. A voice that I definitely recognized.

"Shit!" I climbed off Guy's lap.

"I thought he wasn't coming until tomorrow?"

"I did, too!"

"Go take a shower, I'll cover." Guy scrambled for some clothes.

"Just a minute!" I called to the door. Guy threw on sweatpants and a shirt. His boner retreated rapidly, because what's sexy about your new girlfriend's dad showing up while you're fucking? Still, it wasn't entirely gone as it disappeared into his sweats, still sheathed in the condom.

I ran into the bathroom, closing the door softly and turning on the shower. In an effort to clear the sex smell from the room, I squirted body wash in the bottom of the tub and let the water run over it. That should at least help, right?

I heard Guy open the door. "Mark! Oh my gosh, Heather and Frank, too! How wonderful!" Guy cried, stage speaking so I could hear.

Fuck. The whole family had come early to surprise us. Our room was a wreck. I shuddered to think how many condom wrappers hadn't made it into the trash can. Or what would happen if someone looked *in* the trash can. Whatever was about to happen, it probably wasn't good.

I quickly rinsed off, trying to cool the sexed-up flush on my skin. I wrapped myself in a towel and walked into the room where Guy stood, awkwardly making small talk with my family. The air was tight. Everybody knew something was up.

"Hi!" I said, falsely cheerful. "Let me get some clothes on and I'll give everyone hugs!"

My dad's eyes were furious. I'm not religious, but I prayed he didn't hear what we'd said while we were having sex. Judging by his expression and the lingering smell of sex in the air, even if he hadn't heard, he could connect the dots. Granny Gatto didn't raise no fool. Frank's face was red, eyes trained on the floor. Mom gave me a sympathetic look.

I snatched my only set of clothes and stepped back into the bathroom to change. I was so fucked.

It was when I was hugging Frank that I noticed it. Guy clearly hadn't put on underwear in his rush to open the door for my family, but his dick was done with our drama. Therefore, the condom must have taken the path of least resistance.

The condom hung out the bottom of his sweatpants leg. My eyes snagged on it, and I'm sure I looked like I'd seen a roach or something. Before I could look away, Frank followed my line of vision.

His face went beet red. "Seriously, bro? My fucking sister?"

Guy held up his hands, trying the classic approach of denial. "I don't know what you think is happening here."

"The *condom* is hanging out of your *pants*, bro!" Frank exploded. "We all heard what you were saying to her. You're treating her like a piece of fucking meat!"

There it was. An eerie stillness settled in the room. Dad cracked his knuckles and neck, eyes trained on Guy.

"Consensually?" Guy tried, wincing.

My mother, in all her infinite wisdom, shrugged and spoke. "Well, at least they're doing it right."

It's easy to tell where I got my twisted sense of humor.

That was the match that lit the powder keg.

Frank lunged for Guy. Guy's hands went to shield his own face, knowing the beat-down was coming.

"It's not what it looks like!" Guy objected.

Frank's fist didn't let him finish that sentence. My stomach curdled, and then I was weirdly touched. Frank loved me enough to defend my honor? It wasn't really warranted, but I was pretty surprised at my brother's willingness to come to blows over it.

"What was that, punk?" Frank said between hits. Dad stood back, watching with his arms crossed over his chest and his jaw clenched. Mom clutched Dad's arm. I could tell he wanted to get a swing in there, but he was letting Frank do the dirty work.

My freshly minted boyfriend was getting beaten up by my brother.

"Frankie!" Mom yelled over the fight. "It's just Guy! Why are you so upset about this?"

Frank whirled on his heel to face Mom, gesturing at Guy, who now sat back on the bed. "He uses girls, Ma! He's told me himself, he hits and quits! I'm not letting him do that shit to my sister, when he's always said we're all 'best friends'—"

"I love her, Frankie!" Guy shouted. "I always have. We're just actually getting together now."

Frank's face reddened further and his eyes narrowed. He whipped back around to face Guy. "Easy to do now, huh? You ruined her in high school. Couldn't stick up for her then but you can love her now? You should know better, Kitty. You know how he is."

I felt like the wind was knocked out of me. "You knew? About him being the reason everyone called me a slut?"

Frank dragged a hand down his face, then examined his busted knuckles. "I didn't want to make you feel worse," he sighed. "It wasn't my business. And you two seemed to work it out."

Guy touched a hand to his bleeding lip. "I didn't date her because of you, Frank. I was afraid you'd . . . do what you just did. I didn't want to lose all of you if something went wrong." He sucked in a breath, glancing at me. "And because my dad—"

"Oh, sweetie," Mom said. She stepped away from Dad to hug Guy, grabbing a tissue to dot on his lip. "You're not him."

Right, Eva probably would have told Mom about his dad. Hell, that was probably how they got so close so quickly. Mom doted on Guy how Eva would have, and I think it calmed Frankie's fury. We were most of what Guy had left for a family. We couldn't be fighting like this.

"Is it true?" My dad's quiet voice rang out in the room. "You love her?"

Guy's eyes watered and met mine. He nodded and turned to my dad. "I do."

My dad twisted his lips and looked at the floor between us, grinding his teeth. That didn't look like a major endorsement to me. It was the face he made when he was mulling something over.

Frankie hissed as he tried to make a fist. I went to his side, examining his hand.

"Guess you love me, huh?" I said softly. "You're willing to beat up our best friend for me?"

Frankie chuckled. "Don't get too used to it, sissy."

My arms circled his waist and he hugged me back. "I can fight my own battles. But I appreciate ye," I said in Mom's accent.

"She hasn't pulled any punches," Guy joked.

He and Frankie hugged it out, but Frankie stepped back and pointed at Guy's face. "You're on thin fucking ice, though. And get that condom off your foot, weirdo."

"Okay," Dad said, clearly uncomfortable.

"Why don't we give Kitty and Guy some time to get their

room ready to check out?" Mom said with a wry smile. "We'll go get some coffee while we wait."

My parents and brother filed out, and the door closed. I locked eyes with Guy. "I think I can safely say that is the first and last time I'll call you daddy."

***

"Say cheese!" Mom cackled from the front seat of my parents' SUV.

I had ice on my temple and leg from the accident, which was spread across Guy and Frank's laps. Frank iced his knuckles from punching Guy. Guy iced the left side of his face from Frank punching him.

Frank held up his middle finger with his ice pack for the picture.

"Oh, relax, Frankie. You'll all look back at this and laugh one day."

"Give it a rest, Heather," Dad grumbled. "Let's get the kids' stuff from the car and get our sorry asses to Boston."

Dad, Guy, and I got out at the impound lot where our wrecked rental had been towed. Flurries sprinkled around us, and I shivered against the cold. Dad still hadn't looked me in the eye. Guy got our luggage and refused to let me carry it.

Dad held me back so Guy could walk ahead.

"You'll always be my little girl, Kitty. I know you're growing up, but you always have me. Anything he does wrong, I've got you." He finally turned to face me. "I want you to be happy. Does he make you happy?"

I thought about his question. "So far, yes. Up until the accident, we were just friends. He's been a good friend when he was able to."

Dad nodded. "He left you hanging for a while, Kitty Cat. Years. You didn't say anything, but I noticed."

"I reminded him of Eva dying. He's doing better now, though."

Dad squared with me. "He's part of our family in his own way. But you and Frank always come first. Capeesh?"

"Capeesh," I said, and he pulled me in for a tight hug.

"If he raises a hand to you, Kitty . . ."

"I know, Daddy." I said it seriously, but given the Daddy incident that had just gone down at the hotel, my comedic timing was a little better than anticipated.

He made the face he makes when he has acid reflux at the name. "You and your mother with your sick senses of humor."

"You love us," I grinned.

"More than anything, Kitty Cat. I love y'all more than anything." He squeezed me tighter. "You scared me. I'm glad you're okay. Both of you. And don't worry about the car. That's what insurance is for."

Guy closed the SUV's trunk and headed around to get back in.

"Guy. A word," Dad said.

"Yes, sir."

I got in the car, slowly closing the door to see if I could hear what my dad said to Guy. I couldn't, but I'm not bad at reading lips. One sentence stood out.

"You will treat my daughter with respect."

Chapter 20

Guy

"Over here," I called to Zac. The puck slid across the ice to me. I dusted it off and cracked it toward the net with a wrist shot. It went just wide.

"Think being wifed up is getting to your head, G-Spot!" Mikey taunted.

I shot him a gloved middle finger. Truthfully, we were getting to the end of a hellish practice and I was just plain tired. But maybe I was also tired from staying up a little too late with my head between Kitty's legs. What was I supposed to do? Between our schedules, it was hard to find time to be together. We ended up choosing late nights in each other's beds over good-quality sleep. It all came out in the end, because I slept better with Kitty around, even if it was fewer hours than was ideal.

It's weird how you can picture something for years and be so sure you know what it's going to be like. In some ways, it would live up to that image. In others, it would be completely different.

That's how it was starting to date Kitty. I'd pictured her cheering me on and waiting for me after hockey games. I imagined parties where we'd play beer pong as a team. I imagined watching all of her comedy shows and being so excited to kiss her when she was done.

All those things came true. Some of them were better. Like how I'd hear her filthy sailor's mouth while she screamed for me at hockey games. She doesn't have a high-pitched girly voice, but more of a smooth voice for radio. I could always pick out her angry alto when she let loose some sort of abuse toward the other team. Sometimes I thought if we were short a player we could throw her in a sweater and some skates and get her out there chirping along with us.

I loved how she jumped into my arms as soon as I left the locker room, whether we won or lost. How I had someone to whisper things to at parties, and it was the same someone every time. How we had inside jokes and spent our last minutes before falling asleep making each other laugh. And those after-show kisses were my favorite. I liked to pick her up and plant a big kiss on her until she kicked her feet and squealed.

But there was stuff about dating Kitty that I didn't predict. I underestimated how amazing it would be to have her around more and wake up with someone I loved. I'd spent so long telling myself I wasn't good enough for her because of my dad. But really, there wasn't any getting around being in love with Kitty.

Since we spent more time together, she tested out her joke material on me. She was working on a portfolio for a summer writing internship, hopefully with SNL or one of the late-night shows based in New York. I was always a willing test audience, though she really didn't need me. She knew what was funny and what needed work.

Some stuff sucked. Frank had backed down how much he was talking to me. Even though we made up after he hit me, he still wasn't overly thrilled Kitty and I were an item. I had my friends on the team, but he and Kitty had been my deepest, longest friends. Kitty swore he'd come around eventually, once he saw us sticking together. Kitty was also pretty busy between all the comedy shows, writing new content, and her regular course load. I still had her for all the math help, which we always did after her improv show over a waffle and some tea.

No matter what, I tried to end up in her bed, or with her in mine, whenever I could. We'd lay facing each other and talk about our days. That was my favorite part of any day, taking down all the walls we'd put up and tuning into each other. Kitty never made me feel like a meathead for loving hockey, nor did she put me on a pedestal like the girls who chased after me did. She just supported me, and I supported her.

So yeah, I was a little tired at practice. I was in love. Sue me.

But notably, Kitty hadn't said she loved me back. I understood to some degree. I'd put her through the wringer all those years before, kissed her while I was with someone else, and always treated her like she was a dirty little secret. She needed time with me loving her out loud. She needed to know that I wasn't going to screw her around. I didn't want to push her. She was entitled to some groveling time. She'd always love me as a best friend and in time, I trusted that she'd love me as her everything.

I could tell Mikey's little comment on the ice had some knives behind it. Colton and Violet were a regular thing, and it was getting toward the end of the fall semester. Of our trio, two of us were in relationships.

Mikey found any opportunity to make jabs at Colton and me about dating. That day at practice, Coach had us finish with a bag skate, which is fucking brutal. I knew we had it coming, since we'd lost to Dartmouth the weekend before. I was looking forward to stuffing my face and napping before my evening class, maybe seeing if Kitty was free to cuddle.

Mikey was a hell of a defenseman and generally a goofy guy, but he had a wild temper sometimes. It's probably what made him such a good defenseman. But he despised bag skates more than anyone I knew. He'd also just been grouchy in the last week or so. Between the terrible practice and his attitude, he was clearly agitated heading into the locker room.

"You coming to the Kappa party tomorrow?" he asked as we left the showers.

"Maybe late. Kitty has a show in Boston." I got my clothes

out of my bag. I sat on the bench for a minute, as I never really stopped sweating after practice, even with the shower.

"Could have called that," Mikey muttered. "Colt?"

Colton shifted his eyes to me. "Depends what Violet's doing. I might be going to Boston, too."

"Cool, I'll just hang out with the freshmen you two aren't fucking then," Mikey spat. "I'm sure Zac or Spencer will want to party on campus."

"Actually, I've got a date," Zac cut in.

Mikey spiked his water bottle into his locker. "Are you fucking kidding me? Why does everyone want the same pussy all the time now? Did I miss a memo?"

Colton met my gaze again. It was time for a boys' heart-to-heart.

"You know you're welcome to come with us, Mike," I said.

"I don't want to go to your freshman girlfriend's stupid comedy show! I'm sick of being your fifth wheel," Mikey raged.

I bit my tongue to keep from defending Kitty because I knew he actually liked her. They were friends, too. He was pushing it, but I knew it wasn't really about her.

"Ben, come on, man. Don't be mean about Kitty," Colton said, trying to cool Mikey down. We so rarely used his actual first name that I was jarred by him calling Mikey, Ben.

"It doesn't fucking matter," Mikey mumbled, wiping his skates and slamming them in his bag. "You're both leaving in a semester and I'll be alone senior year. I may as well get used to being without you." His face went so red it brought out more red in his hair.

Colton had been drafted by Tampa Bay and I was off to Seattle. Mikey's a killer defenseman, but he didn't quite have the skills to get drafted before junior year. He was facing potential time in a European league or the AHL until he got his skills up to par. I was going to miss him a lot, and I did have some guilt issues about leaving him behind. And Kitty. That's a whole year more we could have together. When you're a person with a family of one, friends and girlfriends become really important.

So the root of Mikey attacking Kitty was about us leaving, not about Kitty.

"Mikey, you know it's not like that, man," Colton said. "We want to hang out still."

"Then hang out! Go to parties! Stop spending every spare second with your dicks in your girlfriends." Mikey got impassioned again. "And Stelle, you and Kitty need to pipe down. I don't need constant proof as to why you're called G-Spot. She's a loud comer and it's fucking annoying. First it's you, 'Ride my face, Birdy,'" he said with an exaggeration of my accent. Then he imitated Kitty's voice. "'Oh, God, Guy, harder, Guy. Fill up my pussy, Guy.'"

The rest of the team was definitely paying attention now, some of them standing as I did, sensing a fight on the wind.

It was true. Since our first hookup in that hotel room where I didn't want to disturb the entire hotel with our sex, I'd encouraged Kitty to get loud. I loved hearing her scream for me. I lived for it. And Mikey and I shared a wall, so he definitely got the brunt of it.

Still, I couldn't have him blasting us like that. My temper was rare, but I didn't like him broadcasting what our sex sounded like to the whole team. That was private between me and Kitty.

"Don't you fucking dare talk about her like that," I snapped.

"You don't seem to have a problem talking nasty with her. Why can't I? May as well invite me to join. At least then I'd be the one making her scream."

And that was when all hell broke loose. Colton actually threw the first punch, which surprised me. I shoved Mikey into his locker, then held everyone else back. It was nice to know Colton and the rest of the team had me on this one, but I wished Mikey wasn't being such a dick instead.

"Why do you hate Kitty?" I shouted over all the commotion. "She's only ever been nice to you!"

"I hate who you are with her!" Mikey yelled back, checking his lip for blood. "You used to be fun. Now you're Mr. Relationship and you left me behind. Both of you did."

"There are better ways to say that than making fun of what they sound like fucking, Mike," Colton growled. "That's low, bro."

"I'm not going to apologize for loving Kitty or being with her," I said, salty. "But I'm sorry I've been a shitty friend."

Mikey shook his head, looking at the ground.

"Maybe I'm jealous, okay? I can't find what you two have. I'm not cut out for loving someone like you are. Okay? Fuck." Mikey stood up and threw on his clothes, leaving a pin-drop quiet locker room. Before he crossed the threshold, he turned back. "But you'd better get your fucking head back in the game, Frenchie. Seattle's not gonna take you if you keep missing shots."

"Thanks for that," I muttered. I hadn't really been missing shots. I'd scored or gotten an assist in every game we had. I just missed a few in practice. Mikey was just hurting.

Chapter 21

Kitty

We were happy. Time went by too fast. Way too fast.

We both went home for winter break, and I missed Guy so much. Guy surprised me by coming to West Virginia for New Year's until we went back to school, something he'd worked out with my mom in secret. One night, a light snow fell, and we took a walk around my neighborhood, our old neighborhood. The air smelled of woodsmoke and that indescribable but distinct scent of winter. As we neared the house he used to share with Maman, Guy slowed. We stood in the street in front of it, Guy tucking me into his side but not saying anything.

"Is this hard?"

"Bittersweet. It's the last place we were happy. Before it all fell apart." His last sentence was broken. I took off my mitten and wiped the tear that fell down his cheek. "I'm glad we lived here, even if it was just a year."

I nodded. "It was a good year."

He turned to me, pulling our fronts together and locking his arms around my waist through all our layers. "I got you out of the deal," he said, looking down at me. "It doesn't get better than that."

"What if we had only met at Alden?"

"I don't know if I'd have picked Alden if it hadn't been for you," Guy said, nuzzling my nose. "But I'm really glad I did. No matter where you go, Kitty Bird, I'll be right behind you. I can't imagine a life without you again."

He bent, hovering his mouth over mine until I couldn't take it anymore, pulling us together by his coat lapels. His lips were light and soft as the snow falling around us, like we were two figures inside a snow globe. His gloved hands were at my waist and then one at my jaw, cherishing me, surrounding me, making me feel safe. Even though we kissed all the time, he took special care sometimes, building the suspense, soaking up the tension between us. It never failed to give me that roller coaster stomach feeling. Between the snow and where we were and all we'd weathered together, this kiss was magical. I sealed the memory into my head, a sweet moment that was just ours.

I pulled back and watched his coffee eyes. I saw him for who he was to me: the man who loved me, and had loved me all along. He didn't always get it right, but since we'd been officially dating, he'd gone out of his way to make me feel valued. He put his fears to the side and gave me everything he had. He'd shown me a love so deep, pure and unadulterated. It was time for me to put my fears aside, too. I was finally ready to give him all of my heart.

I mirrored his words from the back of that ambulance in Pennsylvania. "I love you, Guy. Like really love you."

Guy let out a little gasp and got the brightest smile. "Kitty. Really? You know there's no pressure. I don't want you to say it unless you're sure."

"Really. I'm absolutely sure. I love you, Guy."

"I love you, too, sweetheart. Oh my God. You love me. We're in love. I love you so much." Guy covered me in kisses, holding both sides of my face. He shouted into the street. "SHE LOVES ME!"

I hadn't said I love you since we got together as a couple. He'd been forthcoming with it from the car accident on, but he had hurt me so much in the past that I needed more time. He had waited patiently, never pushing me, but telling me he loved me every day. I needed to trust that he wasn't going to leave me in the lurch again. I needed to know that what we had really was love. And it was.

Chapter 22

Kitty

Thoughts of Guy leaving ate away at me. He'd catch me at night sometimes, lying awake and worrying about what was ahead for us. He'd be off to the NHL, on West Coast time primarily, and I'd only be in my sophomore year of college. It was inevitably going to be hard.

Of course, our foundation was pretty stable. He was right that his prior love affairs weren't even an issue. They hardly even had a chance to talk to him at parties, because he was like a vacuum attached to me. One unseasonably warm late winter night, we enjoyed a night of beer pong and shit-talking at a frat house. Guy's arm stayed locked around my waist any chance he could get, even hugging me from behind when I was shooting the ball. I knew we were being nauseating, but I was obsessed. The rush of being newly in love clouded any doubts I had.

Guy oscillated between being clean-shaven for a week or so, then rocking the stubble. I enjoyed it, like getting multiple different versions of the same boyfriend. This was a stubble day. We were close to the end of our game, and Guy was intentionally missing shots so Colton and Violet would win.

"I wanna get out of here," he rumbled low in my ear, nipping at my neck. His half-erect dick pressed into my back as he goosed his hand under my shirt to caress my belly. A jolt of pleasure rushed through me.

"Keep it in your pants, Stelle," Colton called as he sank the final ball in our cup. Guy spun me to prop me on the table. I tipped the last cup to his lips and he let some of the beer run down the side of his face.

"Sloppy drunk," I accused.

"No, I just want you to lick it clean," he said, pressing his forehead to mine.

"You're something else tonight, Frenchie."

"You'd better get to it, or else."

"Or what? What are you gonna do to me?" I taunted.

"You don't wanna find out, Birdy," he said, gaze dark.

I tipped my head to the side. "Actually, I think I do."

Guy's eyes blazed into mine. He used his shirt to sop up the moisture on his chin and neck, took my hand, and led me to the door. I waved goodbye to Violet and she rolled her eyes.

"Have fun, you two," she sighed.

He was trying his old tough boy routine, which frankly, was quite fun and one of my favorite things we did. Violet knew I was a sucker for Guy trying to act like he was anything but the sappy puppy he is.

On the walk home, he continually grabbed my ass. Because the night was warm for February in Boston, we didn't have many layers on. Still, it was kind of chilly, and I shivered.

"Keep me warm," I whined.

"If I keep you close, I won't be able to wait til we get home. You have no business looking so good, Kitty Bird."

I wrapped his arm around my shoulder to show him that yes, he could control himself. To prove that no, he could not control himself, he draped his hand over my front and honked my boob.

"I'm glad you haven't gotten tired of me yet," I laughed.

"Tired of you? I'm fucking addicted, Kitty."

We walked a bit longer in a tense silence.

"Let's run the last bit. Come on. It'll keep us warm."

"Fine." We jogged to his apartment. As soon as his front door closed, I was pinned against it with Guy's mouth covering mine.

"Guy, Mikey!" I managed through kisses. Mikey often parked it on the couch for hours at a time, whether he was drunk or just wanted to have a public sleep. It was a whole thing. You always had to check for Mikey before sitting down.

"He's out. Focus. I don't know if I've ever wanted you this bad," Guy sighed, rubbing my center on his hardness. "I want you on the living room floor."

Before I could object, his mouth was back on mine, deeply exploring and seeking me. He carried me to the middle of the living room and laid me on my back. Without breaking our kiss, he unbuttoned my jeans and shimmied them and my underwear down my hips. Within seconds, his hands were on my breasts under my shirt as his tongue engulfed my pussy. God, he was so fucking good at going down on me, but even that intense pleasure couldn't distract me from the fact that we might get caught.

"Guy, what if—"

"Shut up," he ordered.

"But—" I objected, then shrieked as he turned me to my side to slap my ass.

"That's what you get for not doing what I asked at the party," he growled. The glint of joy in his eye and his erection straining at his pants told me how much he was into this game. I sat up and pulled at his button and zipper, unleashing him into my hand. I gave him a couple of firm strokes before licking a drip of precum from the side of his cock.

"Is this better? More of what you want?" I dared. Guy nodded, his eyes going hazy as he pressed his hips forward, putting just the first couple of inches in my mouth. I took the bait, sucking hard and stroking my tongue against him. He put his head back, sighing with a hand in my hair.

"Gorgeous, Kitty," he got out before we heard a key in the door and Colton and Violet's laughter. Our eyes met, wide, and we both rushed to pull our pants up and dash to his room.

"Kitty!" Violet called as we disappeared, slamming Guy's door shut and locking it. My phone buzzed in my back pocket.

I threw it to the side, but not before reading the text.

Violet
Gross. I saw Guy's butt

I laughed.

"Think something's funny, Kitty Bird?" Guy challenged me, stooping down in front of my face. "Clothes off."

Damn, this was the longest he'd ever held onto his tough boy attitude. It was a hell of a lot of fun. If it wasn't fun, I knew I could tell him and he'd stop right away. We'd established a good rapport around how we played, and though we weren't *that* wild, we'd decided to pick a safe word: peaches. We wanted to establish that feeling of security, so we could comfortably push our limits. It allowed us to deepen our trust and was another reason why I loved Guy so much.

I stripped and threw my clothes into the same corner as my phone, watching as he did the same.

"Hands and knees," he commanded. "I want to show you how I'd have done you in the living room."

I did as he asked and looked back at him.

"Eyes forward," he said. "You don't get to see what's coming."

A thrill rushed through me as he knelt behind me, rubbing my ass before landing a quick smack on each cheek. I cried out.

"Quiet," he said, low and cool.

"But you're not being quiet."

"Yeah, but I'm in charge."

Goosebumps erupted all up my back and my stomach tingled with the anticipation of what would come next. He was always chatty and kind of dominant in bed, but it wasn't often that he pulled out all the stops like this. Guy cracked two more spanks against me, and I didn't make a peep.

"That's my girl," he cooed. "Now you get the reward."

He gave me tiny, pulsing thrusts with just the head of his cock. I mewled softly.

"You like that? You got soaked just for me, didn't you, Kitty?"

I nodded, not looking back at him. Since I couldn't see his body, it was the equivalent of being blindfolded, waiting to see how he'd play with me. It wasn't long before his pace became punishing, punctuating his thrusts with smacks on my ass. His callused hands were grabbier, the spanks harder. He railed into me, reaching to the back of my head to grab a fist of my hair. I fucking loved when he was like that, completely wild and undone.

"You like treating me like one of your fucktoys?" I said, trying to provoke him to go even harder. Instead, it seemed to snap him out of it.

"What? Birdy, no." He pulled out of me and helped me to my feet. He sat on his bed and brought me to face him in his lap. "You're the only one that matters."

His eyes searched my face, hands holding my waist, worried. Tough Guy was gone, vanished in seconds. Sweet, puppy-like Guy was back. "You're the only one I've ever loved. You're the most important person in my life. You'd never be that to me. Do you understand?"

I was still recovering from the whiplash of going from delightfully rough sex to this emotional outpouring. "Guy, where is this coming from?"

"I never want you to think I don't respect you. And I didn't disrespect them, but you're it for me, Birdy. When I have sex with you, it's love."

I wrapped myself around him tighter, a koala clinging to him.

"I know," I said, wiping some hair off his forehead and pressing mine to his. "And just so you know, being your fucktoy is fun. I like it when you're rough. I like you kinda nasty, just like I like you sweet. You don't have to hold back that part of yourself to prove you love me. I already know. It's part of how you love me."

He smiled, shaking his head. "You couldn't get more perfect, *ma puce*. You're my perfect person." He paused. "And just so *you* know, no one ever got it as good as I give it to you. You get the special treatment."

I held his face in my hands and kissed him, Guy groaning softly into our kiss as it intensified. We grabbed at each other again, desperate, until he landed a loud, stinging smack on my ass.

"Looks like you'd better be my good girl and get back on this dick," he said with a grin.

And I did, riding him with my tits in his mouth, with his hand on my throat, with him driving up into me with both hands using my hips as leverage, until both of us were screaming and gasping for air, his cum falling back out of me. Guy trailed his fingers through the mess.

"Beautiful," he breathed.

I'd gotten on the pill in the fall, both for my awful periods and so Guy and I could not have a kid. My periods remained painful, but not quite as long and heavy as they were without birth control. Blessing in disguise.

We lay in his bed, sticky with sweat and facing into each other. His massive thighs sandwiched mine.

"Everything's going to be different next year," I said, worry cutting into my post-sex haze.

"It will. It's nothing we can't handle, Birdy."

"How are you so confident? When you moved away last time, you stopped talking to me."

"It's true, but that was for different reasons. I can't imagine not talking to you every day after the way this year has been," he said, stroking my hair.

"But I'll be doing comedy after I graduate. There won't ever be a time where we're not both busy."

"We'll take it one day at a time." Guy kissed me.

"Long distance is notoriously hard, Guy-Guy. There's a reason people fail at it."

And then he spoke the words that couples the world over said when they really believed it would be different for them.

"But they're not us."

Part 3:
The Fall

Chapter 23

Kitty

The summer after freshman year was a lot, to say the least. I got the internship of my dreams at The Tonight Show, rooming with some random fellow interns in some god-awful hole in Manhattan that cost more than a semester at Alden.

The hours were grueling. My friends were the other interns, whether I actually liked them or not. My apartment was basically a place to sleep and that's it. But I was working toward my dream.

Guy had to go to development camp starting in July, and we wanted to maximize our time together. We didn't tell my parents, but he moved in with me from the end of school until the end of June, much to the collective chagrin of my four other roommates. We were putting a hurting on that single toilet.

Still, we did our best. Our place was filthy, literally rat and roach-infested. Guy earned his keep by cleaning while we were all at the studio. Other than staying in shape for the season, he didn't have many responsibilities. As neat as we tried to be, there was no use when my roommates and the other people in our building gave no fucks. Guy turned twenty-one and thus could drink and buy the rest of us booze. He'd sometimes kick trash bags on the street to see if they moved with rats when he was drunk. I hated when he did that. So fucking gross, but he thought it was funny.

"What if I started calling you my City Kitty?" he asked one night while we sat in a park, eating ice cream.

"I'm starting to think you like the actual city kitties more than you like me," I said, referring to the rats.

"Never. But they are a close second," he grinned. "My special little friends."

It was so fucking hot in my room that summer. We didn't have proper air conditioning. Guy bought me a fan when I moved in, and we slept with cold washcloths covering our naked bodies.

"I can't believe you want to live in this squalor with me," I told him late one night. "You're about to be an NHL player for fuck's sake."

"As long as I'm with you, I don't care where we are, Birdy."

We both knew things were about to change. He'd be on the West Coast for about nine months out of the year.

"Counting the days til we play Boston," he'd say. "I'll get you the most public seat on the ice so I can see you screaming for me, Kitty."

"And I'll try to come see you with the Rangers, Isles, and Devils," I promised. "It'll depend on school."

"I'll personally write your professors. Say your grandma died or something," he'd joke.

As soon as his jersey number was settled, he got me a Seattle jersey with his name on it.

"So everyone knows you're mine," he said.

"What about all the other people who will wear your jersey? Are they yours, too?" I teased.

"I'll let you lead the harem," he joked back. "You know it's only you."

Guy did his best to stay present in the early days of our long distance. He sent me a rat plushie to snuggle in his absence, and he got one for himself, obviously naming it "City Kitty." He never actually called me that, but he loved messing with me about his rat friends. We FaceTimed every night, but it was pretty challenging. The time difference, his training schedule, my classes, and shows all added up to give us pretty small windows to talk.

Somehow, it was harder to juggle than figuring out how to see each other when we were on campus.

And, as I'd predicted but hoped wouldn't happen, we ran out of stuff to talk about. We'd tell each other the details of our days, just like we did when we were together, but it didn't feel the same. The physical connection wasn't everything in our relationship, but it was important. I remembered how he acknowledged that things wouldn't be the same when he moved back to Quebec, and we'd just parted ways. There were days when I wished that was the choice we'd made this time around.

Fortunately, his first game lined up with my fall break, so he flew me out to see his NHL debut. He added a checked bag to my ticket so I wouldn't have to leave my favorite hairspray at home. Little details like that made my heart do weird things. It was a turbulent flight, but that swoopy stomach feeling remained when I got off the plane. I stopped in the bathroom to freshen up. I hadn't seen Guy since June, other than on my phone or computer screen. I was worried I'd somehow smell weird or something during my first time seeing him in four months.

I could see his smile at the arrivals gate from yards away. He'd texted me a picture of him in his outfit since he said he'd be "incognito." Hard to miss the tall skinny muscly guy with a baseball cap on. He stood right in the last spot where he wouldn't legally be required to go through security to get to me. He started prancing around as I got close, unable to contain himself. He really was a golden retriever, wagging his tail for me coming home to him. I ran the last few steps to get to him, jumping into his arms and wrapping my legs around his waist. I don't know if I've ever hugged someone so hard in my life.

"I can't believe I've gone this long without you," he whispered in my ear.

"Me either," I gasped under his crushing embrace. "I'm so happy to see you, baby."

I put my nose in his neck, burying my face and breathing him in. He was still the same Guy.

A woman walked by and mused, "Young love," as Guy pulled back and smashed his lips to mine. I turned his hat around backward to get it out of the way and rested my hands on his cheeks, feeling a little stubble.

"Let's go get your bag so I can get you home," he said, eyes sparkling.

He took me to his Tesla, a new purchase since becoming a pro, putting my bag in the trunk. He attacked me once we were in the car, kissing the living daylights out of me. His hands roamed my neck, my ribs, my waist, anywhere he could grab.

"I didn't even ask how your flight was," Guy laughed.

"We've talked enough, don't you think? I just want to touch you and smell you and taste you and do all the things we can't across the country."

Guy put the car in gear, drawing my hand to his lips as we got on the highway. I don't remember a single song on the radio on the drive to his place. I just stared at him. He was really next to me, finally.

Stepping into his huge Belltown apartment in Seattle was like walking into another world. We'd lived in actual filth in New York, and now he had this sexy, swanky bachelor pad. His fridge was stocked with healthy food and there was a bowl of fruit on the counter. His sheets were nice, with City Kitty sitting on top of his pillows. It was like suddenly, Guy was cosplaying as a grown-up. His entry-level contract had been generous, so he had the money. Why not use it?

Guy gave me the official tour of the condo, standing behind me in every room as I took in his new space, anxiously pacing from foot to foot. He'd obviously taken me on tours on FaceTime, but it wasn't the same as actually being in his place and catching all the little details.

"You're quiet, *ma puce*," he said as we looked out over Seattle.

"What do you think?"

"It's great, Guy," was all I could manage.

He deflated for a second. "Great?"

"I'm so proud of you. I am. This is amazing. I just . . . I feel like I don't know you anymore," I said, tears choking my speech.

"Birdy," he said, wrapping me up in his arms and stroking a thumb over my cheek. "I'm still me."

"I know, but your life is so different than mine. How are we going to keep doing this? I'm already struggling with school and keeping up with you, and the season hasn't even started yet."

Guy nodded. "I know. It's hard. I wish it was different. Should we talk less? Would that help you?"

"I don't know. I don't even want to think about it right now. I just want to be with you. I want to enjoy your game and cheer you on and have fun with the time we have."

He held my chin in his hand. "I want that, too. We can talk about the hard stuff. We will. Promise."

"But for now," I said, putting my hands on his chest, "I think we're way overdue for some love-making. I want to test out these grown-up sheets you've got."

Guy grinned, sliding down my body. I thought he'd start pulling down the leggings I traveled in, but instead he threw me over his shoulder and carried me to the bedroom, clapping my ass as he went. He dropped me to my feet just inside his bedroom door, pressing me against the wall.

"I've missed you so much, Kitty Bird. You ready to do this?"

"Is it weird that I'm nervous?"

Guy looked at me. "Nervous, why?"

"What if my pussy smells or something? What if I'm rusty?"

Guy chuckled. "Kitty, if your pussy smelled bad, I'd put on a gas mask and go for it anyway." I laughed at that. "I mean, I'd take you to the doctor later, but nothing could hold me back from you right now."

I giggled, reaching up to kiss him and running my hands under his shirt. Our clothes were on the floor in an instant, tearing and zipping and unbuttoning while our mouths stayed smashed together. All the nerves melted into excitement, my body taking over where my mind drew a blank.

I'd forgotten all the little things I knew about Guy, like how he dropped his head back whenever I first touched him there, or how his pupils went big when he was so turned on, or how he groaned if I sucked his bottom lip. It was familiar and new, native and exotic being with him again.

I started to reach for him after he sat me on the bed and stood in front of me, but he shook his head.

"You first, *ma puce*. Always."

He dropped to his knees and pulled my butt to the edge of the bed, putting my legs over his shoulders. Guy looked back up at my eyes and smiled.

"You're perfect, Kitty."

He kept his eyes on mine as he kissed down my inner thighs, letting me stay sitting up to watch as he teased all around my pussy with his mouth. I let him take his time, having wanted to have that moment for so long. I played with his hair, sweeping it to the side and running my fingers through it, admiring the man that was my always.

Before he could get to the good part, he kissed back up my body, stopping to suck on my nipples. The sensation was heavenly, but I needed him elsewhere.

"You're playing with me," I scolded him.

"I just need all of you at once. I can't decide what part I like best."

"Oh, well, don't let me get in your way," I said with a laugh.

"Don't worry, sweetheart. I'm going to get you."

"Then get to it," I whined, scooting my pelvis forward to encourage him.

He pushed me back on the bed and gave me what I wanted, tugging and licking in just the way I like.

"I love your taste, baby. I missed it so bad," he said, nuzzling my clit with his nose before diving back in. I begged for more, and more, and right there, the pleasure rising and peaking. My ears rang, my pulse pounded, and then I was there, holding onto his hair for dear life as he brought me over the edge.

"That's my girl." He grinned up at me, rising to his feet and jerking his cock. "Ready for me? I can't wait a second longer."

"Get in there, baby."

With one smooth thrust, Guy filled me at the edge of the bed, holding my jaw to make me look at him as he did. That hot, possessive touch would always get me. His jaw clenched, his eyes rolled back, and then he found me again, pushing into me. I sat up on my elbows and rocked my hips to meet him, his eyes wild.

"Fuck, Kitty, I want to make it last."

"Don't," I told him. "Give me everything. I need it all now."

Scooping his hands under my back, he pushed us to the middle of the bed, driving into me with abandon. He was hitting me just right, his cock brushing that perfect spot inside me while getting the outside on the way in. All I could do was hold on for dear life as he gave me everything, squeezing his low back between my legs. He kept trying to say something but failed to get his words out.

"Kitty," he warned.

"Yes, Guy. Go for me."

"You. First," he stuttered out, scraping his hands down to cup my ass for leverage, a move he knew drove me up the wall. I breathed out his name. "Do it for me, sweetheart. Come for me."

And I was gone again, abs burning as I ground my pelvis into him. I came hard, lifting myself off the bed as I pressed my chest into his. He jerked inside me, pulsing and giving me everything he had as he kissed my neck, breathing hard.

"Kitty."

"Guy."

"I can't stop coming," he grunted, squeezing his eyes shut.

"Me either." He collapsed on top of me, both of us still riding the waves of our orgasms.

"I don't want to be without you anymore, Kitty. I love you too much," he said, swallowing as he panted.

"Yeah," I sighed, coming down from my high. He rolled off me and got a towel from his nightstand, sliding it under my butt and then pulling me to lay my head on his chest. His heart thumped under my ear.

It was so wonderful, yet there was something so sad about it all. We'd just be together for a few days, and then it would be over again. Back to life. Back to pretending like I was a whole person when he wasn't around. Back to pretending like what we were doing was enough.

Chapter 24

Kitty

The day of Guy's first regular season game with Seattle, we had breakfast together at his apartment. He was up way earlier than he needed to be for morning skate. I knew he had to be nervous as hell.

He made us omelets, dressed only in pajama pants hung low on his hips. I stood behind him while he cooked, keeping my hands on his skin as much as possible. We'd done plenty of reuniting the night before, not even making it to our dinner reservation. We ordered steak from the same place and ate it on his living room floor in our underwear. After we had our mini-feast, we got right back to exploring each other. In fact, I was sore in various places from all the activity. My abs were especially tired from working hard on top. Still, I already wanted more at breakfast time. I'd do whatever he wanted, though. His body was the one that had to perform professionally that night.

"Nervous?"

"Shitting myself." He laughed, but I knew he was serious. "Just the thing I've worked my whole life to do. No pressure."

"You're going to be awesome," I told him. "Even if you only play for thirty seconds, I'll be proud of you."

He got a funny look on his face.

"Fine. Even if you're a last-minute healthy scratch, I'll be proud of you. They'll want to show off their hot new rookie, though."

Guy's expression finally softened. "Thanks, Birdy." He planted an everything-bagel-seasoning-flavored kiss on me. "What are you going to do while I'm at practice?"

"Probably just wander around your neighborhood, maybe work on some scripts I've been polishing for my portfolio. Have some of that famous Seattle coffee."

We talked about my coursework, and how glad I was to be out of math.

"This new life is great, but I miss being there with you," he admitted. "It's hard wanting to do both."

My stomach turned. I loved Guy so much, and I wanted to support him through all the changes he was going through. And yet doubts kept haunting me, that we weren't doing ourselves any favors by distracting each other like we were. I ultimately couldn't be there for him in the way that he needed, nor he for me. Our love was deep, but there was an undeniable strain in navigating the changes.

"It is hard," I agreed, and left it at that. "Who am I sitting with at the game?"

"My buddy Branson's girlfriend. I've only met her once, but he said she'd be happy to hang with you. She just moved here to be with him so she doesn't have many friends."

"Ah," I said, masking my annoyance. I had strong feelings that I didn't belong among the WAGs, or wives and girlfriends. I had career ambitions beyond just supporting my player. That did nothing for the pile of doubts mounting in my head.

"I'm sure she's great, even if she's no Violet." Guy cocked his head at me, seeing through my bullshit. "Give her a chance, Birdy."

"I will, I will," I grumbled. "You know I'm fucking delightful."

And I am delightful. There's always a type of person who doesn't think so. I can tell within seconds, because almost all of them say, "Oh, you're one of those funny people," after my first joke crack. An instant sign of incompatibility.

"Oh, yes, I'm well aware," he said, pulling out my barstool and standing between my legs. "Can we squeeze in one more delight before we head out?"

* * *

Our seats were a few rows off the ice and to the side of the home bench. Suited up in a brand spankin' new "Stelle" jersey, jeans, and white sneaks, I moved down to my seat. I found a blonde woman with a beer, a soda, a hot dog, a box of candy, and a monster bucket of popcorn. Much like Guy's high school girlfriend, she looked like she came from the Pretty Girl Store.

"Melanie?"

"Hey! Are you Kitty?"

"I am. Great to meet you."

I felt every day of my nineteen years at that moment. Melanie had the air of an Actual Adult.

"Hungry?" I asked, gesturing to her mountain of food and drink.

She snorted. "I get nervous before his games and I eat my feelings. I'm always afraid someone's going to hurt him. You want anything?"

"Hockey is indeed a bloodsport," I conceded. "I'll probably get a soda after they warm up. Guy told me you just moved here?"

"Yeah, from Minnesota. Decided I couldn't be without him anymore." My cheeks warmed. That was exactly the kind of shit I worried about. "I heard you're a talented comedian. How's school going?"

Okay, fine. Melanie was very nice and not snotty at all. She didn't talk down to me for being young, and treated me like I had every right to be there. She knew the pain of being away from the person you loved. She was empathetic and thoughtful. And she never once said, "Oh, you're one of those funny people." She wasn't exactly my kind of person, but I was pleasantly surprised at how well we got along.

"Wait, was I not supposed to wear his jersey? He gave me this to wear," I asked Mel, in a mild panic.

"Typically, WAGs don't, but it's his first game and you're his biggest fan. I think everyone will forgive it," she assured me.

"But... I did do the wrong thing."

"Don't sweat it. If anyone wants to be mean to you, they'll have to take it up with me," she said, nudging me.

Our conversation cut off when the lights dimmed in the arena. A spotlight shone on the Sealpups' tunnel. Guy knew the rookie lap was coming, a time-honored tradition in the NHL. He was well-prepared, stepping onto the ice by himself with confidence and doing some fancy footwork on his skates. His teammates and the crowd cheered for him, the captain knocking the pucks off the ledge for his second go-round. Guy fired off a rocket of a shot with a huge grin.

Pride swelled in my chest, my hands shaking as I tried to take a video. I gave up halfway through and just watched him. I'd obviously seen him play plenty of times before, but I'd never gotten to celebrate him as the star of the show. I sent my shitty, shaky video off to Frank and my parents. Melanie air-dropped me her much higher-quality video, which I then sent off.

"He did great," she said, hugging me to her side. "Branson says he's such a good sport." For someone I didn't know, she somehow knew what I needed. I needed someone to share such a special moment with. Part of me wished my family could have come, too. They loved Guy just as much as I did. Well, maybe not in the same way, but they loved him deeply, too.

My eyes welled when Guy lined up to take practice shots with the rest of the team. There he was. The boy next door made it all the way to the place of his dreams. He defied losing his parents. He defied having his life upended twice in a year. He made it.

After he'd gone through a few rounds of drills, he skated off to the glass in front of our seats. Like I was under a spell, I floated down to talk to him. I didn't realize I was still crying until I got to him.

He held up his glove and I matched it with my hand.

"HI, KITTY BIRD," he yelled like he always did through the glass at Alden games.

"Hi, Guy-Guy," I sniffed.

"You're crying."

"I'm proud of you. You did it."

His cheeks went pink and he laughed, but I could tell he was touched. He moved on to make a joke, I think to keep himself from crying. He wiggled his eyebrows. "You look good in my jersey."

"Yeah, well. Later." There were children around, so I didn't want or need to spell out that I'd only be wearing that later. He knew, though. We both laughed. "Give 'em hell, Stelle."

We snapped a selfie with my phone, blew each other kisses, and he skated off with a wink.

The first period went by in a blur, his first shift on the ice lasting a mere thirty seconds. I knew that was somewhat normal for the beginning of a game, and mentally applauded myself for how much I'd learned about the sport because of Guy. Maybe I did deserve to be a WAG.

Mel's boyfriend, Branson, was in Guy's line, part of the reason they were such good friends. A couple of times, Mel gripped my hand when they were in. Normally, I'd be weirded out by someone trying to bond so fast, but there was something so sweet and pure about her friendship. Mel was a classic Midwesterner, open, kind, and easy to talk to.

Toward the end of the first, Guy took a high stick to the face from one of Vancouver's players. I gasped, my stomach sinking as I looked to see if his face was bleeding.

"Shit, I know what you mean about losing it when anything happens," I said to Mel.

She chuckled. "It never gets easier. Looks like he's not hurt too bad."

And he wasn't. When he lined up for a faceoff in front of us, he gave me a wink. He must have known I was freaking out.

During the second period, he got to drive the puck down the ice toward Vancouver's goal. He popped it to one of his waiting teammates like it was second nature, who sliced it right back to Guy. And just like that, Guy shot it into the upper part of the net.

The crowd erupted, me along with them. I frankly felt like I could piss myself. Tears pricked my eyes as Guy pointed to the sky, for Maman, and then in my direction. One of his older teammates took the puck out of the net as the rest of his line joined him for the celly.

Guy had done something rare and special. He got a goal in his first NHL appearance, a rookie for everyone to get excited about. And he was mine. All frickin' mine.

Chapter 25

Guy

"Hey, *ma puce*. Sorry I missed you again. I just landed in St. Louis. Call me back when you can. Love you always."

It was the third time Kitty and I had played phone tag in twenty-four hours. It had been a week since we'd even had the time and privacy for phone sex.

"Sucks, bro," Branson said as I hung up. "How's all that going?"

I sighed. "Not great. We can't seem to sync up our schedules. How did you and Melanie do it?"

Branson had plans to ask his girlfriend to marry him over Christmas. I was going with him to pick out the ring when he got back to Seattle.

"I got her to move out here as soon as I could. Just have her quit school and wife her up, man." I knew he was half joking, but even the thought was outrageous.

"She's only nineteen. She'd kill me if I tried to stop her from her dreams."

"I thought the same about Melanie, but when push comes to shove, if they want to be with you, they'll do anything."

I sucked my teeth. "Yeah, I don't think that's right for Kitty, though. We always both had big dreams. She's working really hard to make it all work. I can't take that away from her."

"But you could give her a pretty cushy life," Branson countered.

"I mean, yeah, I'd love to have her waiting for me after games and road trips. She's so fucking loud at games, too. It's fun having her there. But she's worked too hard to throw her career away just to cheer for me," I said, thinking out loud. "No offense to Mel, of course. You know I think the world of her."

"I know, man. But have you thought about giving her that option?"

* * *

It took some convincing with Mark and Heather, but Kitty was going to come stay with me during my short Christmas break. The two months between our visits were pretty brutal. Kitty and I just kept missing each other, and it frustrated both of us. We wanted to be there for each other, but it was getting harder all the time. Then when we finally did talk, we'd be happy for a few minutes, then return to our frustration. I still loved Kitty so much, but there was no denying that things were really, really hard.

Kitty had given me shit for not being *that* incognito when I picked her up from the airport in October, so I stepped up my game for our Christmas rendezvous. She doubled over laughing when she caught sight of me. I'd put on my hockey jersey, clearly with my name on it, a fedora, and those glasses with a mustache and a big nose attached to them.

She stopped and took a picture when she was a few feet away from me. I grabbed for her and pulled her into a hard kiss. She had on her strawberry lip balm, so little bits of the cheap mustache stuck to her lips. She cackled, breathless with tears streaming down her face as she picked off the bristly hairs.

"You are my very favorite, Guy Nicolas Stelle," Kitty cooed, her face still red from laughing. She stopped someone passing by to take our picture. A few other people stopped to take pictures with me. I made Kitty stand in with me, knowing those pictures would be on the internet before long. I wanted everyone to know that I was taken. It got old having my DMs fill up with ludicrous offers. I was half tempted to turn them off, but I was always afraid I'd miss some endorsement opportunity.

"You are so unrecognizable," she said as I swept her up into my arms, taking in her warmth and familiar scent.

"I know, right?" It was so good to laugh with her again, especially when most of our recent interactions were riddled with frustration. "How was first class?"

"Guy, you didn't have to do that," she scolded me.

"I wanted to. I wanted you comfortable. It's a long flight." I pressed a kiss to the scar on her temple, leaning down to her ear. "Plus, I need you well-rested for all that love-making."

"We've got a whole four days together, Frenchie. I'm going to be broken by the time we're done," she joked.

The day before Christmas Eve, Branson had a catered dinner party at his house. Some of my other teammates were there with their significant others. Kitty wore a gorgeous green jumpsuit with an open back, reminding me of a sweater that made me jealous not that long ago. She mingled with the other wives and girlfriends, but she kept glancing back my way whenever she could. It wasn't like her to not be confident. She and Mel had gotten along really well in October, but Mel was playing hostess and couldn't be Kitty's sidekick the whole time.

Kitty stuck out as the youngest and the only non-blonde, something of a joke in the NHL circles. Almost every player had a blonde wife or girlfriend. I was perfectly content with my dark-haired Kitty. I walked over to join her conversation, making our defenseman Jace come with me.

"So Kitty, I heard you're into comedy. Are you a big SNL fan?" one woman asked.

"Oh, she's more than a fan. She'll probably be on it someday," I bragged, grazing my fingertips up Kitty's spine.

"That's interesting. Sometimes I wish I could still work. It's just not possible with Ronnie's schedule and the kids," English's wife chimed in. They had two kids under three.

"Oh," Kitty said, trying to seem pleasant. I knew she was struggling. I hated to see her having a hard time.

"So Guy, will you try to get traded to New York if Kitty gets on SNL?"

Kitty and I looked at each other, her eyes blank but smile still pasted on. "We'll see what comes up for us," was all I could think to say. I could tell Kitty was hurt, giving her party smile that only I knew was fake. I gave her side a squeeze and kissed the top of her head.

Branson tapped a knife on a glass, getting everyone's attention.

"You okay?" I whispered to Kitty. She gave me a terse nod and a too-wide smile again before putting her attention back to Branson.

"Thanks everybody for coming tonight. I want to call my girl up here, the one who made tonight possible. Melanie, will you come here?" Branson opened his arms, and everyone clapped as Mel walked up.

"Mel and I have been on a long road. We met in high school, but she turned me down when I asked her out." A laugh scattered across the room. "But then after I got half my teeth knocked out of my head, she said yes. The last year with her has been my best. I convinced her that she didn't need that grueling nursing job and to move out here with me. I can't say enough about how much having her close has meant to me."

Branson turned to Mel, taking both of her hands before getting on one knee, a ring box open in his hand. "And now I'm hoping you'll say yes to something else."

The gasps and shouts of excitement across the room covered up whatever Branson said to Mel, but I felt Kitty go sweaty under my hand. Melanie nodded a yes and Branson swept her off her feet with a kiss. I was so very happy for my friend, but so worried for my best friend on my arm. Champagne flutes came out on trays for a toast. We toasted the happy couple, but I didn't miss that Kitty sucked down her champagne in one gulp. She also picked the skin next to her thumbnail until it bled. I snuck to get a cocktail napkin to stop the bleeding.

The writing was on the wall. She was not happy.

"You ready to go home, *ma puce?*"

"We can stay." Her fake smile flashed. She never used that smile with me. My stomach sank. "Branson is your best friend."

I turned her to me, putting my fingers under her chin. "No, you are." I kissed her, not feeling much of a kiss back. "You don't give that fake smile to me, you understand? We are real. Always. Okay, Birdy?"

Kitty hugged me and nodded. I took her hand in mine and waited for our chance to congratulate the happy couple. Kitty gave Melanie a warm hug that looked genuine, but I saw the sadness in Kitty's eyes.

She was silent the whole car ride home. I held her hand, knowing her conversation with the other WAGs was probably weighing heavily on her.

When we got home, she went straight to the bathroom, closing the door. She never did that. Call it gross, but we were door-open people. But soon I figured out why she shut me out. Vomit echoed off the tile in the bathroom. I knocked at the door when I heard her tears start. I got a cool washcloth and sat next to her on the floor, not sure what to say.

"What's going through your head, Kitty Bird?" I asked, taking the hair tie from her wrist and pulling back her hair.

"I can't be what you need, Guy," she sobbed. I opened my legs and leaned against the bathroom wall, pulling her against my chest.

"What do you mean? You are what I need, Kitty."

"I can't give up everything to be your hockey wife," she said, her eyes red. "I still want things for myself. I don't want to give up my dreams to wait at home for you. And that makes me feel like an asshole."

I shook my head. "I don't want you to give anything up, Kitty."

"But something has to give, Guy. We're stressing each other out trying to stay together and it's only the beginning."

I couldn't hold back anymore. Tears brimmed for me, too. "Am I losing you, Kitty?"

She didn't say anything, just sobbed, looking into my eyes. We wiped at each other's tears.

"I don't want to lose you," she whispered.

We held each other on the bathroom floor, mourning the wall of insurmountable challenges we faced. The only way we could be there for each other is if one of us gave up everything. And neither of us wanted the other to do that.

When it was clear Kitty wasn't going to get sick again, I helped her to her feet. We got ready for bed. We laughed at each other for crying while we brushed our teeth. We were rock bottom pathetic. Then I held her tight to me in bed, thinking maybe if I held tight enough, it wouldn't be real.

Chapter 26

Kitty

I was up early on Christmas Eve, still adjusting to West Coast time. I put on a pot of coffee and looked out over a still-dark Seattle. Guy padded out to the kitchen at around six, rubbing sleep out of his eyes. He didn't say a word, just wrapped himself around me from behind. I twined my arms over his and he kissed my neck.

"I don't even want to say it," I moped.

"Merry Christmas?" he asked, mirth in his voice.

I turned to face him. "No, you goof. Let's have coffee and talk."

We settled in on his couch, facing into each other. We were close enough to hold hands but far enough to give ourselves space. I wanted to be able to study his face while we talked through it all.

"How do you think things are going when we're apart?" I started, giving him an open-ended question to answer.

"Not great," he said. "I want to say that it's not your fault, though. I want to make that clear."

"I know. It's not your fault, either," I said. "Distance is just really hard."

"It is. Harder than I thought it would be," he admitted.

"I think we're kind of torturing ourselves. You deserve to be able to focus on hockey. Our relationship is supposed to bring joy, not stress."

"You do bring me joy, Kitty. You make me so happy. So stupid happy. But it's not the same when we're not together. It's like something gets lost along the way. I still love you, so deeply. I still think you're the love of my life."

I held back tears as he said that. "I think that, too. But we're hurting each other trying to force it. We're both leading half-lives instead of supporting each other."

Guy nodded. "We are."

The next part was super hard to say. "I don't know when the hard part would end, Guy. The distance is going to be a thing at least until I graduate, and then I'll probably be in New York or L.A. At minimum, we're talking two and a half more years. That's a long time of things being hard."

"It is. For what it's worth, I don't want to break up. I just want to have it all work."

I took his hand, the calluses of his palm a familiar scrape. "I wish it was that easy. But you deserve to not be distracted by misery, and I deserve to focus on my dreams, too."

"You're part of my dream, Birdy. I just can't figure out how to make it work right now," Guy said. "I want to spend my life with you. You're my person, Kitty."

"I want that, too. But I don't think we can do that right now."

Guy was quiet for a while. We both knew what we needed to do. Neither of us wanted to say it.

"What do we do for the next few days?"

I shrugged, morose. "What do you want to do?"

"I don't want to be sad the whole time. I want to pretend. I want to love you like it's not the last time."

So that's what we did. After a slow, sweet, passionate session in bed, we cooked Guy's traditional Quebecois Christmas Eve feast. We played around and pretended like we weren't on a sinking ship, dancing in the kitchen like nothing was wrong. A few other couples without family close were coming over for dinner. Guy asked if I wanted to call it off given what we were going through.

We decided the distraction might be good for us. A full table would take our minds off our bruised hearts.

Rather than being stuffed with healthy food, Guy's fridge and pantry were filled with essentials for the dinner menu. Reveillon was to be quite a production. Traditionally, it centered around going to midnight mass. Guy was cutting out that portion in favor of excess eating and wine drinking. Guy spent half the day working on the meat pie, assigning me to the much simpler meatballs. He told me about some of his sweet memories from his childhood, helping Maman and Grandmere make reveillon food. He taught me some French Christmas carols, my horrific pronunciation making him blush on my behalf.

Before the guests were due to arrive, I put on a maroon velvet dress, pulling my hair half up and adding gold earrings Guy had given me the last Christmas. Guy put on a deep blue suit, looking dapper as always. He pulled me into the kitchen and opened a bottle of champagne to settle my nerves. Though I love to perform, hosting is not natural for me. Particularly as a nineteen-year-old serving grown-ups.

"They're going to love you, *ma puce*," he promised with a kiss.

And later, as I looked around the crowded table, warm from wine and stuffed with a crumbly-ass meat pie and cheesecake that one of his friends brought, I felt at peace. Guy squeezed my leg under the table and stood to raise a toast.

"I want to thank all of you for joining Kitty and me tonight, and for being my extended family. And I want to raise a toast to my Kitty Bird, the love of my life," he said, turning to me and taking my hand that was free of a wine glass. "No matter where this road takes us, I'll always be waiting for you, your home base. In a world full of Pepsi and Coke, you're my Dr. Pepper."

Maybe it was the wine, or the sweetness of what he said, or just Guy being my one, but I truly believed that one day, it would all work out.

* * *

Guy and I got up late on Christmas morning. The festivities continued well past midnight, when we shoved some of Guy's very drunk but very lovable teammates into the cars he'd hired for the evening. Though we woke up blissfully naked, Guy had matching pajamas laid out for us. I commented on how sweet it was.

"If I'm going to keep you away from the Gattos, I want to make it special," he said. "I know how much your family loves Christmas."

"We'll call them later, I'm sure," I said. "But thank you for being so thoughtful."

He got an evil grin. "Did you get me presents, woman?" I smacked him.

"Yes, I got you presents, greedy."

"Come onnnnn," he wheedled, tugging me out of bed. Pajama'd up, we sat in his living room around his Christmas tree. We started with our smaller gifts: a sweatsuit for his new team for me and some of his favorite coffee from me. I gave him a biography he'd been wanting to read. He gave me a stuffed flea "for *ma puce*" and to go with the rat that he'd given me.

"Fleas and rats, huh? Very Plague chic."

"I thought it was appropriate. You're a little flea, and I love my city kitties," he laughed. "We go together like fleas and rats."

Guy's minor at Alden was history, so he loved little facts about the past. I was not surprised he worked a Plague joke into our Christmas gift exchange.

"Okay, you know I'm a poor college student, but here's your big gift," I said, handing him a small but heavy box.

"I know I'll love it," Guy said, practically glowing at me. He unwrapped it, the outer box still not giving it away.

"Careful with it," I warned as he slid it out of the box. It was a snow globe with two figures kissing in front of a house. I couldn't make it look exactly the way I wanted, but I got close.

Guy's eyes welled with tears. "Birdy, is this us? In front of my house last year?"

I nodded. Guy turned it upside down, watching the snow swirl and covering his mouth.

"Kitty, it's perfect. Thank you." His voice crackled. He pulled me to him, and I wrapped my legs around his hips. "That was when you said 'I love you' for the first time. I loved that moment."

"Me, too. That's why I wanted to remember it."

We sat in a mini-sea of wrapping paper, our coffee having gone cold in our gift opening frenzy.

"I have one more gift for you. It's a little different. I want you to hear me out before you freak out. Can you do that?"

"Guy," I said, looking at him sidelong. "Now you have me nervous."

He walked to the tree, digging into the branches and pulling out a small box. A box from a jewelry store. He sat in front of me on the coffee table, while I sat on the couch. His hands shook, his long fingers looking out of place on the tiny box.

"Kitty, I meant what I said last night. You're the love of my life and I don't want anyone else. I know everything's a mess now. I wanted to give you this option, in case it's what you need to hear to stay. In case you need to know how serious I am."

Guy opened the box, revealing a diamond ring. An engagement ring.

"Birdy, I love you more than anyone in this world. You're my love, my best friend, my family. If you don't want to work or finish school, you don't have to. I can take care of you. I know we're young. But I know it's you for me. Just you. If you want to start our forever now, we can."

My mouth hung open. I wasn't sure I'd breathed since I saw that tiny box. Guy watched me, waiting for an answer. I gave none. I was genuinely struck speechless for once in my life. Time stood still. Or maybe it didn't. The clock in his kitchen seemed to carry on just fine, tick-tick-ticking away.

"Guy." I was unable to say anything else.

"Kitty, if now isn't the right time, that's okay, too. I just . . . wanted to give you the option."

"Is this what you want?" I asked, finally finding some words.

"I want whatever will make you happy, *ma puce*." His voice was slow, cautious.

The tears came to me. "When did you buy this?"

"A few weeks ago," he said. "I planned to hold onto it longer, but I don't know. After what we've talked about, it felt like I should at least offer you everything I have to give."

"You'd marry me just to keep me?" I asked, still not sure how I felt about that.

"If I could have you here every day, I would. I know it's selfish. I know you want your career. I want you to have what you want. But just in case that's not what you want, I'm here."

"Guy, I don't know what to say. Is that what you want? Me to be a good hockey wife?"

"I want you to be yourself, Kitty. You don't have to fit a certain mold. I'm not comparing you to anybody." He ran a frustrated hand through his hair. "We can stay engaged for a long time if you want. I just want to stay in your life."

It was hard to make sense of the noisy emotions swirling in my head. I was honored, flattered, and thrilled in one way. But moreso, I was horrified that he'd even think comedy would be something I could give up, especially before I'd even gotten started.

"But I can't be myself if I give up everything to come be with you. We can't have it both ways. I can't give 50% at school and 50% in comedy and 50% to you. There's not enough me to go around."

"You don't have to say yes, Kitty. I know this is a lot. I'm not trying to control you. I won't think you don't love me if you say no. But know that I'll give you whatever it takes to make you happy." His lips went into a pout and his eyes rounded. "Even if that means we need to break up for now."

Oh, I didn't like where that was headed. Not one bit. "You're making it sound like it's all my decision, Guy. You know our distance has distracted you, too. That's not fair."

"I'm getting by," he sniffed. "I'm okay to keep going like this. But I get it if it's not working for you."

"Do you hear yourself? It's not just me that's suffering, Guy! Don't pin it all back on me! You're not happy either."

"Well, I'd rather be unhappy with you than unhappy alone," he snapped.

"For the next two and a half years?!" I asked, raising my voice. "We both deserve better than that."

"I'll wait forever, Birdy. No one could take your place."

"Look, I don't want to let you go. I don't want this to be happening. But it is. I won't be happy if I give up my dreams to be with you. You'll feel guilty about it. We'll still be miserable," I pointed out.

Guy put his head in his hands. "This was a stupid fucking idea."

I softened. I wasn't trying to hurt him more, but I wouldn't stand for him making himself the victim while I was the villain.

"It wasn't," I said, taking his hand. He was opening his entire heart to me, and I wanted to be careful with it. "It was a risk, but it shows me how much you value what we have. I do, too."

I took a deep, shaky breath, not wanting to deliver the next part. "But I can't say yes right now, Guy."

He bit his lip, hanging his head. "Okay."

"I'm nineteen. I go to the top school for what I want to do. I still want my dreams. I want to be independent and have my own career. I'd never ask you to give up hockey. And I know you mean well, but it kind of hurts that you're asking me to give up comedy. I need to focus these next few years, and if we're struggling that whole time, it won't help either of us. And I hope you can understand that."

"I do. I want those things for you, too. But I also want you here."

"I know," was all I could manage. Guy opened and closed his mouth a few times, emotion building.

"I'm going to say this, and it might be the wrong thing to say."

"It's okay. I can take it," I said, not really sure if I could. I needed to hear whatever it was regardless.

"Did you think we were doomed from the start? You knew I was moving, and you warned me how hard long-distance would be. Did you really give me everything these past few months, or did you hold back?"

I was stunned, the air sucked out of my lungs. It was a fair question, but that didn't mean it didn't sting. I sat back. His eyes searched the couch cushion as he picked at the coffee table's edge. He still sat where he was when he proposed.

"Did you ever believe in us?"

"Of course, I did. I wanted this to work just as much as you did. I don't want this to be the way it ends."

"Then don't end it, Kitty. Tough it out with me. Stay with me," he begged, his voice breaking.

"Our relationship will keep fraying because we can't give each other what we need, Guy."

"What if your career doesn't work out?"

"What the fuck, Guy! You don't believe in me?"

"You don't believe in us!" he snapped. We stared at each other. We'd never fought, not like that. I was too shocked to cry.

"I'm sorry," he said quietly. "That wasn't fair. You know I believe in you, but comedy is hard, Kitty. Would you come be with me then?"

My stomach turned. It was the outcome I preferred not to think about. "I don't know. Probably? I really don't want that to happen."

"I know, Kitty. I don't want it either. I want you to succeed. But I also want you here."

"I have to at least try to make it first."

He nodded, morose. Then he got more and more agitated, fidgeting.

"What do you need that I'm not giving you?" he burst out, looking manic. "Maybe there's a way to fix it, Birdy." Guy took my hand, rolling his lips between his teeth and swallowing hard.

"Okay. I don't know if I can put an exact name to it, but I'll try." I took a deep breath to steady myself. "I need things to be easy. I know you support me. I support you and cheer for your success so fucking hard, Guy. But I need to not have to talk about everything sometimes. When all we have is talking, we lose the little stuff. The inside jokes. The things that happen from just being together. Sometimes I need to be able to just lay in bed and watch a show with you. There are ways we communicate that aren't talking, or even sex. We have our way of being together. I'm sure you remember how amazing it was to get it back when we met up at school."

Guy nodded. "I know what you mean. It was a rush finding our groove again."

I gave him a sad smile, remembering, and went on. "I'm also missing parts of your life. You can tell me about Branson, but seeing you with him is more powerful. And I love visiting each other, but these are power catch-up sessions. It's not the same as being in each other's lives every day. Does that make sense?"

"It does," he said. "Maybe it can't be fixed."

"I don't want to fade away with you. I think it's possible," I said slowly, trying not to cry again, "that we thought this was our time to try, but it was actually the wrong time."

"So you believe there might be another time?" The infinitesimal shred of hope in his voice was heartbreaking.

"I sure hope there is."

Chapter 27

Guy

My hat was pulled low. Kitty wore a hat, too, covering our splotchy faces as much as we could. We stayed up the whole night, just holding each other, crying, kissing, touching, being together one last time.

I tried everything I could. I begged. I told her she could work on her writing while I supported her, that she didn't have to throw her whole dream away. Still, I knew that wasn't enough. She wouldn't be satisfied until she tried the big dream.

I begged more. I told her I couldn't live without her, because I really wasn't sure if I could. It's real that people die of broken hearts, right?

I begged her to choose me.

In the end, she couldn't agree to stay. I had to accept it. I got us a ride to the airport because there was no fucking way I could drive safely.

"This isn't the last time," I whispered in her ear through my tears. If someone recognized me, it was just too fucking bad. I couldn't say goodbye to her in the parking lot.

"What if it is? You'll find someone else," she cried, her arms snug around my shoulders.

"I won't. I'll wait for you. As long as it takes," I sobbed. "I will, Kitty. I'll wait until the day I die."

"Don't make promises you can't keep, Guy," she hiccuped.

"Okay, maybe I'll fuck someone else, but I won't love anyone else," I half-joked.

"That's more realistic," she said, pulling back with a sad smile and rubbing her thumbs over my cheeks. I held her face in my hands, needing her eyes so she could feel what I was saying down to the core of her being.

"Kitty, I will always love you. I will never stop," I forced out. "No matter where you are, I will be loving you."

She nodded, crying all over again. "You'll always be the one, Guy. I'll never stop loving you."

Always. Never. We were both.

And then we were nothing.

Part 4:
The Ghost

Chapter 28

Kitty

A zombie looked back at me in the dim light of the airport bathroom. I didn't warn Mom that we'd broken up. I didn't tell her that Guy proposed. But when she saw me at baggage claim in our tiny little hometown airport, she knew I wasn't okay.

With a big hug, she just whispered, "I'm sorry, sweetie," in my ear, took me home, and made me a cup of tea while I bawled at the kitchen table.

I held it together for that whole flight home. I felt like I was drugged. I wasn't even old enough for the first-class booze, though the flight attendant was kind enough to offer me some anyway. No amount of Bloody Marys could cure what was wrong with me. I'd walked away from the greatest love I'd ever known, knowing that we both still loved each other down to our bones.

The distance just wasn't worth the stress of it. We both had big things to do and needed the freedom to do them. Long-distance doesn't work if you can't even find a way to talk once or twice a day. We needed connections we weren't getting.

Mom put a steaming mug of tea in front of me. I warmed my hands with it but didn't drink it.

"Tea's disgusting, Mom," I grumbled. "It's just watery leaves."

Mom cackled. "Glad to see you're still funny in your misery. Why don't you tell me what happened?"

Later, Frank knocked on my door. He sat on my bed, where I

was curled up in a pile of used tissues. His tone was gentle, something he rarely employed.

"Hey, sissy," he said, a name he rarely used. "Guy wanted me to check on you."

That started me sobbing again. "I can't believe it's over."

Frank twisted his lips to chew on them. "I know it's hard, but you made the right choice."

"It doesn't feel that way. He still wanted to try."

"Well, he wasn't doing great, either. Not being able to talk to you enough was killing him."

"Yeah, but now we're not going to talk at all," I moaned.

"Maybe you can talk again soon. But you probably do need to grow up a little on your own."

I sniffed. "How is he?"

Frank raised his eyebrows and blew out a breath. "Bad." I whimpered, hating to hear that. "But that doesn't mean you made the wrong choice."

I lay there, lifeless, both of us just sitting.

"Wanna go see a bad movie?" he offered.

I blew my nose. "I'll go if you let me get extra butter."

"Fine."

* * *

Back at school, Violet was my co-pilot through those first awful weeks. She let me stay in when I needed to but also pushed my ass to go out when she could tell I should. She and Colton had split up long ago, even before the prior school year ended. She got annoyed with him and it was just for the best.

Violet let me play all the sad breakup albums on loop. But even those didn't feel right. Guy hadn't wronged me. He was the best thing that ever happened to me. Our timing was just bad.

One night when I was drunk and feeling sorry for myself, I texted Guy while I was in the bathroom at a party. In ever so collegiate melodramatic fashion, I sent him Holy Ground by Taylor Swift. No explanation. Just the song. I bawled as I did it. My makeup was already questionable from being intoxicated, but it was wrecked from my bathroom antics.

I walked back into the party and as luck would have it, immediately ran into Mikey.

"Kitty, long time no see," he bellowed, until he caught my expression. Almost everything Mikey did was loud, whether it was loving or fighting. He softened his voice. "Oh, shit."

He'd already heard from Guy that we broke up. Mikey let me cry on his shoulder and made the executive decision that I needed to go home. Part of me was concerned that Mikey was hitting on me, as that was his typical way of relating to women. But in reality, he was just super sweet.

"I'm sorry y'all had to split," he said as we walked. "I was always jealous of what you two had."

I shot him a skeptical stare. "Really? The king of the casual encounter was jealous of my *relationship?*"

Immediately, I felt bad, because I could tell my words stung. Something else was going on there. I didn't push.

By the time we got back to my room, I wasn't nervous about his intentions anymore. He made sure I had water and ate a snack, staying to chat for a few minutes before he left me to my peace.

"I miss him, too, babe," was all he said when we hugged goodbye.

Pathetically, I turned my phone off silent for the first time in like, ever, hoping I'd hear if Guy texted me back.

When I was posted up in bed, dozing off, Guy responded. He sent the song our moms sometimes put on when they were having their wine nights: Jewel's You Were Meant for Me. They'd both put their heads back on their respective Adirondack chairs and belt out the bridge, Eva in her signature Quebec-tinged rasp and my mom in her gritty country accent.

It was a good memory. Our moms, happy. And the song itself,

sad and longing. Was Guy rubbing in the idea that we were meant for each other?

GUY-GUY FRENCHIE
Miss u Birdy

My drunken tears started up again, cut with hysterical laughter thinking back on the good times we'd had when we lived on the same street. Guy was my person. He was sitting in Seattle or wherever the fuck he was that night, being sad over me, and I was in Cambridge, being sad over him. I hesitated, but I was awake anyway. He was texting. He was on the other end. And I was still pretty drunk.

> Miss you too
> Saw Mikey tonight. He misses you
> Bet he does, that dirty boy
> He try to fuck u
> > Ew Guy-Guy yuck
> > Actually he was really sweet
> Sweet how

What, was I supposed to admit that I was sobbing over him at a college party? Texting him Taylor Swift songs from the toilet while I was supposed to be out living it up and dancing with my friends? Five minutes passed while I debated whether or not I'd be throwing up that night or if it was just me stressing over Guy.

> Sweet how Birdy?!

I started dozing off, the drunkenness outweighing my excitement that we were actually talking. It had been a long month of cold turkey No Guy, my heart hurting every day. My phone rang in my hand.

"Hello?"

"Hi, Kitty Bird," Guy crooned. "You okay over there?"

It was miraculous hearing him talk like everything was fine, not mad or sad. Just sweet Guy. His accent with all of its "d" for "th" sounds. His warm voice. Him.

"I wish you were here," I whimpered.

Guy didn't speak for so long that I thought we'd been disconnected. "Me, too, Birdy."

He paused a lot longer. Embarrassment set in that I was drunk and he was seemingly sober. I was a fool for texting him.

"How was Mikey sweet? Is he hitting on you? Because I'll fly out there and take care of it if I need to." Guy's voice went borderline enraged.

"Oh, calm down, you thug. He was a good friend."

"How?" Guy demanded.

"I was crying over you, okay? Jesus," I ground out. "He saw me right after I sent you that song. He sat with me while I lost it and walked me home. He misses you, too, by the way."

"Kitty, it doesn't have to be like this," Guy pleaded. "Just come back."

"I want to," I said, starting to cry again. "But I can't."

"Do me a favor, then, and don't drunk text me," Guy said, his voice cold.

"Guy," I protested.

"It kills me, Kitty," he ranted. "Every fucking day, I'm miserable without you."

"I am, too."

"Then come back!" he yelled. He'd never once raised his voice with me. The only time he'd ever even been directly mean is if we were playing around in bed and it was part of the game. He wasn't being fair. I thought our decision was mutual, but he was pushing that it was my choice again.

"I can't, okay? We have to choose to be happy alone. Don't be cruel about this. We chose this together."

"That doesn't mean I like it," he snarled.

"Well, I don't either. I wanted us to work out, Guy. I still do. But we need to give ourselves time to grow and maybe later..."

"Maybe later," his voice a quiet, low rumble. "I'm living for maybe later."

"Me, too."

"I love you, Kitty Bird."

"I love you, too, Guy."

* * *

Life went on. The things I wrote that first semester after we broke up weren't overly funny. They were actually pretty dark. Even though I'd told Guy to choose happiness without me, I struggled to be happy without him.

Choose happiness. It was some phrase I'd seen on a mug that some overly optimistic girl in one of my classes carried. I hated it. And yet, I weaponized it and used it on my best friend. The love of my life.

Guys hit on me, but it didn't feel right. I was too wounded. I knew what real love looked like. Why would I waste time with someone who wasn't The One? Guy was The One.

A cute guy from one of my classes, Evan, kissed me at a party. I gave off all the right signals. I didn't *not* want him to kiss me. I didn't push him away. I pushed myself to like him back. But I just couldn't.

When Evan kissed me, I cried. Mikey happened to be at that party, and he shoved Evan against a wall asking what he'd done to me. I just looked at Mikey and shook my head.

"Him?" he asked. I nodded.

Mikey apologized to Evan, who never sat next to me in class or even looked my way again. I appreciated Mikey's big brother attitude, but ultimately, I was relieved when he graduated and got drafted to the Princes' system. The sooner the boys who had known me and Guy as an item were gone, the sooner I could move on.

I did my best to keep my chin up and bury myself in my craft. And mostly, I succeeded.

Eventually, I was able to kiss other men and not cry. I had a good sense of humor going into my first time fucking someone new. I knew it would be weird. My last partner had known every quirk of my body, every single secret about me. How could this guy ever measure up to my Guy?

"Don't compare him," I chanted in my head, but how could I not? The man between my legs seemed to have no idea that the vagina and clitoris are in fact not the same. I ended up taking charge of that encounter, holding my hand over his mouth to shut him up and closing my eyes as I rode him. He thought it was the hottest sex that either of us had ever had. Sadly, that was only true for one of us. I was literally going through the motions and left as soon as I could.

Guy's ghost lurked everywhere, waiting to remind me exactly how good I'd had it.

I lived, but I was haunted.

Chapter 29

Guy

When COVID first hit the U.S., I went into a spiral. I knew Kitty was still at Alden, which isn't that far from New York. I had this panic that she was sick or would die without talking to me again. Hockey was on hold while everything was locked down, so all I had to do with my time was eat, sleep, and worry. I didn't have a partner to hang out with. I just had myself. I was terribly lonely and deeply anxious.

I needed Kitty.

For years, our back-and-forth had only been via text. Little reminders of our friendship, inside jokes, silly memes that we knew the other would think were funny. She, Frank, and I still had a three-way text going, sometimes more lit up than others. But when I developed this fear that she was in danger, I had to call her, breaking out of the text chain.

I was shaking as the phone rang. I was never afraid when a 200-pound man came hurtling down the ice at me with a vision of wedging my body between his and the boards. But the thought of that five-foot-seven woman being in danger put more fear in me than anything could. If I lost her, I'd have nothing.

Her voice was warm on the other end. "Hi, Guy-Guy."

A smile cracked over my face at hearing her, though my words broke. I realized how long it had been since I smiled. "Kitty Bird. Are you okay? Where are you?"

"I'm in Cambridge still."

"We have to get you out of there, Kitty. Are you feeling okay? Are you healthy?"

"Yes, I'm fine. Are you okay? Your team is already a breeding ground as it is."

She wasn't wrong. If one of us got a cold or stomach bug, it was almost guaranteed to make its way around the locker room. We spit and bled all over each other all the time, a veritable cesspool at times.

"I haven't seen anyone in like five days. I hope nobody has it. You're so close to New York, though, *ma puce*."

"It's just been me and Violet holed up together for now. We're okay."

"I'm so worried about you. Can I rent you a car to drive home?"

She chuckled, kind of sad. "Mark Gatto's already on it, Frenchie."

I snorted. "Of course he is."

"He's on his way to get me. I'm more worried about him getting it since he's older. We're going to ride home with the windows down. We'll both isolate when we get back."

My heart pounded. "Kitty, I need to know you're okay. I need to see you."

She was quiet, coughing a couple of times. My panic raced harder. "Birdy, do you have a cough?"

"No, it's just a throat tickle."

I broke down. It was like all my worst fears were coming true. "Kitty, I'm going to drive to see you, okay? I'll stay in a tent in your yard if I have to, but I . . . I need you."

"In West Virginia? Guy, you can't. I'm taking a risk traveling as far as I am. You can't cross the whole damn country."

I couldn't even get words out. The days of loneliness, fear, and handwashing had gotten to me.

"Why don't we make a plan to FaceTime whenever we can? Then we can see each other." She coughed again.

"Kitty, are you sick?"

"Guy, seriously. Hang on."

She hung up, then I got a FaceTime request. I answered right away, wiping my face with the bottom of my shirt. Kitty's face filled my screen. She was wearing sweats, her hair in a messy pile on her head. She lifted her phone so I could see her whole body.

"Hi. See? I'm alive and well. All my parts. Breathing. I'm fine. I'm worried about you now."

I had to laugh. "I guess I got a little irrational."

She gave me a sympathetic smile. "It's okay. Shit's weird out there. How have you been keeping yourself busy? Make any crumbly meat pies?"

Talking to her made me realize just how stark the loneliness had been. It reminded me to call Frank, too. I needed people in my life. I almost always had someone around me, whether it was a teammate or yeah, a hookup. All the stress melted away as we got caught up. Violet passed through her background and said hi at one point.

"Is Violet why you're not freaking out right now?"

"Yeah. We have each other," Kitty said. "It's probably hard for you being alone."

We talked until my phone was hot in my hand and warning me of its imminent death.

"When's Mark coming for you?"

"Two days. Wanna talk again tomorrow?"

And that's how we passed those early days of the pandemic. Heather let the camera roll when they did Kitty's at-home graduation ceremony. Kitty practiced her SNL audition tape on me. We learned stupid TikTok dances together and did pushup challenges. I won. She didn't even try. We synched movies together. The vibe was something like we were in high school and college before we officially got together: really good, really affectionate friends. I think we were both afraid to venture into something more because the problem between us still wasn't resolved. We still couldn't physically be together.

In late July, it all came to an end. The NHL figured out a way to "bubble" teams together, so I had to go back to practice. And Kitty was off to New York, having landed that SNL spot. Even though most recording was remote, she still needed to be close to the studio. I was so fucking proud of her. And in the back of my mind, I felt a little glad she'd said no to my proposal. She made it, just like she knew she could. By August, we were back to occasional stray texts, memes, and jokes. We were back to our distance keeping us apart.

Chapter 30

Guy

The day I'd long dreaded finally came. It was over three years after we broke up.

Kitty was thriving. She was acting and writing for SNL. I was genuinely so proud of my Kitty. We were both doing the things we'd wanted to do our whole lives. At least we'd accomplished the objective for us breaking up.

That's who she still was to me. My Kitty.

I had her few seconds on the SNL intro memorized. She looked over her shoulder, flicking her long, dark hair with a silly look on her face, then laughing and showing her true smile. It was a smile I knew well. It was the one she gave when she was truly happy and comfortable. But the best part was that she wore the bird necklace I'd sent her all those years before in the shot. I wondered if she meant it as a sign to me.

That first summer after she was cast, she went on a standup tour called Wannabe Pop Star. She dressed like a pop star, in a sparkly bodysuit with tall glittering boots, showing off those incredible legs of hers.

I bought a front-row seat for every single show as my weird way of showing support, but I never got up the nerve to go. Part of me said I'd just distract her. Another part of me was just plain scared. What if she didn't still love me the way I loved her? I didn't think my heart could survive the rejection.

Still, I kept my options open. Would she take me back if I could play for New York or New Jersey? I had my agent look into it, to start putting feelers out. I wouldn't be able to move out of my entry-level contract until I was twenty-seven. These were what-ifs for years in the future.

Mostly, I was really dedicated to not distracting her. I had a burner social media account to watch her standup posts. I didn't want her to see my face in her followers, so @funnyfan96 I was. I left nice comments about how funny she was. If someone was mean to her, I turned into a bulldog defending her viciously.

Not that she really needed my help. She was so good, she even got a Netflix stand-up special. I watched it a gross number of times. When Branson caught me watching it *again* on a flight, he intervened.

"You ever going to call her?"

"We talk sometimes," I said, brushing him off. "She knows I'm proud of her."

"Bro," Branson said, looking at me more seriously. "Have you ever talked to anyone about it?"

"What do you mean?"

"I mean like therapy, man." He eyed me cautiously. "You're running through women like water. I heard a rumor you had SNL on while you fucked one of them."

My cheeks heated. It was true. It wasn't my fault that Kitty's show was on during prime fucking hours. It wasn't my fault that I looked for Kitty in every woman I had sex with. Sometimes I'd squint and try to imagine the eyes looking back at me were hers. I tried to mentally trick myself that it was her and not some almost-stranger.

"Guess I need my agent to lock up my NDAs a little tighter."

Branson sighed, massaging the bridge of his nose. "Guy, I'm just worried about you. I'm afraid you're never going to get over her."

"What if I don't want to get over her? What if I know it's going to work out again?" I snapped.

One of our other teammates, Schneider, leaned over. "He doesn't know, does he?"

"Know. What?" I bit out.

"Shut the fuck up, Schneider!" Branson warned.

"What are you keeping from me?"

"Look, I didn't want to be the one to tell you," Branson started.

"Tell me what?!" I demanded, fully yelling.

Branson put a hand on my shoulder. "Deep breaths, Guy."

My eyes searched his, my heart sinking as the realization ran over my body like a cracked egg. "Who?" I whispered.

"Her castmate, Clark Sanders."

I stopped breathing. I thought I had noticed chemistry in their scenes together, but told myself I was just jealous. I pulled out my phone and googled both of their names. Sure enough, there were paparazzi photos of them. Her feet in his lap at an awards ceremony, a laugh coming from her pretty lips. Their hands laced in Central Park. The two of them masked together in a deli.

The worst part of it all was she looked like she was in love. I knew what she looked like in love. I'd seen that face reflected back at *me*.

She hadn't told me. Frank hadn't told me. Both Gattos betrayed me.

The rest of the flight was a fever dream. People talked to me, but I didn't hear them. Branson told our social media manager not to take any pictures of me. He also made me drink water. Coach didn't bother making me put my suit back on to deplane.

When we landed in Seattle, Branson took me home. After he sat with me for a few hours, essentially holding a vigil for my shattered heart, I sent him home to be with Mel and the baby. Being the good friend he is, he refused to leave me alone. He had me pack for a stayover at his place. That's how worried about me he was.

He was right to be worried. I was a walking nightmare. He must have given Mel a heads-up because she was ready for us with a frozen pizza and some wings. She didn't even flinch when I cried into my plate. Not that I could care. I had no shame. I was completely broken.

Kitty was moving on without me. Everything in my whole body hurt.

My playing was abysmal, too. My legs felt like lead on the ice at morning skate the next day. I wiped out of my own accord a few times, and no one said a word. Coach started to bark at me, but someone quickly pulled him aside and mumbled something to shut him up. After practice, Coach called me into his office. I expected the reaming of the century.

Instead, when I sat in the chair in front of his desk, he gave me a sympathetic look.

"You want to be a healthy scratch or an upper body injury for tomorrow, Stelle?"

"Coach? I don't understand," I said, genuinely baffled. "I'm not sick."

"You look like hell."

"It won't affect my playing, Coach," I argued. "I'm not injured. What upper body injury are you talking about?"

"Come on. Don't make me spell it out."

I looked at him with a shrug. I really didn't understand.

"Your head's not on right. I think you need to take a little time off to get it back together. Maybe talk to the team shrink. You could hurt yourself playing when you're like this."

I was embarrassed. Kitty and I had split up three years before and I was still that torn up over her. But while we'd split up, she was always mine to me. Why couldn't everyone get that?

I'd been silent for too long.

"I've been there before, Stelle. I wish someone had given me some time."

"You have?"

"The woman before my wife. She cheated on me, though. You learn to love again."

That statement made nausea churn hot in my gut. I wouldn't love again. I'd only love Kitty.

But I took the time off, and I had a few long sessions with the team psychologist. I'd met with her once before, but it was brief and strictly focused on hockey. This time, I spilled it all out. Papa leaving. Maman dying. Kitty and I getting together. Kitty and I falling apart. My continued hopes that Kitty would come back to me someday. The women I killed time with in between what I hoped was our split and getting back together.

I told her how I really believed Kitty was coming back.

The therapist encouraged me to take the time to mourn all the things I'd lost. She told me it was okay to take some time and space from talking to Kitty as a friend, or to talk if I needed the closure. I couldn't fathom closure, because that would mean it was over. I chose to put distance between us.

She had me write about my feelings. I wrote about how much I missed Maman. I wrote about how I resented Papa for not being able to try harder for us. I looked through old pictures of me and Kitty, and sadly, looked at some pictures of her with *him*. Did I even know Kitty anymore?

But in a way, I felt like I did. We still texted sometimes, when one of us did something noteworthy. We remained each other's biggest fans.

I looked over my shelf filled with hats she'd sent me every time I got a hat trick, along with the snow globe she gave me right before we broke up. Every single time, she showed that she was still paying attention and still cared.

True to Kitty's way of being, the hats were all silly. One, an I LOVE NY hat. Another was a really douchey-looking fedora with a peacock feather in the band. One was so big I had to design a special shelf for it, an oversized cowboy hat. I picked the ridiculous fedora off the shelf and decided I'd start wearing it with my suits for games. She still wore her bird necklace, even while she was with him. I considered that a victory. So I'd wear her hat when I knew I'd be photographed.

Maybe then she'd know how much I still loved her every day. Maybe someday soon, I could figure out a way to win her back.

And never let her go again. Because I only had one more time of trying left in me.

Part 5:
The Return

TALKIE MAGAZINE
EXCLUSIVE REPORT

Talkie has it on good authority that Kitty Gatto and Clark Sanders have parted ways.

The two met on the set of SNL in 2020, becoming quick sweethearts.

"Their on-stage chemistry bubbled over. Clark was completely smitten. Once he won Kitty over, he thought he was set for life," a friend of the former couple says. "He was pretty crushed that Kitty was done."

Sources say Gatto felt the relationship had run its course and was ready for the next stage in her career.

Another source says Gatto was never fully invested. "She always kept her options open," the source told Talkie.

Rumors of a secret marriage and a love nest in the Hamptons were not able to be confirmed, though the pair were often photographed there.

Over the weekend, Sanders was spotted canoodling a new love interest at a club following SNL taping. Gatto hasn't been seen since the alleged breakup, but she'll be back in the public eye soon. She has standup shows on her schedule in the Big Apple at the end of the summer.

Chapter 31

Kitty

"If we want to think about my love life in terms of the Netflix and Channel 1 sensation, the Great British Bakeoff, Paul Hollywood would take one look at my little gingerbread house, stare it down with those piercing blue eyes, and say, 'It looks a bit of a mess.'"

Laughs swelled. I was on stage at Caroline's, one of my favorite clubs for stand-up.

"And it's one of those cases where I'm someone who never should have been cast on this show. The show is fading from favor and they're begging for contestants. Pandemic baking is over. Too many people stopped eating bread and enormous New York Times chocolate chip cookies and went back to diets and salads."

More laughter. I held my body in the explanation posture.

"But Paul and Prue walk up to my bench, and they see a gingerbread house, not even made of proper gingerbread, mind you. It's like half-raw brownie batter with no standing walls. Just frosting and ganache and cookie crumbles everywhere. But like, it tastes *great*."

I waited for the laughter to die as I pulled my stool to the edge of the stage to do some crowdwork.

"Lots of couples in here tonight. Anybody on their first date?"

A couple in the second row raised their hands.

"Oooh, a fresh kill!"

I licked my chops and rubbed my hands together with crazy eyes.

"Let me just get the tough part out of the way for you two. Miss, do you fuck on the first date?"

She gave an iffy "maybe," eyeing her date sidelong. "Depends on the person."

"I hear you, mama. I hear you. And what about you, sir?"

His face went beet red. "Depends on the person."

"Oh, that was slick, sir. She answered first and you just got to mirror her answer. Oooh, this ain't his first rodeo."

I reached in my back pocket and pulled out a condom, tossing it to them.

"Have fun tonight, kids, but lady, watch out with him. He's a little too good."

I scanned the faces looking back at me when I stopped on a very familiar face.

"Alright, hang on. I think we've got a rare opportunity here."

I put my hand over the mic and leaned so my face was past the lights on the stage.

"Guy? Is that you?"

His smile gleamed in the dark and he nodded.

"Will you come up here? Yeah?"

He nodded and stood. I looked to our stagehand, Maurice.

"Maurice, can we get another mic up here? Ladies and gentlefolk, I have a special treat for you here tonight. Please welcome to the stage, star forward for the Seattle Sealpups and my ex-boyfriend, Guy Stelle!"

I pronounced his name the way everyone else does, not wanting to give away something so personal to us. Guy walked to the side of the stage and stepped up to whoops and applause. He wore a short-sleeved button-down and well-fitted jeans that showed off his athletic body. His long-ish hair was smoothed back and parted to the side. A few wavy strands fell out around his face. He looked, in short, as stunning as ever.

I welcomed him with a hug, and God, he smelled so good. Like him. He kissed my cheek to a quick "aww" from the crowd. I pulled the stool back and invited him to sit, and Maurice handed him the extra microphone. I rested my arm on his shoulder, propping my chin in my hand and looking at him.

"So, Guy, you look great. Did your cheekbones get more cut? Jesus. And your hockey butt, big and tight as ever."

Guy laughed, his eyes sparkling at me as he said, "You look beautiful, Kitty."

I flipped my hair coquettishly, but my stomach swooped. I'd always loved the way he said "beautiful." His accent was music to me. I hadn't heard him say my name since the depths of the pandemic: "Kit-tee."

"It's been a minute, huh?" I said, acting like I was interrogating him.

"It has."

I squinted at him. "Did you *know* I was going to be here tonight?"

"I, uh ... maybe?" he said with a wince.

"You don't follow my comedy account," I said, accusatory. "Your face is never in my stories and you're not in my followers."

"Actually, I do," Guy said. "I have a burner account."

My jaw dropped. "Just to stalk my comedy career?!" The crowd looked about as shocked as I felt. One girl had her hands covering her mouth. Another flapped her hands as if to say *this is the most romantic shit I've ever seen.*

Guy blushed and put a hand over his face.

"Are you @funnyfan96?!" I gasped. Guy blushed deeper and bent forward. "You guys, @funnyfan96 puts the sweetest comments on the sets I post. Like that I'm funny and pretty and smart and sexy. And if anyone trolls me, @funnyfan96 is all over them." My heart pounded and my eyes watered. I couldn't hide the quiver in my voice. "It's you?"

Guy sat up and with a look of ultimate embarrassment, nodded. "Jesus, Guy, this is a revelation."

I stood back, taking it all in to the hysterical laughter of the crowd. I took off my jacket and fanned myself.

"You could just, ya know, tell me you miss me."

"I don't want to bother you."

I set my jaw and turned to the audience. They were gobbling this up. Who could blame them? "So to catch y'all up, Guy and I lived on the same street for a year in West Virginia, and his family and my family were besties. Then we started dating in college until he got drafted into the NHL. Okay, so why don't you tell the lovely people here why we didn't work out?"

Guy laughed and so did the crowd. "It just wasn't our time," he said. "You wanted to do this and I wanted to play hockey. Our schedules didn't line up."

"Guy," I said, looking at him pointedly. "I put my life on display for laughs. You can tell them the truth. Surely there's something about me you couldn't live with."

"That is the truth. I never should have let you go," he said. Then just looking at me, he said, "You're the one that got away."

The "aww" that came from the crowd that time was deafening. I doubled over and staggered backward like I'd been shot, laughing because I was embarrassed and crying because it was sweet. He'd never said anything like that during our pandemic rekindling.

"Are you kidding me?!" I shouted away from the mic as I took a minute to recover. Guy's smile was my very favorite one, the one he reserved just for me. The one that was natural and easy but so gleeful.

I stepped back to the mic stand and brushed off my clothes to compose myself. "So like, are you single?" I asked, wiping tears from my red face.

The crowd whooped in approval.

"Pretty much," he drawled.

"Pretty much!" I turned to the crowd. "That's NHL fuckboy speak for 'I still fuck the fans but not one regularly.'"

Guy shrugged and the crowd laughed. He winked at me.

I tucked a strand of hair that had come loose from my ponytail behind my ear. I leaned on the mic stand, putting on exaggeratedly flirty body language. "So what are you doing later?"

He lifted his mic to his lips. "I mean, hopefully," he started, wiggling his eyebrows and pointing to me. He was so fucking charming and funny. The crowd was in the palm of his hand.

"Okay, get outta here. Stop stealing my show. Guy Stelle, everyone!" I held his hand up and we bowed together. He gave me a big hug and another kiss on the cheek before going back to his seat.

When I finished my set, Guy waited at the bar with a beer for me and an open stool.

"You were amazing," he said into another hug, this one longer and more intimate.

"So were you, funny fan! Thanks for coming. It's really great to see you," I said. "And what a surprise!"

"I figured you'd tell me not to come if I told you I was coming," he said. "I really wanted to see you. I miss you."

I took a long drink of my beer. Why did he think I'd tell him not to come? I didn't feel like getting into it with a potential audience around us. "How long are you in town?"

"I booked a room for the weekend," he said. "I knew you had a few sets here, and based on your schedule, it doesn't seem like you live here anymore."

"Oh," I said, somewhat taken aback. It's true, I loosely followed his schedule during hockey season, but he had done research about me. "Yeah, I don't. I'm about to start a job in L.A."

His jaw fell open. "Congrats! What's the job?"

"I got a writing job for a show on NBC."

Guy's eyes lit up. "Seriously? Kitty, that's so amazing! I'm so proud of you!"

"And I bought a house. I close next week," I told him with a grin.

"Oh my God, Kitty Bird! I can't believe it!" He did that thing where he swept me into his broad and tall body and jostled me around like I was a toy. It always made me feel so cherished, a child-like display of affection that was so pure and joyful. "Can I take you to dinner to celebrate?"

I laughed. "Why do I get the feeling you were going to take me to dinner even if I bombed tonight and had no good news to share?"

Guy gave a deep, full laugh. "You know me too well."

He popped on a baseball cap, paid our tab, and we headed out. His fitted shirt gave a delicious peek at his biceps, and his jeans were a goddamn work of art. He touched me as much as he possibly could on the walk over, and I let him. It was so nice to be back in his company, with his familiar scent and his hands moving their old routes over my body.

He was in the mood for sushi, so we slid into a late-night spot not far from the theater district. As I picked my sushi, I kept feeling him watching me. I looked up.

"What?"

"I'm just so glad you're here," he said, eyes soft.

"Yeah?"

We ordered, and he took my hand across the table, playing with my fingers and knuckles until he settled on holding it.

"So I don't mean to crash your weekend in New York, but I want to talk to you about something," Guy started. His expression was vulnerable and sincere in the table's candlelight. "I don't think last time was our only time to try. It was a good start, but it wasn't the end of our story."

I gave a wry smile. "I live in L.A. now, though, and your season is about to start."

"I know. But I have summers off, and really Kitty, I date around but no one makes me happy like you do. You understand me, and I understand you." He looked down at my hand in his, rubbing his thumb over my fingers, then brought his eyes back to mine. "I never stopped loving you. I'll play L.A. and Anaheim a couple times a season, and I can fly you out to see me when you have breaks. I know it's not ideal, but I'd rather have you sometimes than not at all."

"But what's the end goal? You still have another five or ten years to play. Will we be long distance for that long?"

"I don't know right now. But I'll do my best to work around you. I'll never ask you to give up your career for me again," he said. I swallowed hard. One of the greatest deliberations of my adult life was whether I was wrong turning him down when he offered to make me an NHL wife.

"We haven't even really talked in over a year, Guy. You kind of fell off. We don't even know if we're still right for each other. People change," I said, pulling my hand back from his and sitting back. With the upcoming changes in my career, I didn't know if I could handle the emotional rollercoaster of trying with him again. Never really being able to have him. Forever out of reach.

Guy sighed. "I don't know what you had planned for this weekend, and I don't want to take it over if you had big plans. But what if we just pretend for this weekend that it's all going to work? What if we try, just for these three days? Then you can think about it."

I took a beat to think. I thought about what he'd said on stage, and I knew they weren't just lines. With me, Guy isn't an act. He's real. So much had passed between us over the years. So much time, so many memories, so much pain, and so, so much love.

I reached for his hand again. "This weekend. All in. We don't talk about the complicated stuff. I can't have my heart broken like that again. We'll just enjoy each other. I have a couple of dates with friends but the rest of the time, I'm yours."

Guy's eyes went watery. "Thank you. I love you, Kitty Bird."

"I love you, too."

Chapter 32

Guy

"I can't believe you've been keeping up with me all this time," Kitty said, shaking her head as she shoved her last bite of sushi in her mouth.

"I've been so proud of you," I said, dividing the dregs of our bottle of sake between our cups. "You've done everything you wanted to do."

"You have, too," she said, looking at me and glowing. "I'm sorry I don't always keep up with your games. I do check the scores and see if you scored. You almost always get a point somewhere. Sorry about the playoffs last year, though."

She texted me a congrats every time I'd gotten a hat trick, and a few days later, a hat showed up at my door without fail. Even when I stopped talking to her, she pushed on. What she didn't know was that in my head, every single goal, every assist, every achievement was for her.

"That's what they pay me the big bucks for," I deflected.

"I'm curious. Why did you pick now to check in with me?" Kitty's eyes were stunning in the candlelight.

How much was I willing to give away? Go for honesty, or hide my true feelings? In my desperation to keep her when we were young, I don't think I told her about not being able to be traded until I was twenty-seven. Should I tell her I was finally eligible to be traded, or would that get her hopes up too much?

"I, uh, read you weren't with Sanders anymore," I started. "And your standup has been more single-focused, so I thought I might have a chance. We're a little older now, so I thought I might be able to convince you to do long distance again until I can figure out something else."

Kitty nodded, her chest heaving with a breath as she looked around the table. She picked up a piece of ginger with her chopsticks, almost dropping it.

I snorted a small laugh. "You always were shit with chopsticks, Birdy."

"Shut up," she said, flinging condensation from her water glass at me.

"I swear to God, Birdy, I brought you to a nice restaurant and you still can't behave."

"Oh, you're gonna fuckin' get it later," she said, a spark in her eyes.

"Oh, am I? Or are you? You know what happens when you're bad," I said breezily, stroking one fingertip over her knee under the table. "I've missed doing that with you, too."

Kitty drew in a shaky breath. "I understand you've had plenty of candidates to distract you in that regard."

"Don't you slut shame me, Birdy. And besides, nobody holds a candle to you," I said, watching her face flush pink.

"You're just saying that. I'm sure you have girls lubing up their feet for you if that's what you want."

"I'm not just saying that. You're the blueprint, the one I compare everybody to. And you know I'm not a foot guy."

Kitty and I shared a tense glance, the kind that used to end with my mouth on her neck and her nails raking down my back. She took on a slight smirk.

"Ankles, though," she said, raising an eyebrow. She was kidding, but one of my favorite old ways to get her fired up was to nibble at her ankles, then work my way up her leg with my mouth. She has the best legs. One of the reasons I loved her Netflix special so much was that I got to see her legs for an entire hour. I remembered what they felt like in my hands, wrapped around my waist.

"Always an ankle guy," I agreed with a grin.

Outside the restaurant, Kitty stood in front of me, holding both of my hands. The night was hot, the late summer air not cooling much in the evenings. My stomach was a snake pit of nerves. I knew what I wanted to do next, but I wanted to tread lightly.

"Thanks for taking me to dinner," she said sweetly. "And for coming to my show. And to New York, seemingly for me?"

"All for you, *ma puce*." It had been so long since I kissed her that I almost felt like I needed to ask permission. We were strangers in some ways. But when I put my hand on her waist and she stepped in, grabbing my bicep, I knew I was good to go. My other hand went to her neck, using my thumb to lift her face to mine. That always used to make her melt.

Just before I dropped my lips to hers, she spoke. "Is this going to be a mistake?"

"If so, it's a mistake I'm willing to make. Are you?"

Kitty's face lit up with what I'd call her signature devious look. Then with her hand on my neck, she pulled me down to her.

Our lips met again for the first time since she left Seattle for good. It was electric, exactly what I'd been hoping for since I let her go. There were kisses and then there were kisses from Kitty, my one true love. We had a certain rhythm to how we kissed, and it clicked right back into place. We connected, lips sampling three or four times before she licked my upper lip. I slanted my mouth and opened, letting our tongues slide together, sucking back out. I pulled her body close to mine, dragging her into me. I forgot how good she tasted. There was a certain taste that was only hers.

I needed her warmth, even though the night was hot. I backed her up to the brick of the restaurant, cradling her head so it didn't hit hard. I drove my knee between her legs to get closer, Kitty giving a shocked giggle into my mouth. I didn't care who saw us.

In fact, I'd be glad if someone got a picture of us. Then everyone would know she was mine again. Balance was restored in my universe. The years between our being together were generally good years, but there was always a Kitty-sized hole in every achievement, every milestone, and every single day that she wasn't around.

We broke the kiss, Kitty looking up at me dazed and panting. I had an undeniable erection and had basically turned the streets of Manhattan into my personal den of debauchery.

"So you wanna go get ice cream?" And just like always, Kitty had me laughing.

We held hands walking back to my hotel. Kitty elected for us to go there since it was both closer and fancier.

"I think you still probably make more money than me," she said with a wink. "I bet your place even has nice bathrobes and shit."

"Guilty," I admitted. "If you're nice, I'll even let you order a massage to the room."

"Hmm, depends what nice means," she said, looking mischievous. "If I were really a nice girl, I'd sleep in your bed and you'd sleep on the floor like a gentleman."

I snapped my head to look at her. "I think you've been away from me too long. You forgot what nice means."

"You'll have to remind me, then," she said casually, like she wasn't inviting me to do all sorts of fun things to her. She knew she was driving me up the wall. Darkly, I wondered if she was this fun with Clark Sanders. I took a deep breath, mentally thanking my therapist for teaching me what to do with intrusive thoughts. "Are you going to be nice to me, though? I'm a respectable woman. I deserve to be treated like a princess."

Oh, Kitty was playing games. She was waiting for me to bite. I saw an alleyway and pulled her into it, a delighted giggle escaping her. I grabbed her from behind and leaned against a building, pulling her back to my front as I growled in her ear.

"If you want to be treated like a princess, you'd better stop being such a spoiled brat," I snarled. She was silent, gasping, waiting for me to go on. A wave of heat pulsed from her neck, where my lips hovered. "You love being a dirty, filthy little good girl for me. I bet you've thought about it since I've been gone."

"Maybe sometimes," she said, trying to sound airy but for once she sucked at acting. She couldn't pretend to be nonchalant when she was the equivalent of a cat in heat.

I traced my fingers along the top of her jeans. "You know, good girls get rewarded," I said, dipping my hand into her pants and under her panties, cupping her. She was completely drenched. "Are you going to be a good girl for me tonight?"

"Yes," Kitty moaned. So I gave her the reward. I dipped a finger into her slit, coating it in her slick wetness and dragging it up over her clit.

"You're fucking soaked for me, Birdy. Did you miss me?"

"So bad," she sighed, moving her hips to beg for friction from my finger. The fringe benefit was that it made her ass grind against my cock, teasing me at the same time. I flicked the pad of my finger over her nerves. Kitty held my wrist to her stomach, pleading for more.

"Good girl," I said, my finger moving faster. "That's it, Birdy. Let me take care of you."

"Guy," she choked out desperately, strangled.

With one hand down her pants, the other held her to my front, caressing her shoulder and neck, cupping her breast. I pressed kisses behind her ear as she held on to my hips for dear life, her head resting on my shoulder.

"Guy, I've needed you," she whimpered.

"I'm here now, sweetheart," I said. "Let go for me, baby."

Her hips moved furiously again, and she mewled, seeking her release. "Whose are you, Kitty?"

"Yours," she cried out as I felt her pulse against my fingers.

"My perfect girl," I cooed in her ear.

Kitty was mine again. At least for the weekend.

I removed my hand from her pants and slipped my wet finger into my mouth, sucking her taste off. I groaned. "I missed that taste, Birdy. You'll always be my favorite."

Kitty spun around in my arms, facing me and pulling me into a fierce hug. She shuddered as she held me, saying nothing. I stroked a hand over her hair, pinning her to me. Our energy was sexual and primal, but there were undercurrents of the longing and sadness we'd endured being apart for so long. It was spilling over for Kitty like it did for me during dinner.

"I'm glad you're here," she whispered. "Thank you for coming to see me. It's the best surprise. I guess I'm a little overwhelmed."

Her bravado was gone, raw feelings laid bare in the dim light of the alley. She still trusted me enough to show me her most vulnerable self, and that felt nice. All I wanted was to make her feel how much I loved her, and how much I needed her back in my life. I rubbed my thumb over her cheekbone.

"Can I take you home and show you how much I still love you?" I asked, reading the change in mood. She gave me a feather-light kiss that made my stomach tingle. Sweet Kitty was just as much fun as Bad Girl Kitty.

"I'd like that."

Chapter 33

Kitty

The door to Guy's hotel room clicked shut behind us. He looked at me with soft eyes. My heart pounded, the whole scene feeling like one of those visions before a migraine: surreal and distorted. I went from an average New York night to being reunited with my oldest, brightest flame. And him getting me off in a dirty alley? My life was strange indeed.

"Kitty, we don't have to do anything sexual." Guy leaned into the door, respecting my space.

"Says the man who just fingered me in an alley," I retorted.

"I realize that may have been a little much," he said. "I'm sorry."

"I had fun. Nice having our old dynamic back." I pushed up on my toes and kissed him. His lips met me softly, his hand moving into my hair, thumb at my jaw. His eyes opened slowly as I pulled away. Those gentle Guy kisses made me feel so cherished, another thing I'd missed.

"Yes, but we should probably ease into things. Wanna get down to our undies and be skeletons?"

I couldn't help but grin. I agreed and slipped into the bathroom, giving myself a hard look in the mirror. I was me, but there was a certain lightness I hadn't had before my show. I forgot how much Guy completed me and made me whole.

"Get over here, *ma puce*," Guy called from the bed when I emerged from the bathroom. His gaze combed over me as

I peeled off my shirt and dropped my jeans. I felt the need to cover myself even though we'd seen each other naked countless times.

I groaned as I slipped under the sheets, the relief of lying down taking over.

"Feels nice, huh?" Guy said, sliding over to me, placing his hand on my side, and kissing my forehead. I traced my fingers down his arm as our legs tangled together. My muscles instantly oozed with relaxation. It had been a while since I'd had snuggles, particularly snuggles that weren't perfunctory. We were there because we wanted to be.

"So nice," I agreed. I felt nervous and a little awkward, not quite knowing what to say. "So, how have your last few years been? How's Grandmere?"

Guy's face fell. He shook his head. My stomach turned.

"She's gone? When?"

"Last February."

"Why didn't you tell me? I would have been there for you, Guy. In a heartbeat."

He wouldn't meet my gaze. "You were with him."

"That doesn't mean I don't care about you and your family, Guy. What happened to us being a family? Did you tell my mom?"

"It hurt too much, Kitty. I couldn't see you as just a friend anymore. I still can't. You're my everything, and I couldn't deal with being your nothing." I felt like he'd put a pin in my balloon.

"You're not my nothing," I said. "I never stopped loving you, Guy."

Guy moved his hand to caress around my belly button, gaze tracking the movement. "I want this so bad, Birdy." His voice was brittle. "I want you back. No matter what it takes. We only get one life and I want you in mine. My life is only a half-life with you gone."

"I know what you mean," I said. "It's not the same without you."

Guy's eyes finally floated up to mine, the little scar on his upper lip from a puck he took there quivering. "Be with me, Kitty. Don't make me live without you."

I bit my lip, holding back tears. "I didn't expect this. I don't know what to say."

"Say yes. I let you go too easily last time. I'm asking for what I want this time. I want you, Kitty. All of you. No holding part of yourself back so you won't get hurt. I have everything else I want. But none of it means anything if I don't have you."

I wanted him back. Of course, I did. I still didn't know how it was all going to work, though. I couldn't commit the way he wanted me to at that moment. But I needed him.

I placed my fingers on his lips and sniffled. "None of the complicated stuff," I reminded him. "Just being together."

Guy nodded. "Okay."

A moment of tension passed between us, lightning bolts of need crackling in our stare. I wanted it, of course. I wanted to be able to surrender and say yes and just be with him, but I was so afraid of the pain.

But the need surged on.

The need broke me.

I smashed my face to his, pulling our lips together and rolling him to his back. His tongue met mine in a rush, my heart threatening to crack my breastbone with its thunderous force. Guy held me like I was something precious, his hands gripping my ribs, moaning into my mouth. He shifted to have a hand across my back and the other stroking down my spine, so tender and gentle with me.

My hips sought him in a rhythm, grinding my center against his hardness while our kisses tore on. Biting, sucking, strokes of the tongue to soothe. Unfettered desire.

Guy's hands shook as he groped at my bra closure, just like they had the first time we were together. Without breaking our kiss, I reached back to take over, shoving the offending fabric out of the way.

"Kitty," he yelped out in desperation. "I need to see you."

"Not as bad as I need to feel you," I replied, sitting up briefly before shifting down his body.

"Not fair. I need you first," he said, clawing at my arms to attempt to pull me back up.

"69?" I offered.

Guy broke a smile as I lowered the waistband of his underwear, freeing him and meeting that part of him again. I stroked him like my life depended on it, like I needed to touch him more than I needed to breathe. While I waited for his answer, I took matters into my own hands. Or my own mouth.

The taste of his precum on my tongue was a homecoming I didn't expect. I groaned with a mouth full of Guy, not realizing how even little things like that were missing in my life. I felt the rush of blood flow to his dick and more precum that matched his satisfied growl. I needed that. Needed him. Wasn't sure how I'd been without him all that time.

"Kitty baby, you know you go first," he said, darkness tinging his tone. "You'd better do as I say."

I looked him in the eye and spat on his dick in response, adding impossible wetness. I wanted him to give me his worst.

"That was your last warning," he said, tracing a finger along my jaw. "Get up here."

Meeting his fiery gaze, I wiped my lips and crawled back up his body. A powerful smack landed against my backside, a hiss escaping me. I panted in Guy's face, my jaw falling open.

"If you don't want another of those, you'd better sit my favorite pussy in the world on this face."

I did as he asked, mostly because having Guy's mouth back on me in that way was preferable to his spanks, no matter how pleasurable those were. I rested my bottom on his chest, my knees next to his head. Guy inhaled sharply.

"My favorite scent, Birdy," he said with reverence. "For years I've tried to remember everything about you."

"How'd you do?"

"There's nothing like the real you," he said, drawing a finger down my slit and making me shiver. "It's your taste that haunts me the most."

His eyes cut to the headboard. "Better hold on."

Guy's tongue sank into me, and it's like he forgot nothing. He remembered exactly how I liked it, something no one else mastered like he did. He sucked on me, alternating broad strokes of his tongue with teasing flicks. His hands found my thighs, pushing me open wider as my hands gripped the headboard. His eyes met mine, then followed his hands over my breasts, down to my ass. I sighed out his name, overwhelmed as my orgasm loomed. I bucked into his face, fully riding him as a long moan of encouragement left him.

I'd had good times with other guys and even felt bonded during sex, but nothing compared to the sacred intimacy that Guy and I shared. Sometimes it was a treacherous high, but always with a soft net to catch me. Guy was both danger and security. I came, completely breathless in a shaking, quivering rush of emotions.

"Nobody does it like you, Guy. No one," I breathed as I came down.

"Because nobody knows you like I do," he said. "We belong to each other."

He was campaigning for what he wanted, hard. I wanted it, too, but I still didn't see how it could all work. Between that and my orgasm, I was wiped out. I climbed off his chest and laid down beside him.

"Good?"

"You know it was," I teased. "But I need a minute. It's really intense being back like this."

Tears came at me unexpectedly.

"Oh, sweetheart, no," Guy cooed, pulling me into his chest. "Should I have not come to see you?"

"No, I'm glad you're here. It's just a lot," I sobbed, the second time that evening I'd been emotional after an orgasm.

Guy tipped up my chin to look at him, wiping my tears and studying my eyes. "Wanna know something?"

"What?"

"I almost cried seeing you naked again." Guy smiled, but his eyes were sad. I gave a soft laugh. "It's true. It's a lot for me, too. If we need to take a break for the night, that's fine."

I blew out a breath, pulling myself together. "I've needed you so bad for so long."

Guy sighed, too. "You have no idea, Birdy."

We lay there quietly like that for a while: my head on his muscled but somewhat manscaped chest, holding each other tight.

I was almost afraid to ask my next question, like he might make fun of me. "What if we make love? Go slow?"

Guy's sweet chocolate drop eyes met mine. "I'd love that."

Our earlier kisses were fiery and hungry. This was a different kind of hunger. Earlier, our bodies had needs. Then, it was our souls. So much hurt and longing had passed between us, and we needed to honor that. To bury the hatchet.

His lips savored mine. His hands took on a new deference. We listened with our motions. I studied the changes in him and the things that were familiar. I'd been able to read his body like a book before, but it was like new chapters were added. Good chapters, but unfamiliar nonetheless.

"You're still perfect," he whispered between kisses. He descended down my neck and to my breasts, open-mouthed and passionate. I dug my thumbs into his flat brown nipples, his head cocking back. We continued on, touching and feeling, until the time felt just right.

"Want me to get a condom?" Guy asked. "I got tested before this trip, and I haven't been bare with anyone but you."

"My last tests were negative and I'm on birth control," I said. A grin lifted the corner of Guy's lips.

"Just you and me?"

I nodded. "Just us."

In a flurry of kisses, Guy pushed into me. Our words came freely, uninhibited, not profound but meaningful to us.

"I love this."

"God, Kitty."

His hands held mine, pinning them over my head. It gave the advantage of being able to watch each other's faces. I gazed into the eyes of the man who never stopped loving me as he filled me, again and again. The man I let get away. The man I let go so we could have a shot at the lives we wanted. Letting go was necessary, but coming back together was, too. I hoped the weekend in New York wouldn't be the end of us.

We rolled to our sides, my leg wound around his torso. I loved looking so deeply into his eyes, making his presence more tangible.

"Gorgeous as ever, baby."

"More, Guy."

"I'll give you everything, sweetheart. You ask and I give. I'll always take care of you."

And he wasn't just blowing smoke. I knew he meant it. If I let him, he'd give me anything I ever wanted. Guy belonged to me, whether I wanted him to or not.

Chapter 34

Guy

"*Bonjour, ma puce.*"

I woke up before Kitty, but not by much. It gave me the chance to watch her in the morning sunlight that peeked around the hotel room's curtains. I still couldn't believe that she'd said yes. We were spending time together, however fleeting that would be.

I didn't have a formed plan as to my end game. I figured I couldn't get her to fully commit to me again before we left New York. She'd already pointed out that I'd be in Seattle and she'd be in L.A., leaving us in the same predicament we'd always been in. Although, at least we'd be in the same time zone. That would be new. Maybe a point in the "Being With Guy" column.

But maybe I could convince her to at least talk to me more often. Hopefully every day. Then I could work on figuring out how to move close to her. I wouldn't tell her until I was sure it could happen. I didn't want to get her hopes up. My agent, Marcie, had already put some work into seeing if I could trade to New York or New Jersey. Now that I knew Kitty was moving to L.A. permanently, I'd have to change her direction from the three New York area teams to the two Southern California teams.

Marcie was probably going to kill me.

"Morning, Guy-Guy." Kitty rolled her body against mine, letting me spoon her. Her naked body. She'd changed some, as everyone does. She was less willowy and gangly than she'd been a few years before, more like a grown woman. I liked it. My beautiful woman who'd always been my girl. I inhaled at her neck to her giggle. "This feels nice."

"It does," I said. "We could try to have this more often, you know."

"Ugh, Guy, stop campaigning," she sighed. "No complicated stuff."

"You're right, you're right."

"I'll try again. It's nice waking up next to you, Guy," Kitty said, nestling her body closer to mine.

"It is, Birdy."

She reached back and drifted her hand over my cock, which was already hard. "Morning wood, or are you ready to party?"

"A little bit of both. Does that mean you're interested?"

"I think I could be convinced," she cooed. My hand went from her waist up to her breast, where I traced her nipple with my fingertip. Kitty hummed as the peak pebbled under my touch.

"Does that help convince you?"

"Sure doesn't hurt," she said. "But I do have to pee."

I laughed. "Yeah, me too. Meet back here in a few?"

She clapped my butt as she got out of bed. "Meet back here."

After we'd both freshened up, Kitty waited for me in bed. She held her phone, a surprised look on her face.

"What is it?"

"Um, we kinda went viral," she said.

Hell yeah. "We did?"

"Yeah, come look." I sat behind her on the bed and pulled her body back into mine, my legs framing her as she leaned into my chest.

"Holy shit." Kitty paged through links from her agent. One place had written an article to go with a cell phone video of our performance from the standup place. Another Instagram account had pictures of us from inside and outside the sushi restaurant, our steamy kiss fully documented. There were pictures of me reacting to Kitty talking to me, one where I looked absolutely madly in love. "Find you a man who looks at you like Guy Stelle looks at Kitty Gatto," the caption said. Guess there had been photographers, or these days, anyone with a cell phone.

While I was secretly thrilled that I essentially laid claim to Kitty publicly, I figured it might be a little more violating for her.

"Are you okay, Kitty?"

She hesitated. "I mean, not the first time my love life will have been put on display."

"But?"

"You and I have been posted on the internet before, but that was before anyone knew me. Then I was just your little girlfriend. Are you okay? You're used to being with nameless people."

I shrugged. "I'm fine. It's with you, and I love you. But I know it makes our relationship seem more serious."

Kitty's face darkened and she turned over her shoulder. "Did you plan this on purpose?"

Shit. I kind of had. Just the night before, I'd been hoping someone would see us and take a picture, so everyone knew she was mine again. But I was really just going on my instincts at the moment. I wanted to kiss Kitty in public like a normal person could, so I did.

"Or are you using me to get more famous?" she went on.

"Oh God, Kitty, no. Never." I turned her around to face me fully. "Kitty, I'm here because I love you and I want you to think about giving us a shot again. I could give a shit about being famous. I already get enough weird DMs. I just want to love you and play hockey. Whatever else comes along with that is what it is."

Kitty's brow furrowed, but she nodded. She picked at the skin next to her thumbnail, something she did when she was anxious. I drew her hand to my mouth and kissed the broken skin on her thumb. She smiled a little.

"You still do that thing," I said.

"Only when I'm stressed."

"I don't want to stress you out. I want to make you happy."

Kitty's eyes shined as she looked at me. "You do."

"Then let's be happy together." She leveled me with a look. "For this weekend. Let's be happy together for this weekend, and then we'll see."

"Then we'll see," she repeated.

"Can I have some more of you right now?" I asked and she responded with my favorite of her devious grins.

Kitty drew my mouth to hers. I pulled her close to me, wrapping her legs around my back as I settled her onto my lap. We stayed like that for a while, just kissing and feeling each other. My fingers explored the muscles around Kitty's shoulders, a new addition.

"Do you work out now or something?" I asked with a kiss to her neck.

She laughed. "Yes. I finally stopped being a floppy theater nerd. My back hurt all the time and apparently I just had weak muscles. Now I walk and lift."

I chuckled. "I never thought I'd see the day Kitty Bird becomes a meathead."

"You wish," she teased. "You'll always be the meathead in this relationship."

My palm landed on her ass with a smack. "I'll show you who's a meathead. Hands and knees, woman."

"Oooh, okay," Kitty said with a shiver and a grin. I dragged her to the edge of the bed as she set up. Her ass was on display for me, her pussy glistening with her wet. Time to shake things up a little bit.

"Legs wider," I cooed. "I need room."

"You're not *that* huge, Stelle," she joked, but did as I asked. I slapped her butt again, massaging the cheeks in my palms.

"You remember our word?" I asked.

"Peaches."

"Good girl. Don't be afraid to use it, Birdy. I want you to feel good."

"Bring it on."

Lowering my face, I dragged my tongue from the top of her slit to her entrance. Kitty let out a long sigh. But I didn't stop there. Kitty gasped as my tongue continued its journey past her pussy right to her tight little asshole.

"Oh my God, Guy," she whimpered. "Are you sure?"

"I'm sure. Is it okay for you?"

"Yes, oh God," she moaned. I continued and moved a finger through her slit as I worked. She might have been the wettest I'd ever felt her. Kitty was definitely liking it. I skimmed over her clit and she cried out, loud. "God, Guy, right there. Do it again."

My tongue stroked her puckered hole as I pressed her clit again. Kitty absolutely screamed.

"Ready for my cock?"

"Yes, yes, yes," she whined. "I'm about to come, Guy."

"Not til I say so," I rasped. "Crawl."

She moved forward, giving me room. I knelt behind her and held her hips as I drove into her pussy, Kitty giving an enthusiastic sigh. She begged for more, bouncing back against me.

"My perfect, dirty girl," I gritted out. "You want my finger in your ass?"

She whined out my name, desperate to come.

"Don't you come yet, Birdy. Answer my question."

"Yes." She lifted her torso to lean back against me as I thrust into her. I sucked my finger and pressed it into her already-wet asshole, the feeling enough to send me to the edge as well. I could feel the pressure of my dick moving inside her through my finger, an unexpected turn-on. I took her breast into my other hand as her hands laced into my hair.

"So beautiful, Kitty. Such a good fucking girl taking me like this," I hissed as I moved my hand to her throat, not squeezing but holding her to me. She was willingly putting all her pleasure into my hands and I couldn't get enough. The trust we'd built over the years paid its dividends. "You ready to let go, gorgeous?"

"Please," she whispered. "It's so intense."

"Fuckin' right it is. You want my cum, sweetheart?"

"Yes, please, God, yes," she yelled.

"It's time. Come for me, baby."

With an agonizing shout, Kitty fell apart around me as I shot off inside her. I breathed hard, sitting back on my heels as she collapsed in my lap. We laughed, sighing out in disbelief.

"Guy, it's never been that strong," Kitty said, looking over her shoulder in shock. "When did you start eating ass?"

I shrugged. "It just felt right. Your ass looked so good in my face. Thought you might like it."

Kitty flopped onto the bed and I lay down beside her.

"So, what do you wanna do today?"

Chapter 35

Kitty

Guy held my hand everywhere we walked in Manhattan. We'd stopped by my hotel so I could get fresh clothes and shower with my own stuff. It was close to noon, and New York's August heat was thick and sultry. I picked a light cotton dress with some sandals that were comfy for walking. Somehow, my curled ponytail had survived the night pretty nicely.

We waited in line for iced coffee in a small neighborhood shop. Guy got two pain au chocolate with our iced coffees. We gave our coffee names as Jack and Diane, my idea.

"You need two pastries to hold you over til lunch, Frenchie?"

"No. You'll say you only want a bite and then you'll eat my whole pastry. One's for you, *ma puce*."

I smacked him, but still laughed. The barista called out our names.

"Hey, not to be weird," they said, putting our drinks on the bar, "But are you Kitty Gatto?"

"Guilty," I said.

"And this is the hockey player?"

Guy snorted. "Yes, I'm the hockey player."

"Do you mind if I get a selfie? My friends aren't going to believe me."

I glanced at Guy and he nodded. "Sure."

They came around the counter. "Want me to take it?" Guy asked.

"No, get in!" the barista said. Guy hunched down to fit in the frame, giving a crooked but happy smile.

Guy slid his hand back into mine as we left, stopping me just outside the door. He pulled me to him for a quiet but sweet kiss. He looked down into my eyes with a broad smile as he traced his thumb over my lips.

"What was that for?"

"You're nice to your fans. It's cute," he said.

"Well, yeah. I'm not a monster. You're nice to yours, too."

"I haven't gotten to see you be famous, though," he said. "It makes me happy. You deserve everything, Birdy."

My grin could have split my face. "Thanks, Frenchie. Wanna meet some of my famous friends?"

"I don't wanna crash your time with them," he said. "I can go do tourist things."

"I'll double-check, but I'm sure they'll be fine. But we might just gossip the whole time. Your choice."

He gave me a sweet smile. "I'll tag along."

I had a lunch date scheduled with some friends from SNL, meeting up at a dive bar that had great burgers. I texted Tania to see if she was cool with Guy tagging along.

> Hey. My old friend is with me this weekend.
> Do you mind if he comes?
>
> **TANIA**
> You mean that hot piece of ass that you had on stage last night?
> Yeah, bring him. But don't blow up our lunch spot
> with your fame and fortune
>
> Ha. See you soon

Guy came in late, saying he needed to return his agent's phone call. Our recent boost in fame affected his career, too.

Tania, my closest castmate other than the one I dated (ahem), my makeup artist Deandra, and my other co-star James Anthony waited for me at a table, greeting me with boisterous hugs.

"Heard you brought your man meat. Where is he?" Deandra asked, looking behind me.

"Outside on the phone. He'll be in soon."

"Okay, so before he comes in, did you two hook up? Did the stage chemistry carry over?" Tania jumped into interrogation mode.

I sipped the water in front of me. "Has the waiter been by yet?" I asked, changing the subject and fully knowing I wasn't going to get away with it.

"No way, missy. Cough it up. How was it?" Deandra pushed.

I smirked. "He still remembers everything about me."

The table erupted in shouts of excitement.

"But he's the one that tried to marry you when you were nineteen, right?" Tania asked.

"He is," I said after hesitating.

James gagged on his water. "Nine-TEEN?"

"It's complicated. We went our separate ways after that, but we never really stopped loving each other," I sighed. "It's really nice to see him again."

"Is he really the one that got away? We all watched the video before you came," Deandra had stars in her eyes. I swallowed hard and nodded.

"Oh, Kitty Cat," Tania said, grabbing my hand. "Is this going to ruin you?"

"It can't. I'm just about to start with this writing job. He's going back to Seattle. We're just having fun this weekend and seeing what happens, I guess."

"Well, speak of the devil," James said. The door to the bar opened and Guy's tall form filled the doorway. He waved to the bartender like he'd been there a thousand times and was getting his usual. His hand landed on my shoulder when he got to the table. I introduced him to everyone.

"I'm starstruck," Guy said. "Nice to meet the people Kitty loves so much."

"Likewise," Tania said. I kicked her under the table.

"How was Marcie?" I asked Guy.

"Apparently, my little New York trip is sparking New York trade rumors," he said, annoyed. My stomach dropped. Would he really go to New York? Too little, too late, Stelle.

"Have you talked to any teams here?" I asked, trying not to show my panic. We'd finally be in the same time zone, and he was considering moving across the country. Again.

"Not really," he said dismissively. He took my hand casually, draping it between our chairs. He picked up the menu with his free hand. "So what should I get?"

Guy was quiet during lunch, but he laughed often. A lot of it was catching up on set gossip and what everyone was up to. I had an icy feeling in my gut the whole time. Same old shit, different day. Guy taunting me with his presence and perfection while threatening to rip it all away. Again. I focused on my friends, as they were who I came to see in New York.

"Can we all go out after your show tonight? I miss our dance parties," Tania begged.

"Not sure what we're going to get into, but I'll text you," I told Tania. I needed to cuss Guy out in private first.

As we left the bar, Guy turned to me. "What now? We're in the Big Apple together again."

"I've kinda got a headache," I snipped. "I might go back and take a nap."

"Oh. Okay. Should we stop for medicine?" he asked, forever the energetic puppy determined to have a good time.

"You know what? I'm just going to say it." I turned to him. I looked around to make sure we weren't being documented by some onlooker. I hadn't even noticed anyone the night before, so I was extra paranoid.

"What, Kitty?" Guy asked, genuinely surprised.

I crossed my arms. "Did you come here for me or to court some New York team?"

He cocked his head back, eyes widening. "Birdy, no. I came here for you. They're just rumors."

"But you said 'not really' when I asked if you'd talked to them," I went on.

"Well, yeah, I talk to all of them a little here and there. New Jersey was interested for a bit."

I felt like my head was going to fly off. "You could have been in Newark, but you stayed in Seattle? I would have moved there for you. Jesus, Guy."

"Sweetheart, no." Guy reached for me. We'd wandered to the outskirts of a park with a wrought-iron fence. I clung to the fence, picking the peeling black paint. "It's not like that."

"How not?" I huffed.

Guy's eyes went sad. "I couldn't get traded without ruining my contract. But even then, you were with him."

Well, that took the wind out of my sails.

"Why were you talking to New Jersey then?" I asked quietly.

It was Guy's turn to get pissed. He screwed up his face, incredulous. He pinched the bridge of his nose like he was trying to gain his composure, but failed.

"Take a fucking guess, Kitty!" Guy burst out, breathing heavily after the statement. His hands were thrown wide, practically filling the whole sidewalk. His eyes searched mine. "It was for you. Everything, all of it. It's for you. Every woman I slept with, I wished she was you. I watched your show every week just to see you. Branson made me get help because I was still a wreck over you three years later. I was ready to move here for you. But I realized how crazy it was to run after a woman who was very publicly dating someone else. So I stayed."

I didn't know what to say. "Guy."

He rubbed a hand over his eyes, scratching the stubble on his chin. He looked at me, waiting for whatever I was going to say. I pried his hand off his face and took the other one as well.

"I was a mess without you, too. The first guy I kissed, I cried so hard Mikey thought he'd done something bad to me. Almost beat the poor guy up. And the sex, forget it. No one is you. And no one makes me feel the way you do."

Guy wasn't having my shit. His features were scrawled with hurt. "But you had a boyfriend. A serious relationship."

"I did. I didn't know if you and I would ever get a chance again. But it's over now. It's been over. And I never stopped loving you, all that time. I just didn't know what to do about it."

I shook his hands so he'd meet my eyes again.

"I love you, Guy." Guy's eyes rounded, brow furrowed. "Like really love you."

I didn't have to wonder if he'd remember that those were the words he'd first used with me, and then I used with him. I knew he did. He nodded, a tiny smile curving his lips.

"I know, sweetheart. That's why I'm here."

Everything shifted at that moment. He loved me. He knew I loved him. I knew it but had been hiding from it and stuffing it away. He was there to remind me that I loved him. To bring me home to him.

I was stunned.

He studied me for a long time as the realization worked over me, then squeezed my hands. "Wanna go get ice cream?"

Chapter 36

Guy

I actually made her get ice cream. It wasn't like her ice cream question the night before.

We walked the High Line and chatted, stealing licks off each other's cones. Kitty got strawberry and coffee flavor like an anarchist alien, and I got mint chocolate chip like a civilized person. It was hot as shit, and we saw a piragua guy, so we stopped for one of those, too. We shared a lime flavor. Kitty accused me of sucking all the juice out through that tiny little straw they give you.

Kitty had relaxed since our argument after lunch. In fact, she was downright lovey dovey. Despite the heat, she held my hand and leaned into me whenever she could. We wandered in and out of shops. We took silly pictures and just enjoyed each other. It was almost magical.

She stopped me and examined my face. "I think you're starting to burn, Guy. I probably am, too."

"Wanna go inside somewhere?"

"I'm kinda thinking I need a nap. I need to be sharp for my show. It'll take us a while to get back to my hotel, so we'd better get going."

"I've got a better plan," I said. I pulled out my phone to look up a location. "Can you make it another .2 miles?"

"Where are we going?"

"You'll see," I said.

As we walked into the Ritz-Carlton, Kitty was confused. "Are you trying to use their bathroom or something?"

"No, I'm buying you a nap."

"Guy!" she chided me as we walked to the front desk. I ignored her.

"Hi there," I said sweetly to the woman behind the desk. "What's your hourly rate?"

"Oh my God," Kitty mumbled.

"Our what?" the woman tried to stay polite but was clearly struggling.

"Your hourly rate. My friend here needs a nap but we don't need a whole night," I said, smiling but not cracking like I wanted to.

"Sir, this is a five-star hotel. We don't have an hourly rate," the woman said in her best customer service voice.

"Okay, then I'll get a night," I said.

"No, he won't. Sorry to waste your time, miss. Guy, let's go," Kitty hissed, dragging me away.

When we got outside, I finally lost it.

"I can't fucking stand you, Frenchie," Kitty said, trying not to laugh herself. She was already ordering a car back to her hotel.

"No, come on, we can stay here," I said. "It'll be the fanciest nap of your life."

"I need my clothes! And that lady thinks I'm a sex worker now," Kitty whined. "The rumor mill is really gonna be turning."

"How does she know that I'm not the sex worker? I could show you a good time," I said, putting a seductive hand on my hip.

Finally she laughed, doubling over. "You are the most ridiculous person I know, Guy Stelle."

"But you love me," I said, pulling her to me for a kiss.

"Yes, I do love you."

In the car on the way to her hotel, I turned to her. "Hey, can I move in with you?"

Kitty snapped her head toward me. "What?"

"I mean, should I just check out of my hotel and come stay in yours? Then we don't have to keep going back and forth."

"Yours is nicer, though," she argued.

"Okay, then check out of yours and come stay with me."

She weighed that. "I'll have to leave for the theater before you. How about I pack up my stuff and you take it to your hotel while I go get ready?"

I dropped a smooch on her cheek. "You always were the smart one. Did you go to an Ivy League?"

She laughed. "You are extra goofy today, Frenchie."

I looked at her with a soft smile. "I'm happy."

Kitty rested her head on the seat. "Me, too."

Chapter 37

Kitty

I stood backstage at the Palladium, looking over my notes for the show. This was a one-night-only engagement, just something to make a little extra money before I started my next job. And who am I kidding? I love a good stand-up show to a packed house. This crowd was sold out. That never ceased to amaze me. I know I'm funny, but the fact that people will take time and pay money to come see me talk is just wild. A dream come true.

A knock sounded at my door. "Come in."

"A delivery for you, Miss Gatto." A vase of orange and yellow flowers walked in, a stagehand behind them.

She dropped them on the counter in front of me and left me to my peace. The pack of M&Ms stuffed among the blooms told me exactly who they were from. His handwriting on the note told me for sure: Guy.

> Birdy-
> I'm so proud of you and know you'll do amazing tonight.
> I have something I want to tell you, but you might want to
> wait til after the show to read it if you're getting in the zone.
> I'm going to draw a picture below and if you don't want
> to read it, just look at the picture instead.

I snorted out a laugh. The picture was of a Kitty Bird, some comically weird hybrid of a cat and a bird. It looked absolutely ridiculous. And well, I was curious, so I read on.

> When you were on your last tour, I wanted to be there so bad. I didn't think we were ready. I bought a front row ticket to every show, and dared myself to go. I even stood outside the theater in Miami, but couldn't bring myself to go in. I didn't want to distract you, but I wanted to be there for you in spirit. I always want you to shine, Kitty.
>
> If you've ever wondered why there was always an empty seat in the front row, it was my way of being there for you. Tonight, I'll really be in my seat. I can't wait to see you shine and cheer you on.
> Love always,
> Guy

I grabbed a tissue off the counter to try and keep my makeup from running. Maybe I should have waited to read it, but it was also a beautiful confidence boost. Guy had been supporting me through everything, even from the shadows. He never stopped being there for me. I'd tried to support him, too. But buying a hat is not the same as buying a seat to every single show. He was truly my funny fan, for all of my life.

It was overwhelming, the way he loved me so fiercely. We'd been through a lot together, going through seasons where one of us was maybe better than the other. But none of that mattered anymore. More than anything, I wanted to try with him again.

* * *

I'd reached the point of my set where I stopped noticing the heat of the lights. The point where it was just plain fun.

"So, I don't know how many of you saw, but a friend and I have kind of been in the news lately."

A loud whoop and applause came from the crowd.

"Bring him up!" someone shouted.

"We love you, Stelle!" another yelled.

I searched the front row for Guy, and there he was, grinning up at me. "They're talking about you, buddy."

"So this isn't the first time my love life has been on display for the masses," I started. "And that's fine. I'm flattered y'all care. However!"

I turned from where I was pacing. "I saw some comments that said he was funnier than me? He, whose first language is not English. No shade to that. He, who did not finish college. No shade on that, either. I'm very proud of his athletic achievements. But he, who is not a student of the comedic arts, is funnier than ME? Ladies, men taking credit for a woman's achievements, right?"

Girly cheers erupted from the audience. "Because I teed him up for every one of those jokes. Did I not, Guy?"

"You did," he yelled up at me.

I mock-whispered into the mic. "He's just saying that because I put out."

Laughs rose and fell. "But really, he is a funny guy. I'm giving him shit right now, but he's always made me laugh. In fact, I should get ahead of a rumor from today."

I sat on the edge of the stage in front of Guy. "You thought I wasn't going to share this one, didn't you? You don't get off that easy."

Guy's hand was over his face, laughing his sweet "a-ha, a-ha, a-ha" honking laugh.

"So we were out, doing our cute little NYC summertime things. Stopping in little shops. Eating ice cream. Walking the High Line. I said I wanted to take a nap before I came to meet you lovely people tonight."

"And that clever, beautiful, muscular, attractive little fucker sitting right there," I said, gesturing to him in front of me, "walks us into the Ritz-Carlton. Neither of us are staying there, mind you. He tells the lady at the desk," I mimicked his enthusiasm. "'My friend would like to take a nap. What's your hourly rate?'"

I barely got his joke out without laughing myself. The crowd followed my lead.

"Just so you're all aware: I am not actually a sex worker. Sex work is work, though," I raised my eyebrows and pointed out to the crowd. "But my very special friend and I did not need a room at the Ritz to do seedy deeds. If you hear that one, just go ahead and ignore it."

The rest of the show went off without a hitch. A stagehand led Guy, Tania, and a few other friends back to see me after I was done. Guy stood back while I hugged my friends and offered to take pictures of us. I, of course, made him get in them.

"So we going dancing or what?" Tania asked.

I looked to Guy. "You cool with that?"

"Of course," he grinned.

"Y'all go pick a place and we'll meet you there," I said. Tania wiggled her eyebrows at me on her way out. When the door clicked shut, I gave Guy a hard hug. I put his face in my hands, stroking my thumbs at his jaw.

"I read your note."

Guy smiled. "What do you think?"

"I think I don't deserve you."

He gave me a quick peck, looking down into my eyes. "I promise that you do."

"I left you."

"I told you I would wait forever, Birdy. I knew you still loved me." He touched my bird necklace. "Did you wear this for me?"

I nodded. "Every day."

"That kept me going. Anytime I saw you in it, I knew."

We stood holding each other. I breathed Guy in and listened

to the steady drum of his heartbeat under my ear. We didn't need to say anything else. We were *us* again. The warmth that we'd shared for years was back.

We took that warmth with us to the bar, where we danced like fools with my friends. It was something of an elevated dive bar, playing throwback hits. In all our time together, we'd only ever danced in frat house basements. We'd never properly gone dancing. I should have known Guy would be a good dancer since he's so comfortable in his body. It felt like being at a wedding: friends and loved ones all around, goofing off and having fun.

We mixed it up with friend dancing and some coupling off together. We got a little tipsy, but nothing out of control. Just blissful and free. Well, I guess Guy spilled a drink down my front, then made a show of cleaning off my boobs. People took our picture, but we didn't care. I slipped off my shoes because they were holding back my dancing skills. Guy wrinkled his nose at me but then took off his own shoes.

"You can't judge me then do the same thing!"

"If there's glass to step on, I'll step on it first," he shouted over the music. It made truly no sense but we were in hysterics. Those drunken decisions that you know are terrible even at the time.

Luckily, no glass met bare feet. I was just happy to be out doing normal fun stuff with him. We'd both grown, but we still played together in similar ways. I hadn't realized how much Guy was on my wavelength until I had him back.

That whole day had an untouchable joy to it. For that night, I let myself dream. It would all work out. We could have that joy every day. We could make our relationship work.

Chapter 38

Guy

We spent a semi-hungover morning in bed. It was our last morning together, the last day before our bubble was popped and the tide of reality washed back in. We both knew it. We didn't talk much, focusing instead on our bodies. That included intense snuggling and some of our signature love-making. I wanted to make sure Kitty went away feeling to her bones how much I loved her.

We eventually faced the outside world and found a place to have brunch on a patio. It was hot, but we kept the brunch cocktails coming. We were lazy bums having a hair of the dog. Our hands laced and unlaced. We both bore physical signs of our love: love bites and hickeys. After a few cocktails, Kitty fully sat in my lap. I'm sure we looked insane to the other diners and passersby, but I didn't care. I needed as much Kitty as I could get.

We both had to be at the airport at around five. Luckily, we were in the same terminal at LaGuardia. We went through security together and put off going to our gates as long as possible, an unspoken agreement.

But the time came and we had to face it. Kitty stood, holding my hands, tears brimming in her eyes and staring at my shirt.

"I hate airports," she whimpered.

"Why?"

"It's where we say goodbye," she gasped. The sob she'd been fighting slipped out of her. Her wet eyes met mine. "I don't want to say goodbye."

I wiped her cheek with my thumb. "Then don't."

Kitty hiccuped. She laughed, then cried more. "But then what?"

I held her face in my hands, speaking slowly. "Then I'll call you later, and you'll answer. We'll keep talking. We just won't stop. It won't be goodbye."

Kitty's eyes volleyed back and forth between mine. "What will it be?"

I smiled down at her, tears coming to me, too. Mine were happy tears, though. "It'll be us trying."

Kitty's face brightened. Her arms went around my neck. I bent so she could grab me as tight as I knew she wanted. I lifted her off her feet, crushing her to me. She wrapped her legs around my waist, my little koala. I held her up as she gripped my face, bringing our foreheads together.

"I love you, Guy Stelle," she whispered.

"I love you, too, Kitty Gatto." We kissed, but not for long. We were still in public and though we're weird, we're not that weird. I put her back on her feet. "I'll call you when I get home."

Her eyes sparkled, her tears dry. A smile crept across her face. "Okay."

And with one last peck and squeeze, we went our separate ways.

Part 6:
Coda[1]

---

[1]. coda (noun): a concluding part of a literary or dramatic work

Chapter 39

Guy

"I hate that I can't be there tonight," I said into the phone. Kitty was having her housewarming party for all of her L.A. friends and coworkers that night. "I can't believe everyone else is getting to see your house first."

"You'll be here tomorrow. I promise I'll save some fun for you," she said. "How's Anaheim?"

"Oh, ya know," I said, trying to play it cool. "Sunny. Pretty. But I'd rather be with you."

"I know, baby. Hey, thanks for sending those flowers. They look good with all the wood and stone in the house," she said, adoration clear in her voice.

"Are they big? I wanted them embarrassingly big."

"They're enormous," she laughed. "I have to rethink how I'm going to put all the food around it."

"That's what I like to hear."

"Hey, where are you? It's quiet. Shouldn't you be on the bus to the arena?"

Fuck, she was onto me. "No, we got here a little early and I found a quiet spot. I just wanted to talk to you before it was late and you were all champagne buzzed."

"I appreciate it," she said quietly. "I know you like to get in the zone before games. You calling means a lot."

"Anything for you, *ma puce*," I said. "I'll call you after the game, but don't feel like you have to pick up if you still have lots of guests. I know you'll do great hosting tonight."

She gave an exaggerated groan. "Yeah, you know I get weird about hosting. I'll let you get to it, though. Give 'em hell, Stelle. I love you."

"I love you more, Birdy."

* * *

My hands shook as I walked up to Kitty's house. I rang the doorbell before trying the handle. Her porch was so perfectly her: a simple wreath and little yellow flowers in concrete planters. The mid-century modern house was modest, but it was something I knew Kitty had wanted for years. She loved houses that looked like her Meemaw's house. I knew she was especially excited about the pool and hot tub in the backyard. She was obsessed with 1950s California houses. I was so happy she'd gotten everything she wanted. And all on her own. Without me. I knew that was important to her. I could buy her whatever her heart desired, but she wanted to make her own way.

"Just come in!" yelled a voice from inside. But I wanted Kitty to answer the door. I rang again and again, being a pest with the button.

"Jesus, God, what?" Kitty demanded when she wrenched the door open. Her face went from annoyed to shocked as she realized it was me. She looked at the champagne and flowers in my hands. She sucked in a breath, tears making the sound choppy. Her eyes rounded. "You're here."

I grinned. "I'm here."

"Put that shit down so I can maim you," she commanded as she threw her arms around my neck. Of course, she hadn't given me a chance to put that shit down, so I wrapped her up while still holding the flowers and booze. She covered my neck in kisses before putting both hands on my face, like she didn't believe I was real. "How?"

"Coach let me be a healthy scratch tonight," I said, smiling down at her. "I couldn't miss this, Kitty."

The kiss Kitty launched was aggressive and tenacious. I held her tight, elated to have her back in my arms. We hadn't seen each other since New York, and I'd made a lot of changes to make sure I could keep her in my arms more often than not. But I'd tell her that later.

"Come meet everybody," she whispered against my mouth, then dragged me through the door.

"Listen up!" Kitty shouted into the room. Her guests laughed and looked up at us. "This is Guy. He's real. He's actually here."

A cheer went up from the room. "Did you tell them I'm not real?"

"No. They just don't believe that I'm involved with some hockey star," she laughed.

Kitty paraded me around the room, introducing me to her boss, the producer of the show she worked on, and some of her L.A. friends I'd never met. It felt so good to be by her side again, the man on her arm. The man with an arm around her waist. The man glued to her, pawing at her, staring at her because I needed her.

I helped her pour and hand out champagne to all the guests so she could make a toast.

"Come stand with me, Guy," she said after she brought the room to attention. She wound her arm around my back. "Thank you, everyone, for coming over to help me break in my new house. Don't be strangers. Most of y'all know I'm from West Virginia, so I come from a place where I expect you to just show up and insert yourself in my business. If you're here tonight, you are always welcome in my home. I'm new to L.A. and I need all the love I can get. Especially with this guy far away," she said, nudging my side. "It means so much to me to already have such an awesome work family, and friends that I stole from New York. Thanks for being my people. Cheers!"

The room erupted in heartfelt cheers, glasses clinking. I leaned down to Kitty.

"Mind if I say something?"

"Go ahead. Don't embarrass me, though, Guy Stelle," she warned. I clinked her glass to mine to quiet the room again.

"Kitty said I could give a toast, too, as long as I don't embarrass her," I said, beaming at her. "I've known Kitty for a long time. A decade or so now, right, *ma puce?*"

Kitty nodded, blushing.

"I'm sure if you know her, you know how hard she works. She's wanted this for as long as I've known her, and it's been such a joy to watch her grow her talents and succeed. I just wanted to toast Kitty, because I'm so proud of her and who she's become. In a world full of Pepsi and Coke, she's my Dr. Pepper. I love you, Birdy. Cheers."

Glasses were raised again with a few swoons as I kissed Kitty, the taste of champagne on her lips.

"Okay! We're in a room full of writers and creatives, but nobody steal his line! It's mine," Kitty announced, fanning her face. "Now everybody, eat, drink, dance, and have a good time!"

Her friends seemed pretty cool, overall. I don't know what I expected for L.A. I guess something more superficial, but everyone was genuine and kind. Just like Kitty, no one treated me like a meathead. Well, I guess one guy asked me if all my teeth were real, but that's a decently valid question for someone who plays professional hockey. Some even complimented how funny I was in our stand-up appearance from New York. One guy said he'd ask if I could be a guest on SNL.

"Only if Kitty helps me," I said. "I couldn't be funny without her."

While I loved meeting all her people, I was eager to get Kitty alone. It was getting late and I needed to be up early the next day.

When it got close to midnight, I had to speak up.

I took her hand between conversations and leaned down to her ear. "Hey, Birdy, I think I'm going to head out."

"Head out? You're not staying with me?" she asked, her face thoroughly confused.

"Can we talk outside?"

"Uh, yeah," she said, looking scared. I took her hand and led her to her backyard. She had the area around the pool lit with candles and hanging lanterns. A few guests stood outside, smoking and chatting. They didn't pay us any mind as we sat on a lounge chair by the pool. "Did you come here to break off whatever we've got going on?"

"Never," I said. "I actually just wanted to check in with you. We haven't really talked about it since New York. If I can figure out a way to make it all work with us, is that what you want?"

Her face turned pensive. "Yes."

"I need you to be absolutely sure, Kitty. No holding back. No reservations. You fully want this?"

Her mouth arranged into a little pout. "I've fully wanted this since we were kids, Guy. I never would have left if we'd been able to stay together."

My heart fluttered looking over at her. "Good."

"Do you have some kind of plan you're not telling me about?"

"Working on one. I don't want to jinx it and make it end up not working out," I said. "You're coming to the game tomorrow, right? And sitting with Mel? She asks about you constantly. Misses you."

"I wouldn't dare miss it, baby," she said, holding my chin for a kiss. I tugged her closer, deepening it. "You're sure you don't want to stay over?"

I booped her nose. "I don't want you to kick your guests out and I need good sleep. We've got an early practice since the game's at five. You'll still go to dinner with me after?"

"Of course," she grinned. "I'll take you for as many hours as I can get you. And I appreciate you sneaking out tonight to surprise me. It means a lot."

"This house is perfect, Birdy. Everything you dreamed of."

She glowed with pride and gave me a final kiss before sending me on.

Chapter 40

Kitty

"Hey, babe," I rasped out to Mel. I had on sunglasses and a baseball hat. It was 11 a.m., but my party's festivities had lasted well into the morning hours. There may or may not have been One Direction karaoke. It was for the best that Guy didn't stay over. He'd have played like shit.

I felt like shit. But Mel and I had booked brunch as soon as she told me she was coming down for this road trip. She said she needed a little mommy getaway time before she and Branson started trying for number two. She told me to pack my clothes and makeup for the game.

"Looks like the housewarming was a success," she teased. "Sorry I had to miss it."

"You were doing the good WAG thing, seeing Branson in Anaheim. You will be coming to my next house party, though, missy. I'll make sure of it," I said. "If I drink a mimosa, will it reactivate all the champers I drank last night?"

Mel cackled. "I hope so. I already ordered you one."

"And to think, I didn't think we'd get along before I met you. I sincerely apologize for that," I said, scanning the menu for an item that didn't make me want to barf. "I thought I was above WAG life."

"Apology accepted. We all thought we were above it. If anything, I've gotten cooler since I had a kid. I concentrate all my fun into my non-kid time," she said, checking her nails.

I went to pick up my phone out of impulse before I stowed it away in my purse, but Mel snatched it out of my hand.

"Uh-uh. No phones. This is our time to catch up," she said, waving a finger in my face. "And I booked us some fun after this, too."

Oh, Mel. I love her, but I was ready to hang my head over a toilet and take a nap so I could get it together before the game. Maybe watch some bad TV.

I groaned. "What kind of fun? I need a nap."

"You and Branson," she said, rolling her eyes. "Those boys nap more than our toddler. Anyway, Branson booked us a spa day. I could have done it alone, but I want a buddy. You can nap while you get a facial."

I pretended to be annoyed, but time in a nice cool spa in a robe didn't sound so bad. "Alright, I can get on board with that."

"Yay!" Mel shouted, clapping her hands as the mimosas arrived. "So, tell me about the party. Any special guests?"

I narrowed my eyes at her. "Who do you think was my special guest?"

"Oh, nobody."

"You knew, didn't you?"

"Sorry. Branson always spills every secret he's absorbed after we have sex. He's so predictable. But wasn't it a nice surprise?"

I beamed. "It was. It was so weird in a way, having him there with all my people from work and comedy. Like, he fit in so well, but it's just a worlds colliding thing. He and I hadn't seen each other since New York."

Mel gave a pouty lip. "He's so obsessed with you, Kitty. I mention you and he just takes off. It's the sweetest thing. He called you Aunt Kitty to Gunnar the other day."

I blushed. "I've never even met your child, Mel. What's he up to?"

Mel caught me up on the ins and outs of the life of a two-year-old. She was one of those easy friends. We didn't see each other much. Shit, we'd only seen each other maybe three or four times in our whole lives. I felt bad that Guy and I broke up before they got married. She did send me an invitation, but I couldn't do that to Guy. I knew he was in the wedding party. But still, Mel and I were in synch. I could text her about any random mutual interest at any hour of the day and she'd respond right away like we'd just gotten off the phone. Friends like that are the best. Low maintenance, high yield.

Our spa day was pretty magical. Branson had gotten us each a pick-three package. Mel encouraged me to get a manicure because she'd read great reviews of them, and I added a facial and blowout. Then I wouldn't have to do my hair for the game and could take advantage of the plunge pool and hot tub in the lounge guilt-free. Mel opted for a massage over a facial, but I didn't need all that alcohol pushed further into my bloodstream. The day was about recovery so I could be a good hockey girlfriend in the evening.

By 3 p.m., we were pampered and glowing. We got changed and ready in the spa's dressing room. Mel wanted to be at the arena by four.

"Why so early?" I whined. I was being a real pain in the ass. I was lucky Mel has the sunniest disposition of anyone I know.

"I like to watch them warm up! Plus I like to see all the girls who have crushes on them, too," she grinned.

"Evil," I gasped.

"No, it's cute! Reminds me that I snagged a good one. I need the validation for times when he acts like a dingdong."

But by some miracle, we walked into the arena just after four, taking our seats on the glass between the two benches. It was unusual for us to have such good seats, but I didn't think much of it. We cheered as the Sealpups came out of the tunnel, but as I scanned the players, I didn't see Guy.

A light panic flashed through me. Was he hurt? Sick? Why wasn't he out with the rest of the team?

"Where's Guy?" I asked Mel, like somehow she would know.

"I don't know," she said, also concerned.

But then, in a spray of ice, Guy appeared on the other side of the glass. In a black and purple sweater. Like, an L.A. Princes sweater.

My jaw dropped as his glowing grin spread wide. He didn't have his helmet on for warmups, which I gave him shit about most of the time, but this time, it let me look at him better. My stomach was permanently suspended like I was dropping on a roller coaster.

"No way," was all I could say. Mel filmed us with a huge smile, as did someone from the Princes' social media team who materialized out of nowhere. "Are you? Did you?"

Guy nodded. It was only when he motioned for me to stand up that I realized that the shock cemented me to my seat. Someone on the Princes' staff handed me a box.

"Open it," Guy said.

I moved the tissue paper aside to find a Princes jersey with his new number and STELLE written across the back. My hand clamped over my mouth and tears streamed freely down my cheeks.

"You're staying?" I asked, holding my hand up to his on the glass. I could feel all the splotchiness on my chest and neck. Even Guy's face was a little red.

Guy nodded. I was overwhelmed. Guy had figured it out. He left Seattle for *me*. He changed teams to be with *me*. He was giving up his friends so we could be together. I pounded on the glass, wanting to be close to him. He laughed, elated, and pointed toward the tunnel. I tripped over myself running to meet him. When I got there, he lifted me over the railing and held me up, my arms a snug lock around the back of his neck. There was no way I could reach his face when he was in his skates anyway.

"You did all of this for me?" I asked as he nuzzled me.

"I did. All for you. Always. You're everything, Kitty. My life isn't complete without you."

"But Seattle," I said through my tears.

"Seattle doesn't have you, Birdy," he said sweetly. "I'll still see them. The most important thing is you."

I kissed him as both teams gathered around to cheer Guy on.

"One more thing," he said as we broke apart and he dropped me to my feet. Oh, fuck, was he going to propose? There? At the arena? The last time he proposed was in the ultimate privacy. Would he really do it so publicly the second time? He wasn't lowering to one knee, though. He leaned over me. "I don't have anywhere to live yet."

Realization and relief flooded me. "Hmmm," I pretended to deliberate. "I guess you could use my spare bedroom until you find a place of your own."

Guy brought his face closer to mine, danger in his eyes but a smile on his face as he gripped my waist. "Don't make me spank you in front of all these people, Kitty Bird."

"Fine, you want to be my roommate? I'll give you a good deal on the rent."

"Kitty," he warned.

"You want to move in with me?"

"That's more like it," Guy said with a kiss. "And good, because the moving truck comes tomorrow."

"I can't believe you figured it all out, Frenchie. Thank you."

He smooched my forehead and touched my bird necklace. "You're about to get so fucking sick of me."

"Impossible."

Guy and I kissed some more, and then he pointed to the top of the tunnel. "Look up."

My parents and Frank were there, wearing Guy's new jersey.

"I figured they could keep you company while I have to go play," Guy said, kissing my cheek. Wait, my family was there, but Guy didn't propose? Well, moving in with me and changing his whole life for me was a big enough shift. Still, even though we'd only been back together for a number of weeks, there was no doubt that Guy was the permanent destination. He was The One and had been all along. I could have easily committed right then, even if it was in front of an embarrassing number of people. Who else would I be with if not Guy, the man who uprooted his whole life so we could both have what we wanted? The man who waited for me all those years?

Guy and I did a short interview with L.A.'s marketing team, and recorded a quick goodbye for Seattle's fans. It isn't every day that a player changes teams for love and well, we're both a little famous. I didn't blame them for wanting to market the hell out of us.

With a final kiss, Guy lifted me back over the barricade and went out to warm up.

I turned back to Mel. "You knew."

"That's why I had to take your phone. We didn't want you seeing the news before he could tell you." She smashed her body to mine and rocked me side to side. "We'll miss him, but I'm glad he's coming home to you. He isn't him without you."

"We'll just have to visit y'all, and you'll have to come here," I said. "Okay, gotta go attack my family. Wanna come?"

We all moved up to a suite the Princes had reserved for us to watch the game. I felt weird cheering against Seattle after years of supporting Guy, whether quietly in the background or more fully as his girlfriend. So I cheered for both teams, which amounted to a lot of cheering.

My voice was hoarse by the time Guy met us after the game. He wasn't the first out of the locker room, though. It was Mikey. I'd totally forgotten that he was with the Princes until that moment. There were too many players to look at when I tried to follow both teams.

"Hey, screamer," he said, opening his arms and running at me.

I shouted his name as he swept me up in a big hug. "I forgot you were here!"

"Indeed I am. Can't get rid of me now. I'll be on your couch every morning, just like old times."

I laughed. "We may have to talk about healthy boundaries." I looked around the room. "Anybody here for you?"

Mikey's face fell. Fuck. I always put my foot in my mouth with him. "Still unsuccessful there. I do alright, though."

"I'm sure you do," I said, trying to console him and acknowledge his soft spot for the women who fell into his DMs. More power to him. He grimaced and tried to make me feel better about it.

"It's fine. I'm alright. But I think every fight I had with Stelle in college was because I was jealous of you two." Mikey raked his damp hair back. "But hey, you've been a bit of a superstar yourself, haven't you?"

I gave a modest smile. "Something like that."

"Proud of you. I always tell people I knew you back when." I hugged him to my side again. Mikey had always been good to me, even if it was just in his brutish kind of way. "And I'm glad you and Guy figured it out."

"Yeah, well, he did the hard part," I said as a freshly showered and delicious-smelling Guy stepped to my side.

"You chirped yourself out, Birdy," Guy joked when he heard my shredded voice. He leaned down to my ear, and before pecking my cheek he said, "Gonna have to make you more hoarse tonight."

He gave big hugs to my family and then introduced me to some of his new teammates.

"Big fan of your work," one player, Beatty, told me. "My wife's already so happy you'll be around. We love your standup. How are you going to be funny if you're happy with Stelle, though?"

Guy stiffened. He knew that I faced criticism sometimes, the price of being in the limelight. Some of it was about my jokes. Some of it was commentary about my body.

I was too West Virginia. I wasn't West Virginia enough, a sellout. If I existed in a female body and was pictured at an angle that wasn't the peak of flattery, I was pregnant with someone's love child. All my jokes had to be about dating because I was a woman. If I wasn't sad and bitter, I wasn't funny. When I talked about fame, I was unrelatable. If I was too witty, I was unlikable. I'd seen and heard it all.

Guy was prepared. After all, he was the former @funnyfan96. He knew every nasty thing people had to say about me and had a comeback for every point. But here, he was going to have to work with Beatty long-term. He couldn't be his full internet troll self.

"I've known Kitty a long time. She always has something funny to say," Guy said with a forced smile.

"Who knows? Maybe I'll roast his teammates next," I said with a raised eyebrow. Guy squeezed my butt as he stifled a laugh.

"Right. Right. I guess that was a dick thing to say. Nice meeting you. Rachel looks forward to meeting you," he said before walking away.

Guy turned me to face him before we moved to another conversation. "You never need me to defend you, Birdy. I love it."

"But I like it that you do," I said, planting a smooch on his lips. "My big, scrappy bulldog."

We had a nice dinner out with my family, Mikey, Branson, and Mel. Guy held my hand when we weren't eating. It felt like the old days when Guy would have dinner at our house. Everything felt complete. Nothing was wrong. Everything was working out. The puzzle pieces all fit. Guy was really mine to have and had moved mountains to get to me. He said his agent threatened to quit the day he asked if he could arrange a trade to L.A., after all the work she'd done on the New York area teams.

"We'll have to send her a nice Christmas present," I said.

"Maybe we can get her a baby announcement," Guy said, wiggling his eyebrows.

My jaw fell open. "Guy Stelle, if you moved here thinking you were going to knock me up, you are out of your fucking mind. Call that moving company and tell them to turn that truck around."

"I'm kidding, I'm kidding," he said. "I love getting you all worked up."

"You just want me to take it out on you later."

"Maybe," he said, sinking his teeth into a roll with a wink.

My family stayed in a hotel to give us privacy, but would help us move Guy's stuff in the next day. He had a day off before L.A.'s next road stand.

That night, after Guy and I had worn each other out in every position we could think of, we drifted off to sleep together in our home. Not just mine. Ours.

The thing I thought would never be possible had happened. Guy and I were together. We shared a home. We merged the lives we'd built and were finally getting our happy ending.

Chapter 41

Guy

The doorbell rang at 8 a.m. sharp. Kitty groaned next to me.

"*Bonjour, ma puce,*" I crooned. "That's the movers."

"Why so early?" Kitty rolled onto her back, her naked body outside the sheets. I kissed her boobs and her neck until she squealed with giggles. I was hard, but the movers were just going to have to see it.

"You stay here. I'll get the door." I pulled on my underwear and grabbed a pair of shorts out of my suitcase. When I got back to the bedroom, Kitty was in the shower.

Though her house was vintage, the master bathroom was remodeled to be more modern. It still had the 50s feel, but the fixtures had been upgraded to be more comfortable. That meant a nice, big shower with a bench seat and a rain shower head.

"You thought you were getting away from me, didn't you, Birdy?" I said as I crept into the bathroom. "The shower is where we started."

She looked at me sidelong as I got in the shower with her, tracing the water droplets running over her skin.

"Guy, we have company. What if they need to know where to put something?"

I already had her slippery body in my arms, my cock teasing at her pussy.

"They can figure it out," I said, nibbling on her neck to her sighs.

"What if they hear us?"

"Then I guess you'll have to keep quiet, huh?"

I placed Kitty on the bench and spread her legs wide with mine. But before I could get on my knees, she had my cock in her mouth. I let out a loud sigh. Kitty popped off and winked up at me.

"Shhhh," she teased.

"That's it," I said with finality, dropping down in front of her. I clamped my hand over her mouth as I fucked her with mine, her salty-tangy taste overwhelming my senses. I touched myself with my other hand, unable to control my desire. She sucked my fingers into her mouth, pulling hard. That sensation alone was enough to do me in.

I plucked her off the bench and sat down myself, pulling her into my lap.

"Ride." And she did. Kitty's ass was in my hands as she bounced on my cock, holding a vicious kiss so we didn't scream. I aided the rocking of her hips with my hands, curling her clit against my stomach. She came quickly, sinking her teeth into my lower lip as she did. It hurt like hell but it was so hot that I wasn't far behind. I shot up into her, my love, the person I'd always do anything for. Including giving her more pleasure.

"One more," I whispered. "You're gonna give me one more, sweetheart."

"Guy," she whimpered.

"You can," I encouraged her, knowing she wanted to say she couldn't.

I lifted her off my cock, jamming my fingers inside her and pulling her flesh toward me. My name came out as a surprised gasp as I worked her with my fingers. Her mouth was wide with shock as she spilled over the edge, our combined release all over my hand.

"Good girl," I cooed.

"My God," she breathed. And then she looked at me laughing. "This is a little better than FaceTime."

* * *

"Is the moving truck empty?" Kitty asked. The movers were outside, packing up.

"I think there's one more bag," I said. "Will you go get it?"

"Guy, you paid movers," she protested. "They can bring it in."

"Please? They worked so hard, Birdy. I have to go to the bathroom or I'd do it myself."

"Make Frankie get it," she said, flopping down next to Heather on the couch, exhausted and sweaty. Heather patted Kitty's hair to comfort her.

"Kitty," I whined, walking toward the bathroom. "It has my stinky underwear in it. Please?"

She shot me an angry look, but finally agreed and stomped off in an annoyed cloud. The movers were in a line by the truck, checking their phones and chatting amongst themselves. They easily could have brought the bag in, but I told them not to. I'd planted it there just an hour before. Kitty didn't know that, though. I saw from the set of her shoulders that she was getting increasingly pissed off. This was what I wanted: catching her off guard. I knew she expected it at the game the day before, but I wanted this to be more private and just for us. And her family.

She hoisted herself up into the moving truck, the bridge thing already folded up. There was my hockey bag, all the way at the back of the truck. She muttered curses under her breath that echoed around the truck's empty walls. I had to keep from laughing out loud. The ring box fell off the top of my hockey bag when she picked it up.

She hissed out a cuss as she bent to get the box, the heavy bag shifting around to her front. She was seriously struggling. Then she noticed what the box was.

She dropped the bag and turned around. I stood watching her with a smile so big my cheeks hurt, her family behind me. I hauled myself up into the truck and walked to her, taking the box from her and holding her hands.

"Kitty," I said, waiting for her reaction. "I know for sure that you are the love of my life. You're my Dr. Pepper. You're the reason for everything I do. I don't want to live another day without you being mine. Now that we're going to share a home, I want to make it truly ours. To do that, I want to ask you something I first asked you a long, long time ago."

My Birdy started to cry as I steered her so they could see both of our faces. She whimpered out an 'I love you.'

"I love you, too, *ma puce*. So I think you know what I'm going to ask you." Kitty's hands went over her mouth.

I got down on one knee and opened the ring box. She was already nodding but I was determined to ask her properly. "Kitty Elena Gatto, love of my life, will you marry me?"

"Yes. Yes, Guy Nicolas Stelle. You're the love of my life and the only one for me. Yes, I'll be your wife," she sobbed out, pulling me to my feet to hold me. "But I won't change my name," she whispered in my ear as I swung her around. I slapped her butt, to her cackling laughter and Frank's "EW!"

We kissed as I held her up. "I wouldn't expect any different from you, *ma puce*. It's on your terms. Always has been. Whatever you want, I do."

***

After firing off "she said yes" texts to my Seattle friends, Mikey, and the new teammates whose numbers I had, I got a little sad. I didn't have family to text. Kitty's family was with us. I knew Maman would be happy for us, but I'd rather she be able to see it for herself.

We kept working to unpack boxes, Kitty clearing space for me in each room. I'd sold or donated most of my furniture in Seattle, so I mostly just had stuff. It really didn't amount to much. Most things I had were things that reminded me of Kitty. She'd been the center of my life for so long, whether she was actually there or not.

Heather and Mark put together a nice dinner for us: grilled steaks, veggies, and Heather's mashed potatoes that I loved. We chose to eat outside by the pool. Before we started, everyone said a few words to congratulate us.

"You know that I was skeptical about you two," Frank said. "But true to his style, Guy wasn't lying. He really does love Kitty, and he never gave up. And now, I get to have my best friend as a brother, too. And yeah," he said, casually wiping his eye, "That's pretty cool."

"And we know you'd throw a punch for me if he gets out of line," Kitty chimed in.

"Yeah, I still would," Frank laughed.

Mark was a man of few words all the time, so I was especially nervous to hear what he'd have to say. Part of me was a little scared of him.

"I, too, had my doubts about giving up my little girl to some hockey thug," Mark said. "But I knew he wasn't just any player. I knew you were one of the best men deep down, and I had to trust that your true nature would win in the end. You've been like a son to me since you and your mom moved down the street. I'm happy it's official now."

I wiped my eyes. I hadn't expected Mark to call me his son. Kitty squeezed my hand with wet eyes.

"Thanks, Daddy," she said quietly. To Mark. Not to me. Ha.

"Guy, you know how special I think you are," Heather started. "And you know how crazy I was about your mom."

Oh, shit. Here were the real tears.

"But I know what Eva asked of the two of you, and I knew she was right. I knew someday, this would be where we'd all end up. Not in L.A., necessarily, but with the two of you staying together. I knew when you and Kitty split that it wasn't over. You both love each other too much for that. I know Eva's here, Guy. I know she's happy for all of us. Because something made y'all stop where you did, and live where you did. I really believe all of this was meant to be. We love you, bubby. Happy to have you."

Heather pulled me into a tight hug, and though she wasn't my petite storm of a mom, I felt that mother's love. I cried about as hard as I did when Kitty left the last time, then pulled myself together.

I sat and raised my glass. "Gattos, you are the best thing that happened to me and Maman. And something about it does feel predestined. I can't say much more than that. My heart is so full because I have all of you in my life." Tears continually crept out of my eyes and my words were choked. "Thank you for loving me. All of you. It's the greatest honor."

We stood up for an embarrassing attempt at a group hug and continued with our evening. Kitty and I saw them off at the end of the night. When we closed the front door and turned to each other, Kitty was crying again.

I held both of her hands. "What's on your mind, *ma puce?*"

"I can't wait to hate Mondays with you," she said, doing this weird laugh and snot-suck thing at once. "And come to every home game I can. And go to sleep with you whenever you're not on the road."

She took a ragged breath, blowing it out through a small O in her mouth. She looked back up at me.

"But most of all, when hockey's over and my writing days are through, I can't wait to get old together. To annoy each other. To keep laughing together. To see each other out of this life. I can't wait to do it all with you."

I pressed my lips to hers, thinking of the thousands of kisses we'd share for years to come.

"I can't imagine a better life than annoying each other for the rest of it." She beamed and my heart felt full to bursting. "And hey, I know what you can call your next standup tour."

"Oh yeah? What's that?"

"You know how there's puck bunnies?"

She nodded and quirked a brow. "I'm aware of the term. Pretty sure it's been lobbed my way at some point."

"Call your show Puck Funny."

Epilogue

Guy and Kitty,

I am so happy that you're reading this letter. I trusted Heather to give it to you if this moment ever came to be. So if you're reading this, that means it's your wedding day. I long hoped this day would come. Know that I am there with you, and I'm so proud of you both.

I knew from the time that you laid eyes on each other that you were meant to be together.

Kitty, you just "get" Guy. The way you are to him is beautiful. You let him be himself. That's the most a mother could hope for her son. He has the biggest heart. Let him love you the way you deserve. You love him that way, too. If he's screwing up, tell him. If he doesn't listen, tell him I said he has to.

Guy, Kitty is exactly the partner you need. Listen to her. She's smart. Do not take that precious girl for granted. Stay true to her. Don't let your father's mistakes make you doubt yourself. You are not him, nor are you me. You are you, and you're perfect. You have what it takes to be everything she needs.

I hope that as your lives go on, you remember how special your bond is. It will be tested, but you can make it if you try. A love like yours doesn't come along every day. Honor it. Care for it. All I ever asked was that you try, and that led you to today.

And if you choose to have children, Eva makes a great middle name.

All my love,
Maman

ReadMore Press
DISCOVERING THE NEXT BESTSELLER

Would you like a *FREE* WWII historical fiction audiobook?

This audiobook is valued at 14.99$ on Amazon and is exclusively free for **Readmore Press'** readers!

To get your free audiobook, and to sign up for our newsletter where we send you more exclusive bonus content every month,

Scan the QR code

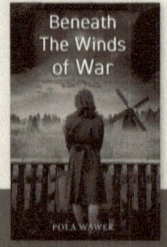

Readmore Press is a publisher that focuses on high-end, quality historical fiction. We love giving the world moving stories, emotional accounts, and tear-filled happy endings.

We hope to see you again in our next book!

Never stop reading, **Readmore Press**

Want more Guy and Kitty?

Thank you for reading Puck Funny! I'd love it if you left a review on whatever platform you prefer.

If you need more of Guy and Kitty's story, sign up for my email newsletter: //dl.bookfunnel.com. You'll receive a link to a sweet and spicy snippet of their happily ever after.

Reading this on a physical page?
Go to https: //www.danigalliaro.com/puck-funny-bonus

Content/Trigger Warnings

Your mental health as a reader is important. Triggers for this story include:
- Reference to off-page domestic violence
- On-page death of a parent
- Discussion of early pandemic
- Fist fights

Additionally, there is graphic sexual content between fully consenting partners. This includes:
- Copious dirty talk, including "good girl" and "daddy"
- Spanking
- Edging
- Face sitting
- Light Dom/sub dynamics
- Anilingus and anal fingering

This book is not a manual on how to practice BDSM.

Acknowledgments

Thanks for reading Puck Funny. This book merges two of my loves: comedy and sports.

I've always been a sports girlie to some degree, but never got into hockey until recently. I became a hockey fan the way many people did in 2022: hockey romance. Thanks to my teams (in this order): New York Islanders, Seattle Kraken, and Carolina Hurricanes.

This book wouldn't be possible without my college improv troupe, the Barely Legal Teens. Yes, I'm one of those annoying people who did improv in college and won't stop talking about it for the rest of my life. Thanks to Ryan for seeing the spark in me and asking me to join. Your coaching, friendship, and encouragement were so meaningful during a tough time in my life.

Thanks also to Alison, Nan, Molly, Monica, Dan, Bill, Bradd, Ted, and Paul. I hope you all are blessed with many carrot deliveries and visits from the phantom ice cream truck.

Thanks to my main female inspirations in comedy: Nicole Byer, Sasheer Zamata, Lauren Lapkus, Betsy Sodaro, Ali Wong, Jenny Slate, Hannah Berner, Taylor Tomlinson, Mindy Kaling, Amy Poehler, and Tina Fey.

To all you crazy cats on BookTok, thanks for being such a supportive community.

To all my ARC readers, especially those who will slide into my DMs and give me the deeper thoughts. There's no feeling like getting to discuss things you made up with people who enjoy it.

To Roxana, for your editing prowess.

To everyone at the 2023 Appalachian Writers' Workshop, thank you for the countless tips on sharpening your manuscript, and for cheering me on when I read you my story about a hockey player falling in love with a West Virginia-born comedian.

To MEV, for helping me come up with Kitty's name and fielding my first flurry of texts when Puck Funny's concept came into my brain. Also for helping me change Frank's name.

To Chrissy, for going with me to Blue Jackets games and having the best hockey commentary in the game. May you have many shots of Starry.

To Nan, for dragging me to my first hockey game in college. I didn't get it at the time, but now I get it. Go Sabes.

To Amy, for reading it from a Quebecois perspective and making sure I don't sound like a fool in French.

To Janney, for once again reading, weighing out constant random texts of "what's hotter?" and playing with me in these little worlds I create. Also HUGE PROPS for combing through the names of people who rode the Mayflower to help me choose an Ivy League university name. You are also the reason the scales tipped toward Guy and Kitty's beach make-out.

To Brooke, for once again reading and always asking for more. Your scene suggestions are clutch. I hope to continue providing you with "dirty hot" heroes.

To my parents, for being the ultimate hype people.

And as always to my darling husband, who helped me come up with a name that would mean "G-Spot" in French but still be a cool-ass name. Who showed up to each and every improv show like Guy. Who moves and loves with the kind of purpose that Guy does.

www.ingramcontent.com/pod-product-compliance
Lightning Source LLC
LaVergne TN
LVHW091539070526
838199LV00002B/136